Fic
Fin   Finch, Phillip
        f2f

f2f

ALSO BY PHILLIP FINCH

Sugarland

Paradise Junction

In a Place Dark & Secret

Trespass

B A N T A M
B O O K S

New York
Toronto
London
Sydney
Auckland

f2f

PHILLIP FINCH

f2f

A Bantam Book / April 1996

Library of Congress Cataloging-in-Publication Data

Finch, Phillip.
    f2f / Phillip Finch.
       p.   cm.
    ISBN 0-553-09718-0
    I. Title. II. Title: f two f.
    PS3556.I456F17   1996
    813'.54--dc20   95-21038
                                         CIP

Published simultaneously in the United States and Canada

Bantam Books are published by Bantam Books, a division of
Bantam Doubleday Dell Publishing Group, Inc. Its trademark,
consisting of the words "Bantam Books" and the portrayal of a
rooster, is Registered in U.S. Patent and Trademark Office and
in other countries. Marca Registrada. Bantam Books, 1540
Broadway, New York, New York 10036.

PRINTED IN THE UNITED STATES OF AMERICA

BVG   10 9 8 7 6 5 4 3 2 1

To Angela and Daniel

With much hope

And all love

PART I

Snowflake

March 24–25

Prologue

Your life is in jeopardy. As you read this, you are within reach of a murderer. Death stands behind you, silent and unseen. At any moment you may feel its chill breath on the back of your neck as it reaches to tap your shoulder . . .

In a short time someone within the reach of this message will die grotesquely and horribly at my hands. (Maybe you!)

You tell yourself: Impossible. Not me.

For you believe that you are unknown and unnoticed. You feel the buffer of distance between yourself and the creator of this message. You are comforted by your privacy.

There is no buffer. The fact that this text has reached you is proof that wherever you are, I may be.

As to privacy, it exists no longer. We have sacrificed it to the cause of convenience; it is our burnt offering to Lord Electron. The digitized details of your existence are in the public domain, available to anyone with a modicum of intelligence and expertise. You are exposed. You are as open to me as a naked whore manacled to the four posts of a bed. At leisure will I probe you. Carefully and unhurriedly will I dissect you and examine you and pick you apart. You are at my mercy.

You are KNOWN.

Knowledge is power.

The power is mine.

You cannot hide.

Reactions?

This was how the killer announced himself, at seven forty-eight P.M. on a Friday evening during the last week of March. He transmitted the text—"uploaded" it—to the public message board of the Verba Interchange.

Verba was one of many thousands of on-line services available to computer users. A few, like the commercial giants CompuServe and Prodigy, were vast bazaars of data and information that served millions of paying customers.

Verba was far from that scale. It was a free service sponsored by a social research foundation in San Francisco, which in turn was endowed by an informal group of software authors and others who owed their prosperity to computers and the electronic revolution. Yet for on-line cognoscenti, it was a popular gathering place. Its users tended to be well educated, at least reasonably affluent, and under the age of fifty. Nearly all of them shared a zeal for the electronic future and a confidence about their own place in that future. This trait alone separated them from most of humankind.

In physical terms Verba consisted of a rack of computer hardware connected to a trunk of eighty-four telephone lines in the foundation's office in San Francisco's south-of-Market district. More than half of Verba's users were San Francisco–area residents, for whom the service was just a local call. In a sense, though, on-line networks like Verba made geography moot. For someone with a computer and modem, an on-line net is as close as the nearest telephone jack.

Every week Verba recorded about eight thousand log-ins—individual entries via outside phone lines. Users met one another within Verba's electronic system, where they chatted, argued, discoursed, speculated, and flirted through the digital medium of computer keystrokes.

Messages posted to the public message board, and elsewhere in the service, were neither screened nor approved. Verba had been conceived as a truly open medium. Its only prohibition was against posting copyrighted material: That was for legal reasons.

While nearly all on-line services allow informal nicknames—known as handles—most require users to register their addresses and true names.

Verba did not. Many users did register, to gain exclusive rights to a chosen handle and the use of an electronic mail drop to receive and store personal messages. However, even registered users sometimes logged in with new handles so as to assume different personas and roam the system as unknown newcomers.

In essence, Verba was a gigantic masquerade party where anyone could enter, leave, or change costume at will.

Thus, Snowflake was completely unidentifiable.

Verba's records would show only that his call had lasted for less than two minutes, just long enough for him to log in and post the message.

Snowflake could have been anywhere.

Snowflake could have been anyone.

Verba's public message board was its most popular area. Superficially, at least, Snowflake's warning resembled many of the other crank postings that often appeared there. It provoked no alarm.

At first, five different users responded to the warning. Although their messages were addressed to Snowflake, they were posted to the public message board and thus were open to anyone.

TO: Snowflake
FROM: Joyboy
Let me get this straight: You intend to kill somebody. And you announce it to the world ahead of time.
Yeah, right.
Also, let me offer a little literary criticism. I mean, ". . . death stands behind you, silent and unseen . . ." Aren't you a little over-wrought?
Nice handle, by the way. You've almost got it right. Just leave off the first syllable. "Flake" would be perfect.

TO: Snowflake
FROM: DeeTeeDude
You are known. You are exposed.
As an ASSHOLE!!!

TO: Snowflake
FROM: Chaz
You are typical of the amoral trash who pollute this otherwise upstanding institution. I suggest that an ad hoc censorship com-mittee institute a method by which such material be screened before it reaches decent and impressionable central processing units.
In fairness, I must admit that I am much intrigued by the image of the unclothed slut. In bondage. Being leisurely probed. Sure gets a rise out of me.

TO: Snowflake and Chaz
FROM: Portia
I remind you both that today's sexist pigs are tomorrow's pork chops.

TO: Snowflake
FROM: Avatar
This is a rather interesting post. You make some excellent points re: privacy. We are indeed vulnerable, and I am certain that sometime, somewhere, someone will take advantage of our vulnerability just as you describe.

Whether you are that person is highly unlikely.

You talk the talk. Do you walk the walk?

The derisive tone of most of the replies was not unusual. Verba's serious users had little patience for puerility. In the jargon of the net, Snowflake was being flamed.

Snowflake logged into Verba for the second time at five forty-eight the next morning. He immediately went to the public message board, where he browsed the messages that had been posted to his name.

A few minutes later he uploaded his second text.

TO: Flamers
FROM: Snowflake
Allow me to reply.
DEETEEDUDE—Your sarcasm is a dagger in my heart. I'll have to return the favor.
PORTIA—When the cleaver falls, remember: You were the one who suggested the slaughterhouse metaphor.
CHAZ—Great joke. You might say it's to die for.
JOYBOY—Overwrought? Just wait; you ain't seen nothin' yet.
AVATAR—I'll take that as a friendly challenge. You can judge my efforts for yourself: I don't believe you'll be disappointed.

Your thoughtful reply is refreshing. Unfortunately, it grants you no immunity. As with the others, you have been noticed.

Snowflake did not leave the system immediately. He remained on line, at the public message board.

A few minutes later the system received a new message.

TO: Snowflake
FROM: Ziggy
Please stop. Everyone enjoys a good prank, but you are injecting a tone of thuggishness that has no place on this board. It is all the more disturbing because you do it so well.
Clearly you are a very clever and intelligent individual. You are capable of much better than this ugly charade. It is a waste of your own abilities and of this wonderful resource.

Snowflake responded at once. Because of the low traffic at that hour, Verba's advanced computer—a Sun Sparcserver 1000—was able to post messages to the board almost instantaneously. Snowflake and Ziggy had begun a cumbersome dialogue.

TO: Ziggy
FROM: Snowflake
This is not a joke.

TO: Snowflake
FROM: Ziggy
Perhaps we should chat. Forum?

Ziggy was suggesting one of Verba's most popular services. In a forum they would converse in "real time," that is, keystrokes made by each of them would appear instantly on the other's screen.

Others could sit in on the conversation and add their own comments. In effect, Verba would create an electronic meeting room for a discussion between Ziggy and Snowflake with the door wide open for anyone else to enter.

TO: Ziggy
FROM: Snowflake
Let's back-channel.

This was also a direct connection, but it would be restricted to the two of them. No other user would eavesdrop. In effect, Snowflake was suggesting that they enter the room and lock the door behind them.

TO: Snowflake
FROM: Ziggy
Why back-channel?

TO: Ziggy
FROM: Snowflake
Let's say I'm the shy and retiring type.

Ziggy was silent for more than three minutes.

TO: Ziggy
FROM: Snowflake
Still out there?

TO: Snowflake
FROM: Ziggy
Okay, back-channel.

Individually they left the public message board and requested the private connection, which was automatically created.

In an electronic sense, Snowflake and Ziggy were now meeting in person.

Snowflake> You're a woman.

Ziggy> My gender is beside the point.

Snowflake> A man would deny it. Yes, definitely a woman. For one thing, you show a feminine indirectness, a feminine hesitancy to engage. A feminine caution. That's good.

Ziggy> Why so?

Snowflake> Caution is appropriate. Out there is a cold, cruel world. In here too. Especially now that I have decided to assert myself.

Ziggy> Please stop that. Nobody is amused.

Snowflake> I repeat—this is not a joke. But you don't believe me.

Ziggy> Pretend I do believe. Are you willing to talk about this?

Snowflake> Keep it interesting.

Ziggy> Why would you want to kill someone?

Snowflake> Because I can. To make a point. To show that it can be done. Also, there are plenty of smart people on this board. I am especially interested in smart ones.

Ziggy> Why?

Snowflake> Because they think they've got all the angles covered.

Ziggy> So you're smarter than everyone else?

Snowflake> "Smart" does not begin to describe me.

Ziggy>   Ah, you're in a league of your own. A genuine master-
            mind.

Snowflake> That's a fact. Take it as you will.

Ziggy>   How do you plan to go about this?

Snowflake> You're asking me to spoil some great surprises.

Ziggy>   Surprises? Plural?

Snowflake> I set no limits.

Ziggy>   I suppose you plan to just reach through the system and
            commit murder.

Snowflake> That is much closer to the truth than you would think.
            The network serves my purposes up to the moment of
            the coup de grâce. Then some personal contact is nec-
            essary for the handiwork.

Ziggy>   How can you touch us? We are anonymous here.

Snowflake> Anonymity is good only until the moment one is
            noticed.

Ziggy>   I don't like you very much. I wish you would stay off the
            net.

Snowflake> Sorry, that ain't a-gonna happen. Actually, I would sug-
            gest the same to you.

Ziggy>   Why should I stay off the net?

Snowflake> Because it has become a dangerous place. And because
            you would be so easy.

Ziggy>   Don't tell me a superintellect like yourself would settle
            for an easy mark.

Snowflake> This has been your second warning. That's two more
            than most people ever get in this life.

Ziggy>   I am ending the conversation.

Snowflake> Undoubtedly the healthiest impulse you've had in a long
            time. However, it comes a bit too late.

Ziggy>   Why is that?

Snowflake> You have been noticed.

The young woman who used the handle Ziggy terminated her connection to Snowflake in an unusual way: She reached across her desk and switched off the power to her computer.

She watched the monitor screen go gray. The computer's low background hum fell to silence.

She had logged hundreds of hours with Verba and other on-line services. Never before had she dumped out of a session so abruptly—so gracelessly. But Snowflake repelled her: She had felt an overwhelming instinct to be as far from him as possible. Turning off the switch immediately canceled his existence in her universe.

Or so she believed.

Snowflake logged off Verba shortly after he lost his on-line connection with Ziggy. Then he immediately reached the service again, this time through an unlisted number that the system's administrators reserved for technical use. Although such numbers are supposed to be restricted, they may be uncovered by someone using a certain degree of canny persistence.

When he connected, the computer's operating system asked for a password. These, too, are obtainable by someone with a certain amount of canny persistence and guile.

Snowflake typed in a seven-character string, and the computer granted him entry.

This time there were no greetings. He was now past all the public screens, and into the system itself.

He went to work, using the computer's operating utilities to search for every message containing the word "Snowflake" and posted during the past fourteen hours.

Changing or erasing the contents files on the Verba computer required the highest level of access: what is known as "root" or "superuser" status. The password Snowflake used did not allow him those privileges.

He was, however, able to alter the electronic label by which the system identified each uploaded message. This information included the date and time on which the message entered the system.

Snowflake changed the date on each file that the computer retrieved for him. These included every message he had posted, and all the responses to his posts. He backdated these files so that they appeared to be one week older than they actually were.

At six fifty-six he logged off.

Four minutes later, at seven A.M., Verba's powerful main computer began two of its daily housekeeping chores.

The first of these tasks was to scan its directories for text files that had been posted within the past twenty-four hours, and to copy these new messages onto a magnetic tape that a Verba technician would later place in a vault.

These files were one of the main reasons for Verba's existence. The network had been conceived as an ongoing social experiment; the directors of the sponsoring foundation believed that someday the tape archive might provide future researchers with an evolving panoramic portrait of on-line computer users during the last decade of the twentieth century.

This morning, as it scanned for new messages, the computer skipped past those Snowflake had backdated. Neither the messages he had posted nor the responses he had received were copied onto the archive tape.

The computer then executed the second of its daily tasks. During its scan through the directories, it had already marked all message files that had a date more than one week old. That morning those files included the messages with the dates that Snowflake had altered.

It now deleted all the marked files, in keeping with Verba's policy that no post should remain on the system for more than seven days. Instantly, every mention of Snowflake vanished from the system.

Snowflake had ceased to exist. But the man who had used that handle again entered Verba's public-access lines shortly after seven A.M., this time logging in under a different handle.

He had written a "bot"—from "robot"—a script program that would automatically dial and log into Verba. Once it was on line, the bot's actions were indistinguishable from those of a human.

Its task was to watch for several users logging into Verba. The bot would track these targets: It would copy their messages so that "Snowflake" could read them later. If the target entered a forum, all activity in that forum would likewise be recorded for as long as that person was present in the group.

To avoid notice, the bot was instructed to remain on line for no more than an hour at a time, after which it would log out. It would then redial the service, enter under a new name, and resume scanning the system. The bot was even capable of rudimentary conversation if addressed.

The bot allowed "Snowflake" to monitor Verba almost constantly, even while he slept. His targets were six different handles, which he typed into the program's instruction set.

The six targets were:

Chaz
DeeTeeDude
Avatar
Portia
Joyboy
Ziggy

Noticed.

PART II

Salome

April 17–26

1

The corpse on the table wore a pulpy red mask. At least this was how it appeared, first glance. Someone had peeled and scraped the skin from around the forehead and nose and temples, from around the cheeks and jaw and chin.

All the skin: ear to ear, hairline to jaw. The exposed flesh was raw and abraded. It set off the lidless white eyes and the slightly grinning rictus of the lips.

Lee Wade stood a few steps to the side as an assistant M.E. positioned the overhead camera directly above the head of the corpse. The camera was in a pod that hung from the ceiling of the autopsy room, and swung smoothly at the end of an articulated arm. Black wire coiled from the pod to a plastic grip that the M.E. held in his left hand.

The camera's flash burst every time the M.E.'s thumb pressed a black button on the grip.

Whap, a head-and-shoulders shot.

Whap, in tighter now, a close-up.

Whap, left profile.

Whap, right profile.

After each shot the M.E. swung the camera for a different angle. He reminded Wade of a portrait photographer at Sears. Quick and mechanical.

Whap.

The M.E. said, "We didn't find any pieces of skin at the scene, am I right?"

"Right," Wade said.

"Killer is probably Asian, then, that's my guess."

"God damn, that's pretty good," Wade said. "Where do you get that?"

"Looks like he's saving face," the M.E. said, so completely deadpan that Wade—thirty-eight years old, a sergeant of detectives in the San Francisco P.D.—needed a couple of seconds to get it.

"Terrific," Wade said when it finally sank in. The M.E. never broke stride, just kept moving the camera, hitting the button, working his way down the body, *whap, whap, whap.*

A microphone protruded from the same pod that held the camera. The M.E. dictated as he moved the pod and popped the flash.

A well-nourished well-developed Caucasian male in his mid-twenties. Rigor mortis is fully established in the extremities. Fixed lividity is observed throughout the dorsal aspect. A circular puncture wound, approximately one centimeter, can be seen at the lower edge of the areola of the left nipple. A similar wound is present in the corresponding position, upper left posterior.

The two wounds were apparently a matched set, from the single thrust of a long, sharp instrument, similar to an ice pick, that had impaled the victim's heart as it passed through his chest and exited through his back.

He had been dead about twelve hours. Found by a jogger, around six A.M., lying faceup at the base of a eucalyptus tree, near the Twelfth Avenue entrance to Golden Gate Park.

Lee Wade watched as the assistant M.E. picked up a scalpel and began the Y-shaped incision that opened the body from chest to pudendum. About forty minutes later, as he was removing the viscera, the assistant M.E. pointed out a bulge in the upper end of the rectum. He opened the tissue and found that the obstruction was a clear plastic bubble about an inch in diameter.

It resembled—and, in fact, actually was—one of those capsules that can be found in supermarket vending machines, holding trinkets that the machine dispenses for a quarter or fifty cents. Its two halves had been sealed by what was later determined to be cyanoacrylate adhesive: Super Glue.

Inside the capsule, clearly visible, was a curled slip of white paper.

The M.E. used a bone saw to cut through the capsule. With forceps he removed the paper and unrolled it: Paper can preserve fingerprints, although this particular scrap was later found to contain none.

Wade stood at the M.E.'s elbow to see the paper. Printed on the paper, in twelve-point Courier type, was the legend:

```
MEATWARE Version 1
4–16
Taken: 17424        05071
Slain: 17441        05086
```

Lee Wade knew that you sometimes found some pretty strange items up there where the sun don't shine. Bits and pieces that are lost when playtime gets out of hand. But this didn't look like it had gotten there by accident. He kept feeling that it had been put in place for this very moment, waiting to be found. Like a message in a bottle.

"This mean anything to you?" Wade asked the M.E.

"Not a clue."

"Me neither," Lee Wade said. "Somebody's playing games. I hate this shit."

The fingerprints were matched to a Donald Arthur Trask, last known address on Chestnut Street, the Marina District. When Wade parked out front, he saw that it was a small block of apartments, three stories, four flats each. Unlike many others in the Marina, it had survived the 'eighty-nine quake.

D. A. Trask was the name on the mailbox of 3C.

The resident manager, in Apartment 1A, was a Mrs. Alexander. As they walked up, she told Wade that Don Trask was a nice boy who lived alone, never made any trouble, paid the rent on time.

She was a plump old woman with gray hair that strayed out of a bun at the back of her head. She reminded Wade of a picture he had seen, Mrs. Khrushchev, when he was a very young boy.

"He have any friends?" Wade said. "Visitors that showed up more than once or twice?"

"I didn't see any friends," she said.

"What about girls? Boys?"

"I never saw anybody."

"Come on now," Wade said. "You've got a first-floor apartment, right between the front door and the bottom of the stairs. And what, just eleven units to keep track of? You telling me you don't watch who comes and goes?"

"Sure," she said. "All the time. That's why I know Donald didn't have any friends."

She unlocked the door and let him in.

The place was simple and tidy. Mostly Scandinavian furniture, Wade noticed, the kind that you assemble out of a carton. A couple of dishes in the sink, a damp towel hanging from the rail of the shower curtain; otherwise everything seemed to be in place.

It did not look like a crime scene. It was not a place where a man had been stabbed through the heart and then had his face pulled off. The victim had not been killed here.

Wade spent about an hour in the apartment, looking mostly for the pieces of paper that would tell him who Donald Trask was and who he knew and why somebody might have wanted to kill him.

There wasn't much. A packet of letters postmarked Valparaiso,

Indiana: his parents. Another packet from Bloomington, Indiana: his older sister. Canceled checks and a couple of unpaid bills, accounts up-to-date.

Donald Trask had owned a TV, a stereo system, a computer that sat on an oak veneer work station in a corner of the living room.

Wade stood briefly in front of the computer. The monitor was switched off, but the machine itself was humming.

He turned on the monitor and watched the screen slowly fade in.

Lee Wade, at thirty-eight, had been born into the last American generation that confronted computers while still adults, not as infinitely adaptable children. The last generation to whom computers were a confounding phenomenon. It was a fish-or-cut-bait situation, he thought—you either got into the damn things or you didn't.

And he never did. Gradually computers were popping up in police work, on a few desks in the squad room. What he had learned about computers was that when you really had to use one, the first thing you did was find a twenty-two-year-old rookie to handle it.

So when the monitor came to life, Wade's first impression was amazement. Because what he saw was flying toasters. These squadrons of winged toasters that kept moving across the screen. It had to be a joke, he thought, something else was bound to happen. But the scene didn't change, it was just toasters, endless flying toasters, and he was amazed that Donald Trask or anybody else would have sat there watching it.

Lee Wade had never heard of screen savers. He didn't know that nobody watched flying toasters, that if he tapped any one of the computer's keys, the toasters would vanish, and he would see what Donald Trask had been doing before he walked out of his apartment and met his death.

Wade did not touch the keyboard. Instead, he turned off the

monitor, then reached around and found the switch of the computer's power supply, and he turned that off too.

The machine's hum stopped. The silence was a void. Lee Wade had lost his chance to understand not only the murder of the faceless corpse on the autopsy table, but so much else that was happening around him, unseen and unremarked.

2

Kate Lavin's editor, a young man named Terrence, folded around five in the morning. Without a word he went to a corner of the editing booth, curled up on the floor, and went to sleep.

Kate took his place in front of the keyboard and kept working. She went without a break for another two hours, calling up shots from the digital memory of the computer-based Avid editing board. Watching them, replaying them, the images running back and forth, sometimes frame by frame: hot air balloons over New Mexico.

She was a small, lithe woman of thirty-three, in jeans and a plain white T-shirt, with a pager at her belt. Her hair was cut short and neat. She had a very pretty face that many people didn't notice all at once. Most who met her for the first time were drawn immediately to her eyes, which were quick and restless and intelligent.

At seven twenty-three, bleary-eyed, she pushed her chair away from the console. She had been in the booth almost continuously for twenty-one hours.

She still wasn't finished. And the rough cut was due in two hours and thirty-seven minutes.

She stood, stretched, and walked out of the booth. She found herself in a carpeted hallway. On one side of the hall were the doors to two more small rooms identical to the one she had just left. On the other side was a broad window that looked into a control room: a dozen monitors, several reel-to-reel videotape decks, audio mixers, and switching panels.

She walked down the hall, through the fire door at the end, and into a darkened TV studio that was nearly the size of a gymnasium.

More monitors and televisions crouched there, on wall shelves and moveable pedestals. Kate crossed the studio, stepping over cables and electrical wires, past the studio cameras, through a double set of doors at the far end of the studio.

Those doors opened outside. She walked out into the morning. Sausalito, California: Gate Seven, bayside.

The air was damp, and the pavement was slick in the parking lot where she stood. Low clouds were breaking up overhead. Straight ahead was an estuary, beyond that the scruffy green hump of Angel Island, and still farther off the San Francisco skyline, blue and gray across the wide water of the bay.

Kate Lavin stood and breathed the cool air. It braced her, put her in place and time again.

A car was pulling into the lot now. The driver was about Kate's age. He parked and headed toward the front entrance of the studio building, a man on his way to work.

The walkway took him a few yards to the left of where Kate Lavin stood. As he passed, he waved at her, said a quiet hello, and also gave a deferential bob of the head. It was the way an employee might greet his boss.

Because the place was hers. She owned it: the bayfront property, the low, wide building itself with the sign out front that said KL MEDIA, and all that the building contained. Full studio and teleconference facilities, including a pair of satellite uplinks. Complete editing and postproduction facilities, film and video.

Ellis Hoile did not scrimp.

It started about a year after they were married, with Ellis surfing the high tide of royalties from his commercial software successes: a graphics program and a database manager that both sold hundreds of thousands of copies. She wanted to make documentary films. Ellis got interested in the technical aspects of production.

He was not a man who could resist electronic goodies. By the time he was finished buying equipment, they owned a video facility as advanced as any on the West Coast. They were in business.

They divorced after four years. Her idea, but Ellis stood aside and let it happen. Though the studio represented much more than half their assets, Ellis had offered it to her in the settlement. He made the breakup easy: probably easier than it should have been, she thought.

She sometimes wondered why he had done this. Perhaps it was an act of love, his gesture to preserve their friendship. Or maybe he had tired of the studio the way he eventually grew jaded with all his toys.

For whatever reason, she had walked away with the studio, free and clear. A manager ran the day-to-day operation, because Kate wanted to keep making films: That was her greatest satisfaction, her pleasure. She was good at it.

She walked back into the building now. She washed her face in a lavatory sink, dried it, and returned to the booth.

Terrence was still curled up in the corner. The clock on the wall read seven thirty-four, and her coffee was cold.

The film was a fifty-one-minute documentary commissioned by a cable TV network. She had promised to feed the rough cut by satellite at ten that morning, to give the client a first look at the product. It wasn't a hard-and-fast deadline, but she didn't like to miss any kind of deadline, and at $1,400 an hour, she hated to waste satellite time.

The film was ready except for a three-and-a-half-minute sequence that would close the first segment. It was a key moment that would set up the rest of the film: She wanted a lyrical passage, set to music, to establish the balloons' grace and beauty.

She had chosen Mozart's Symphony No. 35, the second movement, which like the balloons themselves seemed at once whimsical and majestic. And she had saved some of her most spectacular shots of balloons traversing the desert landscape outside Albuquerque.

But it wasn't as easy as slapping together beautiful music and beautiful pictures. The shots not only should be cut to the pace of the score, but somehow had to match its shifting moods.

This sequence was the keystone of the film, she was sure of it. It had to be right.

Until the late 1980s, what she was about to attempt would have been impossible in two hours. Film documentaries were assembled on Steenbeck editing tables. Editing rooms were festooned with hundreds of film strips, individual shots that had to be examined, run through a viewer, then literally cut and glued onto a working reel.

Electronic film editing—inventions like the Avid, the Rank scanner, and George Lucas's Editdroid—had changed all that. Images captured on film negatives were digitized and stored on computer hard drives, with each frame assigned an individual time code. An editor used a keyboard to retrieve shots, to edit and assemble a sequence, perhaps several different versions of a sequence.

An Avid was based on an Apple Macintosh. The computer handled all the mechanics of editing, but no machine was capable of artistic impulses. That remained a human enterprise governed by human intelligence and intuition and emotion.

And by human energy.

Kate Lavin sat at the keyboard again and tried to force herself past weariness. Concentrate on the work, push aside everything else, focus. She had done this many times. And in a few minutes she was doing it again.

She worked. There was only the work, the shots, and the music. She forgot fatigue, and she forgot time.

Then she laid in the last shot, a long aerial of a single balloon tracking past a sandstone mesa, the camera pulling back to reveal fifteen, twenty more balloons floating over the landscape as Mozart's strings rose, surged, and faded.

She looked at the clock: nine thirty-seven.

She tapped a command, sat back, and watched the sequence from start to finish. Then once more.

Nine forty-five.

She stood, shook Terrence awake, and walked out into the hall. She knocked on the glass door of the control booth, and when a technician opened it, Kate told her, "This sweetheart's booked on the bird, ten o'clock, Galaxy 4—put it up there, I think it's ready to fly."

Then she walked straight out of the building and straight home, where she fell asleep before she got her shoes off.

She awoke to the light trill of her pager. The room was dark. She had to fumble for the bedside lamp before she could read the message.

It was a single word:

PATSY

This had to be Ellis. Whenever he wanted to talk he would send a name, the first name of a girl singer, a different name every time. Bigger the singer—at least, as Ellis saw her—the more important the call. So not only did you have to know your singers, you had to know what Ellis thought of them.

He had been doing this for years with her, no reason why except that with Ellis nothing could be simple.

She thought, Patsy. Patsy.

Patsy Cline. Better not let this one slide.

She tried his voice number. Busy.

The clothes felt like she'd been wearing them for a month. She peeled them off and padded naked into the kitchen. She lived on a houseboat at the end of the Gate Seven pier, a five-minute walk from the studio.

On one side of the kitchen was a sliding glass door. Outside was the black expanse of the bay, the distant lights of San Francisco.

She drank from a bottle of water in the refrigerator and then tried Ellis on the kitchen phone.

She said, "E?"

And he said, "What happened to dinner?"

"Dinner," she said, trying to clear her head. "Dinner! Oh, shit, E, I blew it."

"Yes, you did." His voice was amiable.

"I pulled a marathon in the edit booth—I've been sleeping. It just got away from me."

"I don't mind," he said.

And it was true, she thought: He really didn't mind. Not much disturbed Ellis. In a way it was a wonderful trait, to be so amenable, so impervious to the little peeves and passions that disturbed other people's lives.

On the other hand, those disturbances told you that somebody cared. When you met resistance, you knew something was in there. At least you had a reaction.

More than anything else, this was why she had left. Not the petty annoyances, the eccentricities. But because with Ellis you never knew.

"What time is it?" she asked now.

"Almost eleven."

"Oh, hell," she said. "I'm sorry, E. I really am."

"No problem."

"How about tomorrow night? I could come by, pick up something on the way over."

"Up to you."

"Come on, you want to do this or not?"

"Yeah," he said. "I do. I've got something to show you."

Right, she thought. *And I'm looking forward to seeing you, too.*

"Don't tell me you bought a new toy," she said. She could hear it in his voice.

"Actually, I made this one." He was enthused. "You've really got to see this. The toy to end all toys."

3

Jane Regalia woke a little after daybreak, pulled on an Aran knit sweater, and climbed down from the sleeping loft. She crossed over to the kitchen counter—the cabin was one big room, with the loft overhanging along one side, forming a nook where she kept a small office.

She was in her forties, a slim woman, now going to gaunt. She had always looked younger than her age, but she wasn't sure that was true any longer. It had been a rotten four months, the worst of her life, beginning on Christmas Eve, when her husband informed her not only that he had a twenty-six-year-old girlfriend, but that he intended to marry her and start a family.

She stood at the kitchen window. The view outside extended no more than two or three feet. The fog was in, thick, the way it was every morning and evening up in the hills of the North Coast, bringing with it a chill that penetrated straight to the bone.

She walked outside to where the firewood was stacked, mossy oak in two neat ricks behind the A-frame. The cabin sat alone, halfway up a forested canyon, about a mile from the Pacific and more than one hundred miles up the coast from San Francisco. It was in a clearing surrounded by redwoods. At almost any time the upslope breezes carried the scent of sea salt and earthy moistness and evergreen tang, the cleanest air she had ever smelled.

Even with the fog and the chill, it was perfect. Exactly what she needed: a place to be alone and think, to examine the pieces of her life, decide which of them she was going to reconstruct. And which others she would discard.

She brought in an armload of wood and arranged several pieces on the andirons above the embers in the stone fireplace. She threw on some kindling. Soon fire was licking up around the wood.

Then she walked to the nook beneath the sleeping loft, and she sat at the computer keyboard on her desk.

The computer was already running. A voice mail program allowed her to use it as an answering machine, so she rarely turned off the power.

Within a few seconds the modem was beeping out the tones of a long-distance call to San Francisco. It buzzed and warbled, and then she was connected.

Verba Interchange.

She logged in and immediately entered her e-mail account, as she did every morning soon after she woke, and several times a day afterward. In most ways she lived frugally, but she did allow herself the indulgence of these long-distance charges. The computer was a link to the world. And e-mail was addictive, she had found.

The index of her mail folder showed two new messages from the night before.

The first was from her husband. She opened the file.

Dearest Jane:

Had trouble sleeping last night, and tonight is no different. My mind has been in turmoil. I am afflicted with doubts and guilt. A hundred times last night I wanted to call. I would have, too, except for your prohibition. That seems needless. Of course I understand and honor your request for space and time. I don't wish to intrude on your well-deserved solitude. However, surely the occasional phone call would threaten neither of us.

To tell the truth, I despise this method of communication. It seems so impersonal. I spend half my time correcting typing mistakes. I feel like I'm talking to some dumb machine, and then I fire my heartfelt missive out into the ozone without even knowing whether you have received it. At least let me write a real letter!

Are you well? I have thought of you often, and tried to imagine your bucolic existence. It must be lovely up there.

Let me be completely honest and share with you the reason for my anxiety. Are you "seeing" anyone? I know this is none of my business, but I can't get suspicion out of my mind.

It's been years since we were in Mendocino together. I could drive up this weekend, stay in a motel, of course, what do you say?

Your loving husband,
Albert

She began to compose her reply in the editing window of the mail program.

Albert:

I certainly wish that you had been afflicted with just a few doubts and guilt before you ruined my life. I do not want to hear your voice. I do not want to see your handwriting. If you dare to show up here, you will lose me forever. This is my place. I have found a certain tranquillity here, and if you spoil it with your physical presence, you will have earned my everlasting enmity.

The suggestion that I should account to you for my conduct here is offensive. However, for the record, I am not "seeing" anyone. In fact, that is literally true. The cabin is isolated. I am completely alone here, and unknown. I actually see nobody un-

til I choose to drive into Point Arena for food and to check my
P.O. box.

Your messages always get here. I am very comfortable with this
method of communication. It suits me. And you should be grate-
ful that I have dragged you into the last half of the twentieth
century.

Albert sounded different this time, she thought. Solicitous, almost
fawning.

Doubts and guilt?

Then it came to her. Just a guess, but she knew that she was
right: Albert had been dumped.

She added a final line.

Don't worry, I read you loud and clear.

JR

4

That morning, Roberta Hudgins caught a taxi at the TransBay Terminal. The driver was Mexican, or maybe Guatemalan, Salvadoran—new to the city, anyway, judging from the slack look she got when she told him the address, Tesla Street, off Kearney.

"*Qué?*" he said.

"Telegraph Hill," she said.

He gave it a thought, and in a second his face lit. His right hand started to climb, spiraling up, a corkscrew motion that didn't stop until he reached the headliner of the cab. Way up there.

"You got it, sugar," she said, and he peeled up Fremont.

Traffic was sludgy: The time was a little after eight, the morning rush just starting to peak. This was a couple of hours earlier than she usually made the trip. She hadn't told Ellis Hoile that she'd be late. She knew he wouldn't mind. He might not even notice: Time of day meant nothing to this man.

The driver knew his stuff after all. Fremont to Folsom Street, a few blocks down Folsom, then he was turning left onto the Embarcadero, hustling along.

To her right was the bay, intermittently visible in the narrow gaps between the long wharf sheds. Up ahead was Coit Tower, a cylindrical concrete shaft that rose straight up from the green crown of Telegraph Hill.

Right below the tower was Ellis Hoile's place. She could see it from here, wedged in among the other buildings that clung chockablock to the side of the hill.

She guided the driver off the Embarcadero, up into the maze of the hillside. The streets were steep and narrow. Buildings crouched shoulder to shoulder, right up to the sidewalks.

The neighborhood had once been home to Italian fishermen who walked down the hill every morning to their boats. Family homes and duplexes had lined the streets. But in the past thirty years many of the old houses had given way to condos and apartments, squat cubes that occupied every square foot of their building lots.

Tesla Street was quiet as the taxi crawled up. It was a narrow street, and constantly crammed with parked cars. Halfway up the block she told the driver okay, this is it. Straight above them was Coit Tower, reaching to the sky.

She paid him and stepped out in front of Ellis Hoile's house. From there it didn't look like much, a little bungalow of white stucco. Bars on the windows. Blinds closed, as usual.

Roberta fished the key from her purse and opened the front door. It was solid hardwood, a couple of inches thick, buffed to a shine—a gorgeous door, the first clue that this might not be your standard stucco bungalow.

She walked inside and shut the door behind her. Dark.

She flipped on the lights. Inside the front door, where you might expect a living room, you found yourself, instead, on a broad open balcony that extended the width of the house. Straight ahead, beyond the edge of the balcony, was a panoramic window.

On which the shades were always closed.

Roberta began to go down the black iron staircase at one end of the balcony. The house was built down the side of Telegraph Hill. The lower floor opened up even more, so as you descended from street level you entered the main living area—if you could call it living, what Ellis Hoile did there.

She could smell coffee brewing as she got to the bottom of the stairs. More murkiness down there. The only light was the sickly computer-screen glow that washed Ellis Hoile's face as he peered at the screen, his fingertips poised over the keyboard. He was a man in his thirties, rumpled hair, a two-day beard. Looked like he'd been pulling another all-nighter.

He didn't even glance at her. Something on that screen had his attention. Something usually did.

He was sitting in his cubbyhole. She didn't know what else to call it. At the far end of the main room, beside another huge picture window—where anyone else would put a couple of sofas and a few chairs, face them out toward that view—Ellis Hoile had placed six desks, arranged in a horseshoe shape. His swivel chair sat inside the U.

The desktops were covered. With computers, to begin with, three computers and monitors, and a printer and a fax machine and a copy machine, and electronic equipment that she couldn't name. Plus stacks of papers, books, manuals, stacked so high that they almost formed three walls around Hoile inside. A cubbyhole. Beyond the desks were shelves and more shelves of electronic equipment, video cameras, gadgets, tape decks, and pieces and parts of all these things.

She flipped on more lights down here. His eyes didn't leave that screen. He had to know that she was there, but he just kept staring at the monitor, entranced as always, staring, biting his lower lip.

He was not a people person, she thought. To put it mildly. She told herself that it actually made her job easier, because with Ellis Hoile she didn't have to waste time on small talk. Besides, he was an abnormally smart man. You had to make allowances.

Still, it bothered her, being ignored this way. Twice a week, for the past six months, she had been going there to clean the man's house, wash his clothes, even cook some of his meals—having been hired, crazily enough, by his ex-wife, who had wanted to see the man's life stay on the tracks.

She told herself that by now she should be used to his strange ways, but she also thought that she deserved better.

She went into the kitchen, poured him a cup of the coffee, found a blueberry muffin in the bread box, and put that on a plate. She carried the coffee and the muffin to him on a tray and put it down on the low stack of books near his elbow.

Now his fingers were firing away on the keyboard.

She was about to head back to the kitchen, when she noticed a narrow line of butter-toned light around the edge of one of the window curtains. It set her off somehow: that pathetic little sliver of sunshine in the dark room.

She did what she had been wanting to do since the first time she saw this place.

She walked around to the window, grabbed the curtain, and pulled it back. Daylight exploded into the room.

Roberta Hudgins stood at the window and took in the view. It reached right across the water to the East Bay. Straight ahead the Bay Bridge arched toward Oakland. Light glinted off the windshields of cars on the bridge's upper deck. Out toward Alcatraz a Red-and-White ferry was plowing toward Marin County. In closer were the docks, the Embarcadero, Fisherman's Wharf looking like a collection of carnival bric-a-brac, and then the windows of homes and apartments and office buildings that were just down the hill, seeming almost close enough to touch.

For maybe the hundredth time since she had met him, she had to fight back the urge to ask Ellis Hoile if he wanted to trade houses for a while. Tell him, hey, one dark room is the same as another. Got a three-bedroom off the M. L. King Parkway for you, be perfect, you can board up the windows, feel right at home, you'll be happy as a clam.

She turned away from the view.

Ellis Hoile finally had his face off the screen. He was looking at her over his shoulder. He seemed mildly amused. A thin little smile, anyway: He would not be a bad-looking man if he was ever spruced up.

"Hello, Mrs. Hudgins," he said.

"Uh-huh," she said.

She went into the kitchen and started going through the boxes of food that sat on the counter. Ellis Hoile had his groceries delivered. Twice a week she fixed meals that she put away in the freezer. He wasn't particular: Anything that would go into a casserole dish, that he could stick in the microwave, was fine with him.

She cleared dirty dishes from the sink, put away the groceries, started the dishwasher. She went back into the living area.

It was dark again. Ellis Hoile had yanked the curtain on his million-dollar view.

He was burrowed back in the cubbyhole. Back in that ugly glow. She stood and watched him for a minute, staring at the screen once more, fingers pounding the keys and pausing and then pounding again. In a strange way, he looked happy.

But that was Ellis Hoile. Strange, all right.

5

Jane Regalia spent most of that day on a long hike through the hills behind her cabin. She didn't return to the computer until late in the evening.

She realized then that she had never read the second new message in her e-mail folder that morning—Albert's letter had distracted her.

She opened the mail index now. There it was, the second message: sender, time, and subject:

stoma@verba.org 03:26 Surprise!

She didn't recognize the handle. She wondered if she had encountered Stoma before. Maybe they had once exchanged messages.

No, she thought. Stoma—she would've remembered that one.

She opened the file. It contained a single line—

Give this a whirl

—and the notation that Stoma had attached a binary file to the message.

This wasn't uncommon. Encoding methods allowed users to send photos, line drawings, programs, even music and sound effects, as ordinary e-mail.

The mail program asked:

Do you want to decode and receive the attachment?

PHILLIP FINCH

She typed:

Y

At once the hard disk drive began to click. It worked for several minutes, downloading and decoding the file.

She logged out when it was finished, and her call to Verba disconnected.

She saw that TRY_ME.EXE was the full name of the file that Stoma had sent. The suffix meant that it was an executable: a program.

This had to be a mistake, she told herself. Stoma had confused her with somebody else. This meant that it was none of her business, really. She'd have to send Stoma a message, straighten it out.

But she was curious. And she wasn't sleepy yet.

She decided to open the program, see what it was about.

She crossed over to the kitchen and put a kettle of water on one burner for the cup of herb tea that she usually drank before she went to bed.

Back at her desk she booted Stoma's program with the command:

TRY_ME

The hard drive began to perk, feeding thousands of lines of software code into the computer's memory banks. The monitor screen went black, and in a few moments showed the message:

Want to try me?
(Y)es or (N)o

She typed:

Y

The screen responded:

Good

Again the hard drive activated, and again the screen changed. It dissolved to black for a moment, then brought up an image that appeared to be a steel catwalk against a black background. A single bare overhead bulb illuminated a portion of the catwalk in a pool of light, as if it were suspended in darkness.

It was a computer-rendered graphic, highly detailed, drawn from the perspective of somebody standing on the catwalk and looking toward the light. The catwalk seemed to be made of a perforated metal, honeycomb-like, with a single low railing at one side—the other side was unprotected. The modeling of the shadows from the overhead bulb gave the scene a three-dimensional, photo-realistic look.

A nice piece of work, she thought. If you liked precarious steel catwalks.

Then a man said: "Move the mouse."

The words nearly made her jump: a robust male voice, coming from two stereo speakers that were attached to the computer's sound card.

She didn't move for a few seconds.

Again, the man's voice: "Go ahead, use the mouse."

She put her left hand on the plastic mouse that sat beside the keyboard, and she moved it slightly. The view on the screen shifted, moving forward, toward the bare bulb above the catwalk. She stopped, and moved the mouse a couple of inches to the right on her desk. Again the view shifted, this time panning to the right, as if she herself were standing on the catwalk and turning around.

"Very good," the man's voice said.

She kept moving the mouse, and the view kept panning, until she was facing the opposite direction on the catwalk, toward another bare bulb above, a second pool of light outlining the catwalk in the darkness.

Okay, I get the idea. I'm supposed to be on a metal catwalk. I can move around. I can see where I'm going.

This had to lead somewhere. She pushed the mouse forward and began to move along the catwalk. A scuffling noise came from the speakers—shoes on steel—as she moved toward this second bulb, then through this second pool of light and into its penumbra. The catwalk seemed narrow, and she advanced slowly.

It's only a picture, she thought. But she was still careful not to step off the open edge.

Now a shape resolved itself in the dimness ahead of her: the end of the catwalk, a concrete landing. But she couldn't cross over onto the landing—it was enclosed by what seemed to be a wire mesh screen, forming a cage with a black door frame directly ahead of her, the door itself more of this same heavy wire mesh.

But she didn't know how to open the door. She didn't know if she wanted to.

Because at the far end of the landing, almost lost in the shadows, she could make out the shape of a man. Watching.

"You don't want to just stand there," said the voice from the speakers—maybe it was supposed to be the figure in the picture. "Bad idea."

The voice sounded calm, level, but somehow malevolent.

She backs a few steps away from the wire mesh. The man steps forward, still in shadows. He reaches out and pushes open the wire mesh door and steps onto the catwalk.

Something chills her, the way he moves.

As he gets closer she can see that he carries a club. Maybe a pipe or a baseball bat.

"I would get out of here if I were you," he says, and though she really has nowhere to go—there's just the catwalk and the black emptiness beyond it—she turns and begins to move away from the man, back toward the lights.

Her feet ring on the steel. She moves faster, and the footfalls come quicker. Not just her own. She can make out a second set of footsteps behind her, deliberate, insistent.

He's coming after her.

She runs.

Behind her, the man picks up his pace.

She passes beneath the first bulb, through its glare and into the dim gap between the two pools of light. He's closer, his footfalls louder. Almost on her now as she passes beneath the second light.

And she stumbles. She's pitching forward, slamming down to the steel honeycomb of the catwalk, tumbling.

She rolls over, to find the man standing over her. The overhead light is directly behind him, so he's just a faceless dark form, indistinct but somehow full of menace.

For a moment neither of them moves.

Then he raises the club—it's a heavy pipe, she can tell for sure now—and he raises it above his head, swings it down toward her head, and she screams. . . .

At her keyboard Jane Regalia realized, no, hell, that's not a scream, it's the teakettle.

The kettle was steaming, whistling hard. She hadn't even noticed it until then.

She got up, poured water into a teapot, and stood by the table as it steeped. In her mind she kept seeing the catwalk, the dark figure of the man. She kept hearing those footsteps.

Vile, she thought.

She poured the tea and drank it before she returned to her desk. The monitor screen read:

Try me again?
    (Y) or (N)

She jabbed N. Hard.

Then she deleted the program from the system: even checked the directory to be sure that it was gone.

That night, as Jane Regalia slept, the intruder pillaged her life.

The large program file from "Stoma" had contained a second, smaller program that was automatically activated when Jane Regalia entered TRY_ME.

In the jargon, TRY_ME had been a Trojan horse. The small program it concealed was a "daemon." The daemon immediately found a place in the computer's electronic memory, and copied itself into a sector of the hard disk, where the system stored hidden files. It had remained intact even after she purged TRY_ME from her machine, and lay dormant, monitoring the system for the precise conditions that would activate it.

That happened at the moment the computer's internal clock reached 04:00.00. Instantly, the daemon reacted by temporarily altering the system's internal settings—an operation that required milliseconds—so that input through the modem would be received as if it had been typed at the keyboard.

The rogue program then set the modem to answer any phone call on the first ring. It searched for, and silenced, the modem's speaker. This, too, was a near-instant altering of software switches.

For the next thirty minutes anyone phoning into the computer from outside would have full access to the machine and its stored files.

Jane Regalia slept on, oblivious.

Two minutes later, a call connected silently. Only the flickering of red diodes on the face of the modem signaled the event.

The caller was the man who used the handle Stoma, sometimes Snowflake. He was now operating the computer as if its keyboard were in front of him. He had reached through the phone line to control the machine.

He began scanning her files and directories, copying them directly into his own computer.

Jane Regalia had embraced the concept of the computer. She used it for dozens of tasks, from correspondence, to analyzing her diet, to balancing her checkbook and paying her bills.

Along the way she had entrusted to it some of the most private, most telling details of her life. They were facts and feelings, statistics and thoughts.

They were her secrets—this was *her*.

Now, as she slept, the intruder began scanning her files and directories, copying them directly into his own machine.

This went on for nearly half an hour, the disk drive working, yielding up what she had stored there in the certainty that it was safe from prying eyes.

Then he disconnected and was gone, without a trace of what he had done.

6

Kate Lavin showered, brushed her teeth, and carefully blow-dried her hair. She grabbed a blouse and a pair of slacks from the closet—wondering what was right to wear for a late dinner with an ex-husband—then put back the blouse and slacks and took out a green silk dress, DKNY. Telling herself, What the hell, why not?

She and Ellis had been divorced for a year, married for four years before that, and had known each other more than half their lives.

And she still wasn't sure what they meant to each other.

She knew that Ellis was special. She had always been attracted to extraordinary people, and Ellis Hoile was at the top of that list.

He could make her laugh. He could dazzle her, he could awe her, he always taught her something. He was never far from her thoughts. She sometimes worried about him—which was funny, because Ellis in many ways was supremely capable.

Ellis was part of her life, and always would be.

His feelings were less clear to her. He cared about her in his own way. He depended on her in his own way. But he was not made for devotion or loving attention. He was not made to be needful. It was just not in him.

Kate slipped on a pair of pumps, spread on pale lipstick. After a moment of hesitation she dropped her diaphragm and a tube of Orthogynol into her purse. She had spent the night with him a few times since the divorce, never planned, something that seemed right at the time. She had no idea whether it would happen again that night.

This was another way that divorce complicated things: all the decisions about how she and Ellis were supposed to act, what they were supposed to ask of each other.

Getting divorced had been easy. *Being* divorced was a lot thornier.

She knew that Ellis didn't torture himself this way, trying to figure out the relationship. He would spend hours tracing circuits on a board until he had the thing pinned down and grasped, but in matters of the heart he was happily vague. He was much too willing to let it be.

This was something that you had to accept if you wanted to be close to Ellis Hoile. You learned to live with unanswered questions.

She unlocked the big front door on Tesla Street, using the key she had carried during the five years she and Ellis had lived together there. He had never asked her to return it.

She carried the food downstairs. He was there in the living-room-turned-workshop, sitting near the window, watching a monitor while his left hand moved a control on a black metal cabinet: a device she didn't recognize, with dials and digital displays.

But she didn't take in the details, because she also saw, hallelujah, the curtains pulled back, the big, beautiful bridge filling that window.

He turned away from the monitor screen and looked up at her, then rose to greet her. He wore rumpled khakis a size too large, and a plaid shirt. When she kissed his cheek she saw that he had shaved.

You would not make much of this in any other man, maybe. Presentable clothes and a shave. But for Ellis Hoile it was pulling out all the stops. He was even giving her, for a few hours, the view from this room that she had loved so much.

She said, "Looking good, E, very sharp."

"Sure thing," he said. And then, like a kid in a grade school play suddenly remembering his lines: "You look great yourself, Kate."

"Thank you, Ellis."

She brought the bags of food into the dining room. The table was already cleared, except for two place settings of her old china and silver. Ellis had been ready to give her this in the settlement, too, but she had insisted that he keep all the furnishings. She knew that he would never replace most of them, and she had hoped that maybe owning the right dishes and towels and furniture would somehow keep him in a half-civilized state.

On the kitchen counter was a bottle of Chandon in an ice bucket—probably from the case she had left behind—and two tulip-stemmed glasses. She opened the bottle, poured some wine into the glasses.

He followed her into the kitchen and took one of the glasses when she gave it to him.

She drank from her own.

"This is very nice, E," she said. "I appreciate it, I really do. I'm charmed."

He gave a boyish shrug.

The wine felt good in her. Silly, maybe, but seeing that china on the table made her feel almost nostalgic. It also made her feel as if she belonged there for the next few hours.

She was glad she had brought the diaphragm.

He helped her spoon the food from the take-out cartons onto their plates. They sat and ate. Fast. She was hungry, and anyway, Ellis was not a man for ceremony, especially at the table.

She ate plenty, took a second and then third glass of the wine. She felt good, relaxed and warm.

With someone else, at that moment, she'd have reached across the table and squeezed his hand. They would have gone to the sofa, sipped wine and talked, and probably more.

But with Ellis the etiquette of the situation was different.

She said, "Okay, hotshot, let's see this new gizmo."

She followed him back into the living room—God, her incredible living room, which since her departure had become an incredible jumble, more cluttered every time she saw it—over to a workbench near the window.

He sat at the black box beside the window. The box was a metal cabinet about the size of a briefcase, painted in a black crinkle finish. Two digital LED displays, a set of switches and knobs.

Two video cables ran to a long antenna on a tripod, pointed out the window. Another set of cables ran to a PC, and the computer was connected to an NEC multisync computer monitor. The NEC showed . . .

. . . *The Partridge Family,* she thought, *are you kidding me*?

"This is a modified Van Eck video scanner," Ellis said. "I found the plans in this ten-year-old Dutch journal, and it sounded great, until I saw that Van Eck left out some of the crucial components.

"But I got around that. It generates an oscillation, you combine that with the electromagnetic radiation off a TV, any kind of cathode ray tube, it restores the horizontal and vertical sync so you get the video back."

This meant almost nothing to her. She could see that the picture was a little grainy, like broadcast TV when you were nearly out of range. The horizontal hold looked like it was starting to slip; Ellis fiddled with one of the knobs, and the picture pulled into place.

She said, "Where's the audio?"

"No audio. This comes off the CRT, it's just the video."

"So we're sitting here watching *The Partridge Family* with no sound, like a couple of brain-dead assholes."

"No," he said, and he was grinning, pleased with himself, "we're watching the radiation from a TV where some other brain-dead assholes are watching *The Partridge Family*. There's a big difference."

He could see that she didn't get it.

"But look," he said, "if that doesn't grab you, we'll check in somewhere else down the hill."

He stood at the window. He was holding what looked like an infrared remote control, and he began tapping a button there. The antenna began moving, very minutely, on the tripod.

She could see now that the antenna sat on a two-way power-head tripod. She had a couple of them at the studio. Two actuators controlled the tilt and pan of the camera—or, in this case, the antenna—in response to the commands you punched on the remote. That much she understood.

The Partridges went away on the screen. Now it was just fuzz. Ellis kept moving the antenna, glancing back and forth between the monitor and the window.

Another image appeared on the screen. Larry King, moving his mouth. She could barely make it out at first, but Ellis tapped the remote a couple of times, the antenna shifted almost imperceptibly on the tripod, and Larry snapped into focus.

And two thoughts came to her at once as she realized what was going on.

First, he had not opened the curtains to give her the view, damn him, he just wanted to see where the antenna was pointing.

This upset her, but she didn't have time to dwell on it, because at the same time she realized exactly what he was doing.

The antenna was aimed into a home. Through the walls. Ellis was actually eavesdropping on the picture from somebody else's TV.

"So far I'm good out to six hundred meters," he said. "But I can improve on that. Use a super-high-gain antenna. And I've got some ideas for the circuitry. The big thing is refining the search algorithms. And frequency discrimination—I've got some ideas on that too. I'm pretty sure I can get the reach out to fourteen hundred meters, no problem."

Fourteen hundred meters, nearly a mile.

"This is impressive, E, it really is," she said. And she meant it, the idea that he could have created something like this.

He was moving the antenna again. She went over and stood beside him. The antenna was aimed at an apartment house, down near the bottom of Telegraph Hill. Almost immediately he got another picture. Robin Leach, *Lifestyles of the Rich and Famous.*

A few more taps of the remote. He was scanning across the top floor of the apartment building.

Tap tap. Rush Limbaugh.

A few more taps. Video game, Super Mario Brothers.

More taps. Male-on-male porn tape.

She added: "But I have to tell you, I don't get the purpose."

"Come on," he said. "Come *on,* you have to get it."

Tap tap. Tap. A commercial spot, Jane Fonda's new workout video.

"If you're trying to make a point," she said, "that there's a lot of people out there filling their heads with dreck every night, well, I've got news for you, nobody's going to argue with you on that one."

"I'm not trying to make a point," he said. He was watching the screen, tapping. *Celebrity Bloopers and Practical Jokes.* "This is observation."

"Yes," she said, "you're observing a lot of dreck."

"No. I'm observing people. The old heads, back in the sixties, they had this saying—you are what you eat. Bullshit. You are what you watch, that's a hell of a lot closer to the truth."

He sounded intense; this was unusual, to see him wound up about anything.

He said, "Show me what you put on the screen in front of you, what you watch and what you turn off, inside of a month I'll know what kind of person you are."

He stopped long enough to tap MTV, Pearl Jam, onto the monitor.

"That might not have been true twenty years ago," he said, "when all we had was three broadcast networks and everybody was forced to watch the same crap. But now we've got cable, we've got videotapes, our choices are a lot more refined and a lot more distinctive.

"Wait a couple of years, you'll have five hundred channels and the Internet coming down a fiber-optic line into your living room. Then I won't need a month to figure out who you are. Let me know what you choose to watch for just a day, I'll have you nailed."

A few more taps. Now the screen showed . . . numbers. But she could barely make them out.

He left the window, fiddled with a couple of the dials on the console of the black cabinet.

Those numbers looked much clearer now. She could even see the black arrow of a cursor gliding across what looked like an IRS Form 1040.

She realized what she was watching. Not TV or cable; it was a computer monitor. Somewhere down the hill, someone was using one of the computer tax programs that let you file an electronic IRS return.

She was watching a stranger do his taxes.

Down the hill, the stranger scrolled up to the first page of the form. She could read the names, a husband and wife, and their address and social security numbers. She read the names and birth dates of their two children, and their incomes.

It was like looking over somebody's shoulder.

No, worse: It was like peeping through somebody's open window.

And even worse than that, when she thought about it. Because somebody who doesn't pull the shades down should expect a little scrutiny from the neighbors. This poor sucker was just sitting in a room, behind four walls, believing that he was alone.

She turned away from the screen. She couldn't watch any more. She felt as if she owed those people a call tomorrow, an apology.

"See," Ellis said, "it's not all dreck."

Okay, she thought, *I get it now.*

But I still don't get why .

He was working the remote again, moving away from the tax return. She didn't want to see any more though. The scanner scared her. It seemed dirty—just seemed wrong.

Ellis apparently couldn't get enough of it. She wished that he would leave the thing, turn it off, and take her into his arms, kiss her, and lead her to bed.

But he was engrossed in the device.

She had gotten used to this all their years together. She had learned not to take it personally.

She decided she would wait for him, at least a little while. She wandered around the room, into the horseshoe formed by his computer desks.

Among the computers she found a machine she hadn't seen before, about the size of a desktop PC, but without a monitor, no disk drives . . .

. . . a telephone handset, a coax cable screwed into the back of the chassis, what was this, and what was it doing at his work space?

He glanced over and saw her looking at it.

"Another new toy," he said.

"You didn't make this one," she said.

"No, that was an acquisition."

"You mind if I ask?" she said. Almost before she could get the question out, he said, "That's a cellular test set."

"Cellular," she said, "like in phone."

"Right," he said, looking a little abashed, as if she had caught him at what he wasn't supposed to be doing. "A test set, the cellular companies use them, cops, too, sometimes. Basically it monitors usage, it identifies the serial number of any cell phone involved in any call you pick out, tells you what cell it originates from. I've got an antenna on the roof; it works great at this elevation, I've got a clear shot at calls involving any cell within line of sight."

Line of sight, she thought, that would take in at least half the city, much of Marin County and the East Bay, halfway down the San Francisco Peninsula. . . .

"Don't tell me this is legal too."

"Not exactly. But I had a friend who owed me a big favor, I pried it loose from him. It's a real gas, the things it'll do."

"What for?" she said.

"The companies want to know who's using their equipment at any given moment. The cops, well, you can imagine . . ."

"I mean, what are *you* doing with it?"

"It's a game," he said to her. "I guess you could say it's my newest phreak. People, the ultimate phreak. You pick out a cellular call, any one. You try to figure out who the people are, as much as you can. Sometimes you start with just the phone number. Or they might say something that helps. Sometimes they'll key in the code for their voice mail, that's always interesting, once you can hack in there."

She couldn't believe this, the grin he got, the delight. Listening to other people's voice-mail messages.

"Anyway, you take it from there," he said. "You try to learn everything you can about them. It's amazing what's out there, just in the public domain. You wouldn't believe it—real estate trans-actions, all kinds of license applications, death claims, the header information off credit reports—everything's in a database somewhere. Then, along the way, if you get a social security number, that's it, with that you can get almost anything."

He was getting enthused in spite of himself.

He said, "You can put together *dossiers* on people, things they didn't even know about themselves."

"Tacky, Ellis."

"And you don't have to be Sam Spade either, just sit down at a keyboard and call the right numbers."

"Cheesy, Ellis."

"It's something to do, that's all."

"When did this start?"

"Last summer sometime."

Just after the divorce.

"What do you do with your data?"

"Nothing. Just see how much I can compile. It's an exercise."

"You ever meet these people?"

"Hell, no." He sounded shocked. "Why would I do that? That would be against the rules."

"There are rules?"

"Of course."

"Who makes the rules?" she asked.

"I do."

He waited a few seconds for her to say something more. But she didn't—what could you say?

He turned back to the remote control and the monitor screen of the video scanner. Another tool for eavesdropping, she thought, what was going on here?

She walked over to him; he kept watching the monitor. She stood close to him. Touched him on the shoulder.

She said, "Written any software lately?"

"Not really."

"One of your hacker buddies once told me that you wrote some of the most beautiful code he had ever seen. Ellis writes code like diamonds, that's what he said."

"Could be."

"I know you were the best techie I ever worked with in the video business."

"I had my moments."

"You are, for sure, the smartest person I ever knew. Or ever will know."

He turned to her.

"What are you trying to tell me, Kate?" he said.

She gestured toward the device, and let the movement of her hand carry back toward the computer, what was on it.

She said, "Why are you wasting your time on this?"

He shook his head, a gesture that could have meant anything. I don't know. I won't tell. It doesn't matter. None of your business.

She said, "Don't you care about anything anymore?"

For a moment his face took on a terrible, lost expression.

"I guess not," he said.

He looked toward the monitor. He started moving the antenna again.

"You," he said without looking at her. "I care about you."

"The eternal afterthought," she said. "That's me."

She bussed the back of his neck, grabbed her purse, and started up toward the front door.

"Where are you going?" he said.

"Home."

"Don't," he said. "Please stay."

The sound in his voice almost—almost—pulled her back.

But she shook her head.

"Got to go," she said. "Got to."

And she walked up the steps and out the door.

7

After Kate left, Ellis Hoile turned back to the monitor. Once more he began working the remote control, moving the antenna on the tripod, one picture sliding out of the frame of the monitor, another sliding in to replace it.

Looked like Eddie Murphy onstage, grinning, mouth silently moving. But the vertical hold was slipping. Eddie kept getting tilted, contorted.

Ellis Hoile tried locking the picture in with a couple of taps at the remote. But his hands were shaking. He couldn't see right either.

His vision had gone liquid. Ellis Hoile's eyes were filling with tears.

He put down the remote control, and he went into the kitchen. First he ran some cold water in the sink, splashed it in his eyes. Then he dried his face, poured coffee, spooned in sugar, took a sip, and another.

He held the mug in his hands. The familiar actions steadied him.

Another sip of the coffee. Better now.

He took the mug over to one of the computers. He sat, and brought a program up on the screen.

A few keystrokes set the modem to dialing. Several seconds later his screen showed the message:

Greetings,
   You have connected to the Verba Interchange.

His fingers began to move on the keyboard. For a couple of minutes he had to force himself to concentrate on the screen in front of him.

But a couple of minutes was all. Before long he was lost again, immersed, alone in the timeless darkness.

8

It was late at night when Charles Obend opened his desk drawer and pulled out a computer modem.

He was alone in an office that he usually shared with three others. They were all junior associates in a firm of insurance claims adjusters outside Kansas City.

The modem trailed a long phone cord and a wide, flat serial cable. He fastened the cable to a receptacle in the back of his desktop computer. Then he got up from his desk to plug the phone cord into a jack across the room. He was a man of about medium height, somewhat overweight, hair thinning at age thirty-two.

The phone jack connected to the firm's outbound 1-800 service. Charles Obend returned to his chair, and in a moment the modem was pulsing tones; a few seconds later Verba's welcome screen was on the monitor.

Charles Obend was not a registered user at Verba, but he was a regular, and he almost always took the same ID. He typed it in again now:

CHAZ

And then the command:

visit VFB

The system answered:

You are now entering the Virtual Fern Bar: a meeting place for professional singles, wannabes, and the otherwise hopeful.

Discretion, honesty, and subtlety are suggested. However, as in real life, you are on your own.

The system announced his entry, then listed seventeen users who were already in the forum. Most were unmistakably male. Three or four seemed to be women—the standard proportion for this forum on a Friday night—but Charles Obend strongly suspected that most or all of *those* were men too: out for a few laughs, getting their cheap thrills, or just looking for a little attention.

Gender hacking.

Nobody seemed to notice Charles Obend. He sat back and began to read.

It took a while to get used to the pace. Like a real singles bar on a Friday night, this was a crowded and noisy place. Usually at least two or three users were typing at the same time, involved in different conversations. Messages got interrupted, then restarted a few seconds later.

Tonight, as ever, most of the chatter involved sports, cars, and computers; and, of course, women. Charles Obend thought that Verba's Virtual Fern Bar was actually more like a virtual men's locker room. He had never met a woman there, not that he could verify. But he was there most nights anyway.

One difference from real life was that in VFB you could tune out the people you didn't want to hear: The system would filter any number of users you designated. Charles Obend sometimes did this so that he could follow a single conversation out of the jumble.

Tonight he felt like filtering all of them.

Then the screen showed:

Sherm>   Yo, Chaz.

Three different conversations intervened before Charles Obend could get his keystrokes on the screen:

Chaz>   Yeah?
Sherm>   Back-channel, pal.

Charles Obend was feeling a little surly tonight. He answered:

Chaz>   Do I know you?

More scattered chat got in the way. Then:

Sherm>   Back-channel.
Chaz>   Go away.
Sherm>   You won't want to miss this. I promise.
Chaz>   Give me a break.
Sherm>   How do you mean that?
Chaz>   If you insist on hitting on guys, there are other forums
           where you'll get a warmer reception. Be my guest. Okay?
           But this is not the place.
Sherm>   Back-channel. You won't be disappointed.

Who is this jerk? Charles Obend thought. But he collected himself and responded:

Chaz>   Okay, for a minute.

A few seconds later they were in a private channel.

Chaz>   What can I do for you?
Sherm>   I hope you can begin to think of me as Suzanne. Because,
           you see, that really is my name. Susie Q is my handle.

Chaz>   Sure it is.

Sherm>   You're skeptical. Should I log off and log in again using
           the correct one?

Chaz>   No. That's okay.

Sherm>   If you can think "Susie Q" every time you see "Sherm"
           it would help us get to know each other.

Charles Obend didn't answer right away. He wasn't sure how to
take this.

Sherm>   Probably I have startled you.

Chaz>   You could say that.

Sherm>   I sometimes come to VFB as a male. I like to look around,
           but I don't want to be bothered. Besides, there's a sort
           of exhilaration in alternate gender identity. Does that
           make sense to you?

Chaz>   I think so.

Sherm>   I'm glad. I've seen you here before. I always look for you
           when I arrive. I've seen you in other forums too. You
           seem like a very nice person.

Chaz>   Thank you.

Sherm>   I always enjoy reading your messages. I feel that I know
           you quite well already. Some would say that's not pos-
           sible, just from reading someone's words. But we reveal
           ourselves in the words we use—not only in what we say,
           but what we leave unsaid. Don't you agree?

Chaz>   Yes, I do.

Sherm>   I'm glad you feel that way. I would like to know you on
           a one-to-one basis.

Chaz>   Why?

Sherm>   In this life we make many acquaintances but very few
           intimate and meaningful contacts. When the chance

> presents itself, we should not let it pass. Do you also feel
> that way?

Charles Obend, sitting alone in his office in Kansas City, did feel that way. He felt it very keenly at that moment. He wasn't completely convinced that Sherm was a woman. But he believed that given enough time, he would discover the truth—that no man could pull off that charade forever.

He certainly wanted Susie Q to be real. And he understood himself well enough to know that if he passed on this one, he would think about it for a long time. Always wondering.

He answered:

> Chaz>   Yes. I do.
> Sherm>   I'm glad to hear that. Why don't you tell me a little about
>   yourself?

Something within Charles Obend made him hesitate. It was not so much caution as an ingrained reserve. He had never been very good at self-exposure. He knew that he tended to keep people at arm's length.

He also knew that it was a habit he had to overcome. Otherwise he might spend a thousand more Friday nights alone at a keyboard, reading strangers' words on a cathode ray tube.

The screen showed:

> Sherm>   You might think of it this way: Under the circumstances,
>   you have very little to lose and much to gain.

True, Charles Obend thought. *So very true.*

And he began to type.

9

Kate Lavin didn't go straight home after she left Tesla Street that evening.

As she drove across the bridge, into Marin County, she found that Ellis Hoile kept surfacing in her thoughts.

His first words to her, in a corridor of Redwood High School in Mill Valley, had been: "Want to call Marrakech?"

They were both sophomores then. Her family had just moved to Marin County. He was a punkish, swaggering kid: *trouble*, not at all the twerpy little Math Club nerd you might expect. As a freshman he had dropped a double bombshell into the guidance counselor's office, first when he turned in his IQ screening test after twenty minutes, swearing that he was finished, then again when he broke 180 on that same test.

Although, as he said later, the numbers tend to be meaningless when you get up into that range. The samples are so small. . . .

That year, she and Ellis took poetry and physics together. Ellis, when he showed up, was simultaneously bored and brilliant. She herself was going through a Sylvia Plath phase, and saw Ellis as the new Baudelaire, maybe even the new Lou Reed.

That was the poetry.

In physics he was just bored. About a month into the course, they studied atmospheric pressure. The teacher explained how a barometer worked. Then he called on Ellis to tell the class how you could use a barometer to determine the height of a skyscraper.

The idea was, you read the barometer while you're on the bottom floor, then go to the roof and read the barometer again, and the difference in the two readings will tell you how high the building is. This was the answer that straight-A students had been giving in physics classes for the past fifty years.

What Ellis said was, "I would drop the barometer off the roof and time how long it takes to hit the ground. You plug that factor into the formula for the acceleration of a falling body, you'll find out how high the building is."

The physics teacher forced up a tight little smile. He said, "That's very clever, Ellis, but I think there's another way to do it."

"Well, sure," Ellis said. "You find the building superintendent, and you say, 'Hey, I'll give you this nice barometer if you tell me how high your skyscraper is.' "

At that moment she fell in love with him.

He wouldn't even look at her though. She thought there must be something wrong with her: It didn't occur to her that the guy who could break up Mr. Willis's physics class might have no idea how to approach a girl.

That day she walked up to him after class and said, "I think you're great, you're such a beautiful person, how come you hate me?"

And he said, "Want to call Marrakech?"

He reached into one of the big pockets of the combat fatigue pants he was wearing, and he pulled out a little blue box with buttons, almost like a home-made telephone. Later, she learned this was its actual name. The Little Blue Box was a tone generator, similar to a Touch-Tone phone, except that it was capable of wonderful feats that no telephone could do. The Little Blue Box could open up long-distance phone lines around the world, free of charge. It could get you into the secret innards of the system—the Bell system—and once you were in there, you could run wild.

They did call Marrakech that day, from a pay phone in the cafeteria. Ellis knew the number of a pensione where the old drugged-out hippies stayed. He knew the numbers of a bordello in Paris, an Italian restaurant in Hong Kong, a pay phone in Red Square.

Ellis was a phreaker: an explorer, somebody who liked to peek into corners that other people wanted to keep hidden. You might hear a computer hacker say, "I phreaked Mutual of Omaha last night," meaning that he had used his computer to slip into the company's computer banks. Nothing malicious, just get in there and poke around, see how the big boys did things.

Freakers in general liked to push the limits, determine exactly what was possible. And that was Ellis, all right. While he eventually lost interest in opening Ma Bell's closets, he never quit trying to test the system. Any and all systems. Seeing how they worked, how much he could get away with. A phreaker forever . . .

And now with a new project. "People," he had said, "the ultimate phreak."

She knew she wouldn't sleep with Ellis on her mind, so Kate drove to the studio. It was quieter now than in the daytime, but still alive, softly pulsing with its own energy: an existence that was oblivious of her internal disarray.

The studio and the work did not care whether she was able to put Ellis Hoile on the shelf.

She spent about half an hour at her desk, catching up on her backlog.

Then she went to an editing suite, where she sat alone and reviewed the working versions of two projects in progress. This consumed nearly another hour.

She still wasn't quite ready to face the houseboat.

PHILLIP FINCH

She returned to her office, to the computer on her desktop. There she booted the communications program. A few seconds later the Verba welcome screen greeted her.

She typed in her ID and password.

The handle was from her teenage years, one of her favorite rock singers. She had chosen it for its ambiguous gender: She didn't wish to be immediately marked as a woman, though she didn't wish to masquerade as a male either.

The singer was David Bowie, whose own stage persona had been somewhat ambiguous during the phase when he performed as "Ziggy Stardust."

The Verba system greeted her now:

Welcome, Ziggy

10

The greeting card talked when Stephen Leviste opened the front flap.

It was his family, saying: "Happy Birthday, Stephen, we love you, happy returns and many more, happy happy birthday, happy birthday, Stephen," four voices that started in unison and finished in an overlapping jumble.

He closed the card, then opened it again.

The message played once more.

It lasted ten seconds—he was timing it with his new birthday present, a digital wristwatch.

The card measured five inches by eight. But it was a little heavier than an ordinary greeting card, and about a quarter of an inch thick.

He found a slit that let him pull out the guts of the card: a miniature speaker and wafer microphone, both connected to a circuit board about an inch square, powered by a button-sized battery.

The price on the back of the card was $7.95. Counting taxes, that would be eight bucks and change for a complete digital recording/playback device that contained enough nonvolatile memory to record ten seconds of audio at a capture rate of—he guessed—around eleven kilohertz.

He was impressed.

However, ten seconds of memory was not enough for what he had in mind.

While he considered his dilemma, he chewed Milk Duds from a box.

Actually, he thought, ten seconds would be about enough if he could record exactly the *right* ten seconds.

That gave him an idea.

He found an old cassette recorder that he had bought at a garage sale, a dollar and a half. He opened the case, and used a pair of wire clippers and a small screwdriver to remove the VOX—voice-operated—switch.

The greeting card's recorder was mounted on a white plastic frame. He de-soldered the speaker wire and spliced it into a microphone jack. He replaced the contact switch circuit with the VOX switch from the old tape recorder.

The recorder would now switch on only when it heard a voice or a loud noise. A dial tone would do it.

Once he had cut away the excess plastic, the rest of the tiny recorder—circuit board, the wafer mic, and the power supply—all slid easily into the box of Milk Duds.

Which was now empty.

He placed the box against his telephone so that the microphone was flat against the side of the phone. He lifted the receiver, punched the buttons 1-2-3-4-5-6 in quick succession, and replaced the receiver.

At that moment the bedroom door opened. His mother stepped into the room.

She handed him an envelope—no, he saw that it was a cardboard diskette mailer.

"That just came for you," she said.

She glanced at the front of the birthday card, beside him. She smiled. She didn't seem to realize that it had been eviscerated.

"Isn't it darling?" she said. "I saw it at the card shop at Tanforan, I thought it was just darling."

On impulse, she bent down, kissed him on the top of his head, ruffled his hair.

People still did this to him. He was now two days past his

twelfth birthday, but he looked younger. His hips and shoulders, his voice, his face, could all have belonged to a ten-year-old boy.

A ten-year-old girl, for that matter.

He hated it.

He hated looking like a ten-year-old. He hated having adults poke and pinch and tousle him, the way they did with little kids.

She smiled and closed the door behind her.

Stephen tore open the mailer and looked inside. It contained two unlabeled 3.5-inch diskettes labeled TRY ME DISK #1 and DISK #2, and a printed slip of paper that read HOT WAREZ!!!

No return address. He thought it must have been sent by one of his friends. But not a real good friend. A real good friend would have known that Stephen had outgrown copied software—warez.

Anybody who *really* knew him would know that Stephen Leviste was now into hacking, and that as a hacker, what he needed was not warez, but codez.

He put the diskette aside, slid the minirecorder from the Milk Duds box, and plugged the output jack into the sound card at the back of his computer.

He toggled the minirecorder to play.

The monitor screen in front of Stephen immediately displayed a wavelength graph that represented the ten-second output from the recorder, now stored on his hard disk as an audio file. The peaks in the graph showed him that, as he had guessed, the little wafer mic picked up sounds through the thin cardboard of the box—in fact, the box seemed to act as a sort of sounding board.

He played the file again. This time a small window in a bottom corner of the monitor showed the numerals 1 2 3 4 5 6 as each tone sounded.

The program had analyzed the tones to identify each button he pressed, in the correct sequence.

Now another experiment. With the phone still on-hook, he began pressing buttons again, at about what seemed to be a normal speed. He did this for ten seconds, and found that he had pushed twenty-four buttons before time ran out.

He tried it again, this time a little faster: twenty-six buttons in ten seconds.

Once more, but slower: twenty-two buttons.

Someone using a pay phone to make a long-distance call would first dial the digit 1, plus area code and number. Eleven button-pushes. The caller would then key in the credit card number from a long-distance service, usually fourteen digits.

In all, twenty-five key-pushes. Ten seconds, if it was done in a hurry. And people were always in a hurry.

Otherwise, time would run out and the Milk Duds recorder would miss the last few digits.

Stephen didn't want that to happen. He didn't care about the phone number that a caller might dial—it was useless to him. He wanted those credit card numbers: sometimes known as service access codes.

Codez.

11

Several days of fog and drizzle kept Jane Regalia housebound. When she finally woke to a sunny morning, she celebrated by spending six hours outside her rented cabin, using a spade to turn over a small garden plot.

It was punishing work. Even with gloves it raised blisters on her hands almost at once, and immediately broke the blisters. But the earth was rich and she imagined summer mornings, not too far off, when she would carry armloads of her own corn and tomatoes and squash into the kitchen.

She kept at it until late afternoon. Then she went into the cabin, sat at her computer, and logged into Verba.

The service addressed her as it always did:

Greetings.

You have connected to the Verba Interchange.

Verba is a social and technological experiment dedicated to the free exchange of ideas and information. You may conceive of Verba as a boundless public hall. Within this system are people whose interests and knowledge range across the spectrum of human experience. We invite you to encounter them, as they are invited to encounter you.

Please type the identifier by which you wish to be known during this session. It should be no more than twelve characters in length.

She typed:

Portia

The system immediately responded:

The identifier you have chosen is reserved by a registered user. Please enter your password or press >Control<-I to enter a new password.

Jane Regalia had been registered on Verba for almost two months. She typed a password and the system answered:

Welcome, Jane Regalia

Last log-off: 17:44; 04/25/94

Remember, Verba is your service. It is what you make of it.

She then typed:

visit WI

The command moved her instantly onto one of Verba's permanent forums. The greeting screen listed it as:

On Our Own: Women Independent

Eight other users were on the forum channel when she entered. She recognized most of them. She was one of about a half dozen who gathered there nearly every day in the late afternoon.

She had first entered the forum about two months earlier. Some of the others had been regulars there for much longer than that. Few had ever met face-to-face, yet they believed that they knew one another very well.

Several of the regulars greeted her arrival.

Nancy-T>   There she is—about time.
Carrie>   Hugs from all.
Michiko>   We've been waiting.
Salome>   I was afraid you weren't going to make it today.
Portia>   I've been out and about. Sorry, Sal.
Salome>   You're always worth waiting for, dear.

Jane Regalia sat back and began to read the exchanges. They weren't quite up to their normal level today, she thought.

She kept watching the screen. Occasionally she glanced out the small window in front of the writing desk. The monitor mostly blocked her sight, but when she shifted in her chair she could see the narrow driveway that ran from the cabin, down the canyon to the Coast Highway.

On the network, Michiko told about discovering a 900 number on an old phone bill.

Michiko>   It was one of these dial-a-porn numbers. Three weeks
            before our marriage broke up, we're spending hundreds
            of dollars a month in counseling. At the same time we're
            supposed to be learning how to be intimate again, he's
            getting off with some hired slut over the phone. It was
            more than a year ago, the marriage is finished, so I
            shouldn't care anymore. But I do. It ruined my day. In
            fact, I'm still p.o.'ed about it.

PHILLIP FINCH

Jane Regalia responded:

Portia>	Sometimes it's the little things that get you. I have a leaky faucet in the kitchen that keeps reminding me what a dummy I've been.
Carrie>	Call the landlord, get it fixed.
Portia>	He's in Boston, and if I kept ragging him about every little nuisance, he'd have me out of here. That's not the point anyway. My husband always fixed the little nuisances. The faucet just reminds me how much I turned over to him, things which I now have no clue about.
Salome>	It makes you feel powerless.
Portia>	Yes.
Salome>	And reminds you how far you have to go before you're really independent.

Right again, Jane Regalia thought. In some ways Salome was Portia's favorite of the group's regulars. A little too strident and bitter, sometimes. But Salome understood. Sal *knew.*

Jane Regalia answered:

Portia>	Yes, yes, yes.
Salome>	So you learn how to do it yourself.
Portia>	Seems so imposing. All that man stuff.
Salome>	No, it's easy. That's one of men's secrets. They act like it's such arcane knowledge, how to fix a faucet or tune a car, a thousand things like that. Men like to make a big deal of it, so we'll think they're indispensable. But the truth is that anybody can learn.
Nancy-T>	Men weren't born knowing.

·   ·   ·

The killer watched these exchanges as they appeared on the screen of a portable computer that he held on his lap.

```
Nancy-T>    Men weren't born knowing.
Carrie>     If they can learn it, anybody can.
```

Now his fingers moved on the keys, and the screen displayed the words as he typed, the screen cursor gliding, the characters spilling out from behind it:

```
Salome>     Right. How hard can it be?
```

He paused a moment, then continued:

```
Salome>     Hey, just noticed the time—I've got to get out of here.
Portia>     So soon?
Salome>     Duty calls.
```

The system announced his departure:

```
Salome has left the group.
```

Jane Regalia read the exchanges for the next half hour. Mostly she stayed in the background—"lurking," in the argot of on-line users.

Carrie kept complaining about her divorce lawyer. Someone named Jaybee—Jane Regalia didn't recognize the handle—told an interminable story about being hustled in a singles bar.

Neither of these topics, divorce lawyers and singles bars, concerned Jane Regalia.

Not yet anyway, she told herself.

The blisters on her hands were hurting. She got up from the chair, went over to the kitchen cabinet where she kept some Tylenol, took two tablets with a glass of water.

When she came back, Aurora was cracking jokes.

Aurora>   Why do so many women fake orgasms?

At that moment, as she was about to sit down again, Jane Regalia heard a noise outside, an engine, somebody driving up from the highway.

She leaned to look out the window and saw a van pull up outside. It was brown, the shade of tobacco, no signs or markings: a minivan, the kind you usually saw carrying kids and groceries. But this was a cargo version, with no windows in the passenger compartment.

She went to the door.

Carrie>   I give up.
Aurora>   Because so many men fake foreplay.
Michiko>   Nudge in the ribs to Portia.
Nancy-T>   No response from Portia, I see.
Carrie>   Portia is our resident straight arrow. Isn't that right, Porsh?

There was a pause while they waited for her to answer.

Inside the cabin, Jane Regalia was screaming.

The cursor blinked, motionless, on her monitor, and on the screens of the seven other machines that were connected to her through Verba.

On a computer, a motionless cursor is the sound of silence.

Now words began to move again, almost tentative:

Michiko>   Portia?
Aurora>   Hey, girl, it was just a lame little joke.
Carrie>   Portia? Are you out there?

They all waited about ten seconds for a response.
    Then on the network they read:

Portia>   Here I am. UPS truck came by.
Carrie>   And how did Mr. UPS look?
Portia>   She was named Janet.
Aurora>   A quick lay is like a cop. They're always around, but you
           can never find one when you really need one.
Nancy-T>   Tell us the truth, Portia. Don't you ever get a little,
           ummm, shall we say, restless up there in the North
           Woods?
Carrie>   Not our Porsh.
Portia>   Don't want to be rude, but I'd better log off. I want to
           call a plumber. I'm going to get that drip fixed. The fau-
           cet, not the husband.
Michiko>   Tomorrow, then.
Portia>   Maybe not. I was thinking of driving to Oakland for a
           few days. I have an old friend down there I haven't seen
           for a while.
Carrie>   A friend, she says.
Nancy-T>   My. Portia does get restless after all.
Aurora>   Exactly what gender is this friend?

On the keyboard of Jane Regalia's computer, a man's fingers typed:

Portia>   That's my little secret.

12

Kate Lavin spent that afternoon in the city. She headed home by way of the Embarcadero, driving with the top down on her Miata.

The route carried her past the foot of Telegraph Hill. She found herself looking up the hill, toward the house below Coit Tower.

The shades were drawn again on the picture window, she could tell. She thought of Ellis holed up inside. In the days since their dinner, she had talked to him once by telephone, on business, for about half a minute. She hadn't seen him—it was the longest they had been apart since the divorce was final.

And now, without even thinking about it, she was turning off the curving Embarcadero, a left turn up the hill.

Just an impulse. She didn't fight it. She kept thinking about him behind those curtains. Thinking that she would stay only a few minutes, just long enough to see that he was okay.

She wedged the Miata into a space that was almost directly across from the front door of 2600 Tesla, got out and started up the walk.

She stopped just short of the door.

She thought, *What are you doing?*

Look in on him, she told herself, you must be kidding. You know he's okay. In his own fashion. Ellis can look after himself. Always has.

She didn't move. She kept staring at the front door, thinking of him alone in there.

And she turned away. It took an effort, but she did it.

She told herself, A break is a break, you've got to make it stick sometime. Might as well start now.

She got into the car and drove away without looking back.

13

Jane Regalia drifted into consciousness.

Not right away. It was gradual, an ebb and flow, until she finally crossed the threshold of awareness. Then she awoke. She began to absorb sensations, impressions.

She was sprawled facedown.

Her face and ribs throbbed where he had punched her, kicked her, while overpowering her in the cabin.

She was in utter darkness.

She moved her head, and the floor rasped against her cheek. She reached a hand to touch it.

She found that it was rough perforated steel, a honeycomb pattern.

Her hand groped, and found that the honeycomb stopped a few inches from where she lay. Beyond that . . . nothing. Emptiness where a solid floor ought to be.

It came to her, where she had seen a steel honeycomb not long ago.

She became aware of a pressure at her face. She brought a hand up, and felt heavy tape, layers of tape, across her eyes. This was why she couldn't see. The tape wrapped around her head—she couldn't begin to pull it off.

From some distance, a man's voice said, "I'll bet you've had better days."

His words sounded confident, almost mocking. She also picked up a light, quick echo of his voice. She could sense from the sound that they were in a large room. And that the floor was far below.

"Where am I?" she said. She surprised herself a little, being able to talk.

"That's immaterial."

"What do you want?" she said.

"We'll get around to it," he answered.

When his words ended, there was just silence. She fought to stay calm.

More silence for a few seconds: maybe longer, hard to tell.

He said, "You can smell fear, did you know that?"

She was almost glad to hear him. The sound helped restore some sense of place and distance, give her some breathing room in the blackness.

He said, "I always thought it was just a phrase—the smell of fear. It's true though. You really can smell fear. Under the right circumstances. I found that out the other day, I actually smelled fear."

A short, dreadful pause. Then he barked a short laugh.

"Not my own," he said, "if that's what you were thinking."

Another pause.

And now a new noise.

Tup . . .

Tup . . . *tup* . . .

Footsteps.

She could not just hear them—she could feel them through the steel where she lay.

He was coming toward her. She raised her shoulders, and sat up to face the direction of the steps.

Tup . . . *tup* . . . *tup* . . .

Sounding almost brisk, not hurried, but businesslike.

Very close now, almost on her. He stopped.

"Get up," he said from a few feet away. "C'mon, get up, you're okay."

She shook her head in refusal. Then she felt a cold, hard touch at her cheek, and she brought her hand up there.

Her fingers touched a broad blade, flat against the side of her face.

"Careful," he said.

Her fingers moved along the blade. It was huge. She realized that he was holding a machete against her face.

The blade withdrew.

"Get up," he said again, and this time she stood. Her right hand found a low metal rail: She grasped it for support.

"You know where you are," he said. "You've been here."

She could picture it: a steel catwalk with a single low railing along one side. *Can't be,* she thought. But she knew that it was true.

Her guts clutched. She wanted to retch.

He said, "There *is* a way out, you know. There has to be, otherwise it wouldn't be interesting."

She stood immobile, letting the railing take her weight.

"So move," he said.

She was rooted.

"Come on," he said. "Jeez, most people would at least *try.*"

She felt stricken. Even breathing took an effort.

"You want an incentive?" he said. "Stay alive for the next two minutes, I let you go. Hundred and twenty seconds, hell, you can do that. Then you walk out of here. You can believe me on that or not, but it's true. Chance of a lifetime, you might say.

"Or die right here, right now, it's your call," he said.

He would kill her, she thought. She was sure of it.

She chose life, even if it was only seconds more.

She turned, switched hands on the rail—it was on her left side now—and she began to edge down the catwalk, shuffling away from him.

"There you go," he said.

She kept her hand on the rail, using it as a guide, sliding it along as she moved.

She began to move faster, trying to put distance between them.

He called out: "Thirty seconds down. Minute and a half to go."

He began walking toward her. She could hear him coming.

She moved a little faster, trying to match her own steps to his. Keep space between them.

His steps became even brisker.

She tripped, caught herself, kept walking. Faster.

She broke into a half-run. His footsteps became more rapid too. They were quick and sure, banging on the steel surface of the catwalk.

TupTupTupTup

Faster. Louder.

Closer.

And now the machete began to ring, a quick series of banging noises. He was rattling it along the railing—she heard the ringing, she felt the blows through the rail, tingling her palm.

The rattling was closer. She thought of the blade coming her way, cool and sharp and deadly.

He was overtaking her, just steps away.

He was there, within arm's length. She could hear his breathing. . . .

She bolted. She ran headlong, desperate, anything to stay out of his hands.

And it must be working, she thought, because the ringing had stopped, and she could not hear him follow.

And she ran, her legs churning . . .

. . . she ran, her shoes slapping against the catwalk . . .

. . . she ran, until she put her left foot down and it found nothing, no steel, nothing, it just treaded air, and then she was pitching forward, catapulting, out of control.

Falling.

.　　•　　•　　•

The killer watched her run headlong into empty space at the far end of the catwalk.

He thought that it was remarkable. The way she ran as hard as she could, kept running hard right until the moment she had no more floor beneath her feet.

See, you could not fake that. Even in the movies, a stunt man would prepare himself, subtly hitch his stride, before he flung himself off the brink.

It was something in the human makeup, he thought, some involuntary twitch that restrained you from completely abandoning yourself to gravity that way. If you knew what you were doing, where you were heading, what was going to come next.

But if you didn't know, if you were running blind and you just flew off the edge . . .

Well, that was something to see.

Oh, man. The way she raced straight for oblivion. The way she launched off the edge, completely unaware. Then screamed and flailed and tumbled before she finally fell out of sight.

You could not fake that. You could not see that anywhere else, under any other circumstances. This was rare stuff.

One thing you could say about the game of murder.

It was real.

She fell, she fell, she fell.

Hurtling blindly downward, in an unknown place, knowing that agony and maybe worse awaited her when she finally met the earth again.

It was only a second or two, but the moment was infinitely expandable, it seemed to stretch on endlessly.

Then she hit. And then the pain came, pain and the knowledge that one way or another she was very near her end.

She smashed against a concrete floor.

The hurt exploded over her, waves of hot red and hot white pain that rippled across her vision before they subsided. She writhed but she could not get up. She just lay there, in agony, before the pain overcame her.

She wondered briefly about *him,* what he was going to do next. But mostly the pain crowded out thought.

She lay there for a time that she could not even guess. Finally his steps sounded. Nearby, and approaching. Somehow he had made his way down to her level. Wherever she was.

The sound of his feet stopped beside her head.

He said, "That last step's a bitch, huh?"

He hooked his arms under her shoulders and began to drag her. The pain surged again, and she screamed with a force that nearly deafened her.

Now they were at a staircase. She could feel the hard ridges in her back as he tugged her upward. The pain exploded, too much, unbearable, and she fainted away.

The tape was gone from her eyes when she blinked awake.

Bright. A couple of strong lights on stands, glaring at her. She tried to raise a hand, shade her eyes. But it took a great effort, too much. She let her arm drop to the floor.

She was in a room, a bare room with concrete walls and floors and ceiling. He was there, bending over an object on a tripod.

She almost pitied him when she saw what it was.

A video camera.

Pathetic, she thought. *And very, very sick . . .*

Her clothes were in a pile on the floor, looking as if they had been torn off. She realized that she was nude. She noted it abstractly. Just another detail. She was beyond caring.

She did not react even when he left the camera, walked to a corner of the room, then turned and came toward her.

He had picked up the machete again.

He stepped toward her.

Then he raised it up and swung, it flashed down toward her, and that was the last she knew.

PART III

Ziggy

May 6–May 9

14

Rain pelted the windshield of Lee Wade's Crown Victoria as he headed up Telegraph Hill. After a dry, warm winter—low snowfall in the Sierras, predictions of water rationing come summer—spring had turned sodden.

Wade drove slowly, looking for a parking spot. Nothing. He finally ended up in the cul-de-sac at the end of the street, barely wide enough to turn around in. The curb was painted red, no parking at any time. He drove the Crown Vic up onto the sidewalk, straddling the curb.

Then he got out, locked the car, and started walking. He wore no hat, carried no umbrella. Real cops definitely did not carry umbrellas.

After nearly two weeks, and a court order, Pacific Bell had come through with the user records for Donald Trask's home phone. They had faxed over a tidy computer-generated list of every call made from the number for the past three months.

Wade and his partner were trying to visit every local number on the list, a way of piecing together Donald Trask's life, and maybe his death.

Most people were not aware that telephone companies kept records of local calls. For a long time the police—even the FBI—had been unaware of it. The telco was full of these little surprises.

Lee Wade stopped on the sidewalk, looked the place over, then strode up the front walk and pressed the buzzer beside the front door at 2600 Tesla.

Nobody opened the door, and Wade could not hear a bell or buzzer or anything else inside. Rain streamed down his face. By now his hair was matted wet.

He held the button down a good three or four counts now, and that got some action. After a few seconds the door opened.

The guy who opened the door was a white male in his mid-thirties, medium height, medium build. He looked mildly annoyed, but a little disconnected too.

Lee Wade had his shield ready in his left hand, the shield and the ID card in a black leather foldover that he held open as he said, "Hi, Lee Wade, SFPD homicide."

Lee Wade watched closely. It was always interesting to see how the word "homicide" struck home, especially when it came unexpectedly.

But this one was different. The guy who had opened the door—brown eyes, black hair showing a few flecks of salt, two–three days' beard, dressing like he was determined to show the world how little he cared about looking good—this slob on the other side of the doorway acted as if he hadn't heard.

His expression didn't change a bit.

"I'm looking for Ellis Hoile," Wade said as he slid the shield back into his jacket.

"That's me," the grunge said after a couple of beats.

"Can we talk for a couple minutes?"

Another couple of beats. The rain was streaming down Lee Wade's face.

"Why?" the grunge said.

"We're conducting an investigation," Wade said, implying the authority of the department, the great machinery behind that plural, *we*.

Wade added, in case the guy had missed it the first time, "A homicide investigation."

The grunge who claimed he was Ellis Hoile acted as if the words were coming to him from a great distance. As if his body were there in the doorway but his mind were somewhere else that was much more interesting.

Wade wondered if he had interrupted some serious boffing.

Or maybe some serious drug using.

"What do you want?" said Ellis Hoile.

"Can we talk inside?"

"Why?" said Ellis Hoile. Again.

Something flared inside Wade. He was usually very composed, polite, he knew regulations, how to deal with the public. He could even be genial. But Ellis Hoile and that numb-nuts expression on his face set him off.

"Because it's raining the fuck out here," Lee Wade said. His voice still quiet, but with an edge that nobody could miss. "Because I look like fucking Joe the Geek standing out here with water running the fuck off of me."

Ellis Hoile glanced at the sky as if he were noticing the rain for the first time.

"Sure," he said, and he stepped aside to let Lee Wade through the door.

Wade stepped inside, and was almost sorry he did, because when Ellis Hoile shut the door, it was dark inside.

Dark made Lee Wade nervous. Sharing strange dark rooms with strangers, he very much disliked that: He wanted at all times to see where he was and what was going on around him.

"I don't suppose there's a light switch anywhere," Wade said.

Ellis Hoile acted like he had to think about that for a little while. Then he walked over, found the switch, and they had light overhead.

Wade said, "Thank you. You know a man named Donald Trask?"

"No," Ellis Hoile answered, almost without a pause this time.

"Think about it."

"I don't have to. I know who I know."

"He called a phone number here four times during the month of March."

"I don't know Donald Trask."

"Maybe he called somebody else here. Anybody else live here, take phone calls here?"

"No," Ellis Hoile said, "I live alone."

Then he asked: "What number was he calling?"

Lee Wade took out the photocopy of PacBell's printout, copied the number down on a notebook page, saying, "It's in the name of Ellis Hoile, it's listed at this address," and he tore out the page and handed it over.

Ellis Hoile glanced at it and said, "That's one of my data lines, hold on."

Abruptly he turned, walked away, and went down the stairs that descended from the wide landing. Wade went to the edge of the landing and watched as Ellis Hoile reached the bottom of the stairs and went straight to one of the computers on the desks downstairs.

The only light down there being the glow of three computer monitors, Lee Wade noticed, *three* computers.

The whole incredible room downstairs looked to Wade like an electronics warehouse. He stood there, thinking, Jesus, does the guy really live like this. . . .

Ellis Hoile's fingers flashed on the keyboard, just the two index fingers, a quick blur. Wade had never seen anyone type so fast.

Without looking up from the screen, Ellis Hoile said, "What number was he calling from?"

"I can't tell you that, it's confidential," Wade said, though that wasn't really true: He just didn't like giving away too much.

"Oh, yeah, police business, confidential, *right*," Ellis Hoile said, sounding sarcastic. Wade really didn't like this guy.

He searched a second or two through the mess on one of the desktops, and came up with what he wanted much sooner than Wade would have expected. It was a small, silvery disk, a CD.

Ellis Hoile slipped the disk into one of the computers.

A few more taps at the keyboard. Almost instantly he said, without looking up from the screen, "That would be Donald Trask on Chestnut Street."

He read off the correct phone number.

Lee Wade took a couple of seconds to digest this.

"How do you know?" he said.

The CD popped out of the computer, and Ellis Hoile held it up.

"Every residential listing in the western U.S. on CD-ROM. You're local, he's probably local. And he's the only Donald Trask in the area code."

"How about that," Wade said.

Ellis Hoile didn't appear to notice. He was at another machine now, his fingers working again.

"Let me try to match that number," he said, and almost immediately he said, "Oh, you mean DeeTeeDude."

"How's that?"

"His handle, DeeTeeDude, all one word," Ellis Hoile said, and he spelled it out, saying, "That's what he called himself on Verba. He was also DoomDude, he used two handles, he didn't think I knew that, but I figured it out."

"You lost me," Wade said.

Then Ellis Hoile explained it to him, the Verba Interchange and how it worked, taking it slow when he saw that Wade really had no idea. He did it in about five or six sentences, precise and distilled, choosing his words.

The dopey demeanor could fool you, Lee Wade thought. This was no dope. Far from it. He was plenty quick once he got focused.

Wade said, "How often did you talk to him?"

"I never did."

"I got phone records that show three calls to your number, over an hour each."

"No doubt you do. If you checked my records, you'd find three or four to his number too."

"You talked to him six or seven times," Wade said.

"His computer called my computer. My computer called his. I never spoke to him. He wanted to play Doom. He was a fool for Doom. There's a forum on Verba where you can hustle up opponents for various games, he was always trying to find somebody to play Doom with him."

"Doom," Wade said.

"A game. You play it alone, it's this space trooper against the aliens and zombies. You play it by modem, then it's space trooper against space trooper with the aliens and zombies thrown in for laughs. That's how DeeTeeDude liked to play it, in DeathMatch mode."

It almost got past Lee Wade. But he caught it, and he asked Ellis Hoile to say it again, just to make sure he'd heard it right.

Uh-huh. DeathMatch. That was what he said, all right.

"You never met him," Wade said.

"Not in person."

"Never talked to him."

"Not to hear his voice." Ellis Hoile sounded as if he were making an effort to be patient, like someone who hates going over old ground.

"Never even knew his name."

"I logged him in as DeeTeeDude. Good enough for him, good enough for me."

He was looking levelly at Lee Wade, unblinking. Maybe it was the look of someone who had nothing to hide.

Or maybe of somebody who thought he had all his bases covered.

Wade reached into his jacket and brought out a business card. His name and office phone, official seal of the City of San Francisco.

He held it out.

"You think of anything else, give me a call."

"Sure." Ellis Hoile took the card.

"You never asked me what happened to him," Wade said. "Everybody asks. Most people can't stop asking questions when I show up."

"He's dead, somebody murdered him, you're trying to find who did it. No other reason you'd be here."

Wade nodded.

"End of story," Ellis Hoile said.

"That's one way of looking at it."

Wade started back up the stairs. Ellis Hoile stayed down there with his machines. When Wade got to the top of the stairs, Ellis Hoile was seated again, staring at one of the monitors. It was like Wade was already out of the house, out of his life.

But Lee Wade wasn't quite finished.

From the top of the stairs he said, "I forgot to ask. When the two of you played, you and Donald Trask, who usually won?"

Ellis Hoile turned in his chair and looked up.

"I smoked his ass." He grinned like a twelve-year-old. "Every time."

"Every time?" Wade said. "You never lost to him even once?"

"I rarely lose to anybody."

"You're pretty good at that game, huh?"

"I'm good at all of them," said Ellis Hoile.

15

At ten that morning Kate Lavin flew to Burbank for an afternoon meeting with one of her regular clients, a cable network with offices on Wilshire Boulevard.

When she flew back that evening she had a commission: a one-hour documentary on the vanishing Central American jaguar, to be shot mainly in Belize. Kate won the job with the promise that yeah, sure, her crew would find and photograph one of the cats on a night prowl.

And the not-so-rough cut would be ready within three months. *Of course,* she thought, *no problem, we do it all the time.*
Right.

She liked this kind of edge work, pushing herself, testing the limits. This was how things got done, when you challenged your own comfort zone once in a while.

She boarded her return flight at six-fifteen. She felt strong, capable, the buzz she always got when she'd had a good day. But something happened during the seventy minutes before the Air West flight touched down again in San Francisco.

She felt herself deflate.

She told herself that it was just a chemical letdown, the slump that always comes when you've been running on adrenaline all day.

A pretty good explanation, she thought. Except that she'd been slumping like this, on and off, for more than a week now. And not just at the end of the day. It might hit her in the morning, it might keep her tossing in bed, it might catch her unaware in the middle of the day and ruin the next few hours.

She knew that this slump was probably not just an endocrinal deficit. She thought that she had to do something about Ellis Hoile.

Then she corrected herself.

Not about Ellis. About me.

That's the real problem, she thought. Ellis's feelings and acts weren't the point anymore. Ellis was in the past. So decreed. The question was her own life, now that Ellis was out of it.

Move on, she told herself.

A cold rain was beating hard—pounding, wind-driven—as she pulled into the parking lot off Bridgeway. She put her head down, walked through the pier gate, then nearly the whole length of the boardwalk that extended out into the bay.

Her boat was two slips from the end of the pier: a one-story structure with walls of cedar shake, sitting on a wide, flat fiberglass hull that rode low in the water.

The structure covered nearly the entire hull. As she stood now at the edge of the dock, she was able to reach the lock of the sliding glass door that was the main entry. She turned her key in the lock, pushed the glass aside, and stepped inside out of the rain. She slid the door shut behind her, locked it again, and pulled the curtain that blocked the view from outside.

The place was dim and cold. Right away she went through the boat, flipping on light switches, turning up the thermostat on the electric heat, shedding her wet coat and hat and shoes. She stopped in the kitchen to open the freezer. Inside were at least a dozen paper trays wrapped with plastic: single-serving entrees packaged by a local deli. These days she almost never cooked.

She reminded herself that this collection of meals for one was supposed to look smart and efficient, not absurd.

She pulled out one that was marked lasagna, stuck it in the microwave. She poured a glass of red wine and brought it with her as she stripped in the bathroom and stepped into a hot shower.

She could feel wind buffet the boat, rocking it, tugging at its moorings. Rain smashed against the windows.

She stepped out, toweled fast, stepped into a terry-cloth robe, blow-dried her hair—her short cut needed just a minute or two.

In the kitchen, the lasagna was ready, waiting. She slipped a CD into the player—Haydn string quartets—and brought the food and the wine to the living room. She sat cross-legged on the floor with the plate of food in front of her on a coffee table, and she began to eat.

Even with the lights and the heat and the warm meal and the music, the place still felt empty. Not so much a home as a way station.

And then, with the wind still rocking and the rain still pounding outside, someone knocked on the glass door.

It was loud: three sharp, decisive raps.

They sounded like a man's.

16

Half a continent removed from the tumult on the bay, Charles Obend felt a surge of elation.

He was logged into Verba, engaged in a back-channel chat with Susie Q.

And tonight, for the first time, she was telling him that she wanted to meet him in the flesh.

At first their electronic acquaintance had progressed faster, and with more promise, than he had dared to hope. The night after their first encounter they had chatted on line for nearly half an hour. Then an hour the next night.

Susie Q>   Describe myself? I am optimistic, kind-hearted, ebullient. I love a good joke. The man who can make me laugh is halfway into my heart. I am perhaps too trusting. It's an easy way to get hurt, but I wouldn't have it any other way. What good is life if we erect walls around our emotions? Better to have loved and lost, etc., etc.

Physically, I am a touch over 5-7, a little taller if I'm in high heels. (Which I am frequently. They're instruments of torture, but I do like the effect.) Red hair, green eyes, long legs. My build . . . I'm not afraid to wear spandex, let's put it that way.

Susie Q—Suzanne Quillen—was a manufacturer's rep in Boston, twenty-eight years old. Like Obend, she was single, without children. They shared tastes in music, food, baseball, and movies. He had been astonished to learn that she, too, had a passion for classic American cars of the sixties: She actually drove a 'sixty-five Pontiac GTO.

He had felt an instant rapport, and a longing.

She had uploaded to him a digitized graphics file, electronically scanned from a photograph. It showed a slim young woman who, if not beautiful, was certainly as attractive as anyone Charles Obend had ever dated. Her eyes suggested a certain winsome sadness, a quiet unfulfilled desire. . . .

Charles Obend's longing deepened into a real ache.

Neither of them had suggested speaking by voice. Most on-line users agreed that the intimacy of a telephone conversation actually inhibited contact. People felt more free to express themselves when they sat at a keyboard.

Then, several days ago now, Charles Obend took a step that he had never before attempted with any on-line contact. He asked Susie Q for an "f2f"—a face-to-face meeting.

Chaz>	I would really, really like an f2f soon. Will happily fly to Boston or pay your way out here. I'm free and solvent.
Susie Q>	Maybe one day.
Chaz>	I'm a nice guy.
Susie Q>	I know that.
Chaz>	Then why the reluctance?
Susie Q>	I'm the shy and retiring type.
Chaz>	I certainly understand that. And you can't be too careful these days.
Susie Q>	Exactly.

Since then they had chatted once. Susie Q had been busy, traveling on business, she said.

Even so, she had seemed slightly distant, somehow less eager than at first.

But tonight she was turning all that around.

Susie Q>   Hello, Charles. This has to be quick—I'm in a bind for time tonight. But I want you to know that I have some news. I'm being sent to San Fran on business tomorrow. Ordinarily I would catch a nonstop flight. But I have the option of flying to K.C. and taking the red-eye from there. USAir has a connection that would give me two hours on the ground at KCI, what do you say?

Chaz>   Yes!!! [grin grin]

Susie Q>   Okay, Flight 540 from Boston, tomorrow night. Arrives a little after midnight, can you make it?

Chaz>   Any time, any place.

Susie Q>   Is that a yes or a no?

Chaz>   Sweetie, that is a big yes.

Susie Q>   Good. I'm glad. How will I know you?

Chaz>   By my look of intense anticipation.

Susie Q>   Tell me. How will I know you?

Chaz>   I'll be wearing a burgundy suede jacket and, say, a blue baseball cap. How about that?

Susie Q>   That works.

For a few seconds Charles Obend paused.

He didn't want to press her, but he needed an answer.

PHILLIP FINCH

Chaz>   One question. Why the change of heart?

And the cursor on his machine replied:

Susie Q>   Patience, dear Chaz. Patience. Soon all things will be clear.

17

Kate pulled back the curtain and saw him standing at the edge of the dock, standing straight even in the wind and rain, wearing a slick yellow anorak with the hood pulled over his head, and matching rain pants.

He was looking back toward the end of the pier. The hood obscured his face.

Then he reached out to rap on the glass again, and he turned his head to find her looking at him.

He stopped his knuckles a couple of inches short of the glass. And he smiled.

The details registered with Kate rapidly, subliminally.

He was about her age.

Maybe six feet tall, good posture.

Looked directly into her eyes.

A nice smile.

Nice face, what she could see of it.

Very nice smile.

He was yelling, gesturing toward the end of the dock, still smiling but shouting to be heard. She couldn't make it out.

She unlocked the glass and slid it open a few inches. Right away rain smacked her face.

". . . this the public anchorage?" he was yelling.

"No," she said, and she gestured over his shoulder, behind him. "Gate Three, they've got daily rates."

At the end of the dock she saw a sailboat that hadn't been there when she came home. It was bobbing and heaving, but it seemed secure. It was large, at least a forty-five-footer, a serious seagoing vessel.

"Terrific," he said, loud over the wind, still with a rueful little smile.

"You'll be all right there for a few hours," she said.

He nodded.

"Anyplace near here to get a meal?" he said.

She shook her head. Not after dark, not at this end of town. Downtown Sausalito, and the restaurants, were at least a mile down the road.

The rain beat hard in her face.

"Even a cup of coffee?" he said, the wind nearly swallowing his words. "I lost my generator last night, should've put in at Bolinas when I had the chance, it's my own damn fault."

He kept using the singular.

She said, "Are you alone?"

The words, really, just jumped out of her. But at the moment it seemed important, the question of whether he would have to sit, solitary, in the dark, rocking boat, cold and hungry, while he waited for the storm to pass.

Only later did she realize that he must have spent many nights alone on that boat. It would be routine if he sailed single-handed.

"Yep," he said.

The rain battering her face.

"You want some coffee?" she said.

"Yep." A speculative grin was now forming behind that hood.

She slid the door open and he stepped in.

She moved aside as he entered, and had to reach past him to shut the door. Then she stood watching as he pulled off the anorak, slipped out of the rain pants, tugged off his boots. He was trim but solid in a T-shirt and shorts.

Taller than she'd thought. A couple of inches over six feet.

One thing she noticed as he was peeling out of his gear: His eyes didn't go searching the place, trying to size things up. A nervous man might have done that. He did not look nervous.

He did give a quick glance. It caught the lone meal on the coffee table, which told him all he needed to know.

"Looks like we're a pair of orphans in the storm," he said.

She told him her name and put out her hand.

He took the hand. His grip was friendly, held just long enough.

He said, "Jonathon Wreggett. I am in your debt."

The way he said it, somehow he made the phrase sound real, sincere, not at all stilted.

He had a way of hitting all the right notes.

He followed her over to the counter and stood talking with her while she steamed water for cappuccino. He was on his way south from the San Juan Islands, off British Columbia, where he had spent the past three months. San Francisco Bay was a stopover on the way down to Cabo San Lucas.

She said, "Canada in the winter, Mexico in the summer, that's original."

"I'm a contrarian," he said. "Avoid the crowds."

She liked this guy.

They sat in the living room and talked. He was from back east, Massachusetts. He had been doing this for more than a year, sailing single, no ties. He left the impression of having money, certainly at least the means to live this way; but he didn't get into details, and she didn't ask.

He made her laugh about five times before they got to the bottom of the cappuccino. She realized that she felt at ease with him. Part of it was because *he* seemed at ease in a stranger's house: confident but not overbearing.

She heated another meal from the freezer, and this time she foraged for a salad to go with it.

They talked through the meal and into another cup of coffee. He asked her a few questions about herself, but not much, as if he didn't want to push.

They both seemed to notice at the same time that the rain and wind had stopped outside. The night was calm.

She was sorry to see it. The storm had been their excuse for being together, and now it was gone.

He brought his cup to the kitchen sink and said, "I probably ought to get my boat out of here."

"Right," she said.

"Public dock is down this way, huh?"

"About half a mile south along the waterfront, it's easy, you'll find it."

He was at the door. Picking up his slicker, slipping on his boots. She went over there, reached, slid the door open for him to leave. The air outside smelled clear and clean off the bay.

"This has been nice," he said. "Ah, that's a weak way to say it. But it has been. Very nice. It's times like this that I miss, being out on my lonesome."

And then again that grin, slightly crooked, as he added, "But if I'd had more like this, I might not be out there at all."

He stepped out onto the dock.

Simultaneously she said, "Good luck," and he said, "Thanks again." He walked a few steps down the pier, then turned back and found her still standing at the door, watching him leave.

He seemed ready to speak. But he didn't. He gave a slight, final wave of the hand, then turned away for good and continued up the dock, into the night.

18

The body washed up sometime before daybreak. It lay several hours in a mudflat within the shadow of the Martinez-Benicia toll bridge, which spans a northern strait of San Francisco Bay.

The body had come to rest nearly thirty miles from where it was thrown into the water, two weeks earlier. Actually, though, it had drifted more than four times that distance, the currents pulling it back and forth in the bay, until a combination of the high winds and a cresting spring tide had finally beached it and then abandoned it in the mud, where it was found by three high school boys who hiked down to the water with fishing poles and an ice chest full of beer.

They noticed it because one of them decided to investigate the loud buzzing of flies and a putrid stench.

He followed the sound and the odor to their source, and stood a few feet away, blinking and waving away flies and wondering what he had found.

Two weeks of putrefaction, two weeks in the bay, where it was set upon by scavenging birds and crabs and fish, had rendered the body almost unrecognizable.

Finally, though, the boy understood what he had found: It was human—a woman—or had been.

But it had no head. And the arms had been cut off at the elbows, the legs truncated at the knees.

The boy turned and retched into the weeds.

The body was taken to the office of the Solano County medical examiner.

Solano is one of eight counties that are usually said to comprise the unofficial region known as the San Francisco Bay Area. Within those eight counties are more than seventy-five discrete municipalities, each with an independent police force and its own set of criminal files.

Computers and telecommunications have given those counties and municipalities the tools to pool important information on crimes that cross their borders. In the end, however, those electronic tools are still dependent on human effort and subject to human foibles.

In the case of the decaying, dismembered body, the Solano County M.E. did not perform an autopsy until another day and a half had passed.

When he did, he identified it as a woman in her late forties. At one point he found a transparent plastic capsule lodged in the trachea. Inside the capsule was a square of white paper.

The paper was marked with the heading "meatware" and contained a series of numbers that the M.E. considered meaningless.

A clerk in the sheriff's department—whose job description included several different tasks—delayed by four days entering the county officers' report into the regional law enforcement database through which the Bay Area's cops share information.

And then the clerk entered an incorrect key word into the case header. This is the summary on which data searches were based: It was the equivalent of losing a file by placing it in the wrong cabinet drawer, and it meant that Lee Wade's partner passed over the report when he did a routine scan of murders in other jurisdictions.

Four more days passed before this error was caught and corrected.

In all, nearly ten days were lost before the information about the body—and about the plastic capsule and its contents—finally reached the one person who needed it most.

And by then it was too late.

19

Stephen Leviste had plans on Saturday morning. It was his first free day since his birthday, and he wasn't going to waste it.

His father, who worked at a product support desk for a software publisher down in Menlo Park, faced at least a half-hour's commute after he got off at five.

His older sister had gone to San Francisco with friends, and probably wouldn't even be home for dinner.

His mother, a real estate agent, had a series of showings booked for an out-of-town client all afternoon. She hadn't yet told him that he couldn't leave the house, and he wasn't going to give her the chance.

When he heard her moving around the bedroom, dressing, he took his sister's Walkman from her dresser and slung it around his neck.

Then he slipped downstairs. As he opened the front door, he called back, "Bye, Mom, have a good one, see you for dinner, huh?"

He closed the door behind him. Moving fast, he grabbed the bicycle leaning against the porch rail and pedaled away, down the hill.

The Levistes lived above the town of Pacifica, a few miles south of San Francisco, in a suburban neighborhood that was draped along the west side of a ridge that sloped down toward the ocean.

It was a steep ridge, and Stephen picked up speed very quickly as he headed downhill, away from the house. In a few seconds he was out of shouting distance, so he braked, slowed, relaxed.

He was gone.

.   .   .

By noon he was aboard the SamTrans bus, headed for the main terminal at San Francisco International Airport.

The first thing that struck him when he got off was that nearly everyone he saw was an adult. The few kids all seemed to be with parents.

He figured he'd better do this fast, before somebody started wondering about him.

He walked through the terminal until he found a row of six pay phones against a wall. Only two of the phones were open, and he went to one of those.

He picked up the receiver, mimed dropping in a coin—he had to stretch to reach the slot—then punched several numbers, and after a few moments he began to talk.

He pretended he was talking to his mother.

While he talked, he pulled the Milk Duds recorder from his shirt pocket. He set the box on the sill around the base of the pay phone. The edge of the box was touching the phone chassis.

"Okay, fine, I'll be home in a few minutes," he said into the receiver. Then he hung up.

Before he turned away, he reached into the box and pushed the red plastic switch that prepared the device to record the first loud noise.

Then he walked away from the phone and found a seat on a bench. From there he could see the phone.

Nobody seemed to notice him. Nobody paid any attention to the box of Milk Duds.

Several minutes passed before somebody used the phone. A woman with gray hair, he couldn't even guess how old.

He could tell right away that she wasn't going to be fast enough. She picked up the receiver—that would trigger the recorder—and by the time ten seconds ran out, she was still fumbling to get the phone card out of her purse.

After she left, he went back to the phone, went through the little charade again, and reset the recorder.

A few minutes later a businessman-type came to the phone. But Stephen saw his hand tap the keypad only seven times—a local call, no card involved.

When the businessman was gone, Stephen took the box down to a phone at the other end of the terminal. He didn't want to be noticed.

This time somebody hit the pay phone right away: a woman in a shirt and blazer and a leather attaché case. She picked up the receiver and banged out a long string of numbers from memory, rapid-fire.

Bingo.

When she was gone, Stephen retrieved the box, plugged the output jack into the Walkman, and recorded the tones onto a tape. They sounded clear enough when he played back the tape.

That was one.

He stayed in the terminal for nearly two hours, recording what he was sure were at least three or four good tries, with half a dozen possibles. He might have continued, but a security guard seemed to be watching him.

He walked out of the terminal and caught the next bus for Pacifica.

He didn't get a chance to play the Walkman tape right away. He was just dumping the recordings into his computer's memory when his mother got home, barely enough time for him to replace the

Walkman in his sister's room. As penance for rushing out the door that morning he had to clean the basement, his mother's favorite rainy-day assignment.

Dinner was ready by the time he had finished cleaning. Then his sister came home, went to her room, and started yelling that he had been into her things, a standard rant. . . .

Finally he got to his room, shut the door behind him, and opened the sound file of the tape, the series of beeping tones that the Milk Duds recorder had picked up.

The decoded numerals kept appearing on the screen, going into a word-processing program. Stephen had left several seconds of blank tape between each ten-second Milk Duds recording, so he had no trouble sorting them out.

When the tones had ended, Stephen began editing the strings of numerals. He deleted all the phone numbers, then deleted all the strings that hadn't been finished within the ten-second limit.

He was left with five complete, valid, verifiable access codes. Every one was good for up to a month of free long distance, until the cardholder opened his or her monthly bill.

He had to tell somebody about this.

He turned on his modem and connected to Verba.

At the welcome prompt he paused to consider which of his handles he should use. He had at least four or five at any time.

Stephen Leviste had been reading since he was three years old. He had read *Old Yeller* when he was six and had finished all of Dickens's major works the summer he turned ten. He had charged through Evelyn Waugh within the past few weeks.

Waugh had, in fact, provided him with one of his favorite handles. It was from *The Loved One*, the name of a porky, obscene undertaker.

Steven typed it in now:

Joyboy

Then he typed:

visit MAG

The Manga-Anime Gallery was supposed to be devoted to discussions of Japanese cartoon and animation art. In the last few weeks, as a sort of sideshow, it had become a hangout for assorted hackers, crackers, phreakers, and warez pirates: the computer underground, and those who aspired to it.

Stephen wanted to brag about what he had done that day, and he thought that the Milk Duds hack might be an entree to the clannish crackers, who scorned dilettantes and warez kidz, but who were always looking for ways to steal phone service.

This evening, though, Stephen found himself alone in the gallery. Apparently the cyberpunks had crowded out the animation lovers, and then had abandoned the group once they had it to themselves.

Stephen logged off Verba.

He was about to turn off the computer, when he spotted the diskette that had arrived on his birthday. HOT WAREZ. A little boring, but maybe worth a try.

He stuck it in his disk drive and checked the directory. TRY_ME was the command that would boot the program.

He was about to do that, when his mother came to the door.

"Bedtime," she said.

"Mom, really . . ."

"Bedtime," she said again, firmly now.

He had come close to real trouble once today already—her patience would be thin.

PHILLIP FINCH

While she watched, he popped out the diskette and laid it on the machine, switched off the modem and the monitor and then the computer itself.

He changed into pajamas, brushed his teeth, kissed his parents, and went up to his room.

He went to bed with the lights out, fully expecting to climb out in a few minutes and boot the computer again. Check out that diskette.

But the bed felt good. For the first time all day his head stopped working. He gave up thinking about codez and warez and the diskette and all the rest, and he slept.

20

Kate Lavin's Saturday morning began badly. She awoke loggy after a fitful night. Then, later in the morning, she had to cancel a staff meeting to kick off the jaguar documentary; the freelance director she wanted to use called to say that her car had been stolen overnight, she wouldn't be able to get to Sausalito.

Kate walked over to the studio anyway.

The place was busy.

In one video control booth, a director was calling shots on a syndicated sports interview program that taped five segments once a week from a studio set.

In the second booth, a local filmmaker worked postproduction on a documentary of his own—the studio's facilities and its staff were all available for hire, by the hour.

The three editing suites were all occupied with editors and producers who were cutting a series of TV ads for a hamburger chain, an in-house safety training film for an oil refinery, and public service promos for the California Highway Patrol.

Kate stepped into each suite in turn, to stand and watch for a few minutes.

Everyone was working hard and well. Doing exactly what they were supposed to do, she thought. Which meant that there was really nothing there for her.

She went into her office, logged into her e-mail account on the computer, and found nothing—she had already checked the messages from her machine at home less than an hour earlier. She signed off on a short stack of paperwork that required no more than ten minutes.

It left her with a clean desk and an open day, and no plan to fill the empty hours.

She started across the parking lot, back home.

Her mind felt dull and somehow distanced from the sunshine and the briny smell of the bay and the pavement under her shoes.

She could feel the day getting away from her.

She hated the idea of being adrift and aimless. She craved direction, a place to go, a reason to be there.

With Ellis that had not seemed so important. Ellis was content to follow the seemingly random threads of life. Not in a lazy way either: He was quite capable of focusing, almost to a frenzy, on a task with no apparent point, hitching himself to it and letting it take him where it would.

Ellis asked—demanded—only that the pursuit be interesting. When it stopped engaging him, he might walk away from a month's work.

He might even walk away from a marriage, she thought.

In any case, Ellis would certainly know what to do with a free Saturday.

She forced him out of her mind. She thought that she could at least pretend to have something to do, a place to go. The day was slipping away from her; life itself seemed to be slipping from her grasp, and that could not be allowed.

Back in the houseboat, she pulled on a sweater over a shirt and shorts. She went outside, around to the stern, to the fiberglass kayak she kept lashed there. In a minute or two the little boat was bobbing in the water, and she was climbing in, pushing off into Richardson Bay, headed toward the shallows at the north end of Sausalito's waterfront.

Richardson Bay is about a mile wide at its mouth, where it empties into San Francisco Bay, and it extends three or four miles into Marin County. With Sausalito on its west shore, Tiburon and the enclave of Belvedere on its east side, it is surrounded by some of the nation's most desirable and expensive residential real estate.

She and Ellis had kayaked together out there during their marriage, when they'd both spent long days at the studio. The kayak was a friendly craft in a way: Almost anyone could climb in and immediately start going places, muscling it along.

But doing it well required technique bordering on art. At times, during the last few months, she had thought she was really getting there, when the kayak seemed to skim the water, almost leaping ahead with each stroke of the paddle.

Not today though. Even in the quiet estuary she seemed to be fighting the boat and the paddle—and fighting herself too.

Ellis, though he was no athlete, had mastered the technique. He had paddled with a narrow-eyed intensity, his face set hard, his strokes precise. Calculating the optimum method, he told her.

Leave it to Ellis, turn physical exercise into a mental challenge.

She headed for home now, about three-quarters of a mile distant. She stroked, pulling, off rhythm. She hated to wrestle the kayak this way. The dock was within sight now. She could make out her place, wedged in among the others along the north side of the pier.

And off to the left, tied at the end of the dock, a large white ketch-rigged sailboat.

He was there—Jon Wreggett—standing on the dock, then hopping off onto the houseboat, walking to the stern, reaching to pull her up and lifting out the kayak.

This was the part she hated, hauling the kayak out of the water. It didn't weigh a lot, but it was ungainly, and the stern of the house-

PHILLIP FINCH

boat sat just high enough to make a long reach for her down to the water.

But he made it look easy, one quick move and he was lifting it out, turning, setting it where it belonged.

He started lashing it down.

"You're good," he said. "I was watching."

"Either you're trying to snow me, or you don't know what you're talking about."

"No. Really. You have the moves. I can tell."

Just like that he had the kayak secured. Nothing to distract him now, he was giving her his attention. She felt sweaty, disheveled.

"I guess I have my moments," she said.

He stood looking at her, seeming tentative, she thought—she hadn't noticed that in him before. She thought she ought to say something, fill in the gaps, so she said, "I didn't expect to see you again."

"Yeah, here I am," he said, and then—almost as if he were in a hurry to get it out—he said, "I've been thinking about it, I've been thinking it would just be incredibly stupid if we never saw each other again. I realize we just met, but it really felt good. I thought you were great, just a flat-out winner, it was all I could do to make myself walk away from here last night."

For a second he almost looked like a kid, a nervous boy disgorging a speech.

"What am I supposed to say to that?" she asked.

"Say you'll go sailing with me."

When she hesitated, he added, "I'm not talking about any round-the-world voyage. Let's not rush things. I was thinking of"—looking back over his right shoulder—"right there, looks like a nice little anchorage. We could go ashore, walk around, I'd have you back in a couple of hours."

He was looking at the big shaggy hump of Angel Island, off

Tiburon, just beyond the mouth of Richardson Bay. It was a couple of miles away.

"I guess that's not exactly rounding the Horn, is it?" she said.

"Take things a step at a time, like I said. But it looks pretty."

"It's beautiful—that's a state park."

He said, "Then how about it?"

There was a quiet copse of eucalyptus halfway up the west side of the high hill that dominates the island—she could see it from here. More than once she and Ellis had spread a blanket up there, alone on a weekday afternoon. They had made love and then dozed with the hillside and the bay and the Golden Gate spread out before them. . . .

"When?" she asked.

"Tomorrow? Maybe noon or so?"

She didn't answer right away. He stood before her, waiting, patient and composed.

"Why not?" she said.

21

That night Charles Obend parked his Camaro in the short-term garage, in front of Concourse A, Kansas City International Airport. He left the car and walked toward the concrete stairway that was the only pedestrian exit for the garage.

He walked into the concourse building. It was nearly empty: a few minutes before midnight. Charles Obend went directly to the USAir Arrivals video screen. Flight 540 from Boston was on time, due at 12:18 A.M. He had about twenty minutes.

The concourse restaurants were all closed. But Obend found a newsstand, where he bought a Snickers bar. He brought it with him to a bench in front of the glass-enclosed portal of Gate 9.

He sat, unwrapped the candy, and began to eat it while he waited.

He could see the plane as it taxied toward the gate. Obend stood and straightened the blue baseball cap on his head.

In a minute or two the first passengers made their way up the jetway ramp. Two men in their fifties, rumpled business suits. A college-age girl in cut-off jeans and Docs, running into the arms of a boy about the same age. Obend kept watching as the rest of the passengers streamed out in a brief rush.

Not many of them, just twenty or thirty in all—the plane must have been flying almost empty.

Then no more passengers came through the door. The jetway was empty.

Missed her, he thought. *She's around here someplace.* He looked around. But he saw nobody who even came close to being a twenty-eight-year-old, five-foot-seven redhead.

Obend waited a few more minutes, until the three flight attendants appeared on the ramp. Then he walked quickly up the concourse, to the baggage carousels. He hurried up there even though he knew that didn't make sense: She was just supposed to be passing through, so she wouldn't be picking up baggage.

And she wasn't, either.

The gate was empty when Obend walked back there. He turned away, left the building, and headed down the concrete stairway.

At the bottom of the stairs he started toward his Camaro. The garage was half empty, and quiet. Nobody else around.

No, someone was standing by a blue four-door, about ten or twelve spaces up the row where Obend was walking. Man in a black overcoat, wearing black gloves, resting a black nylon camera bag on the hood.

And holding a video camcorder in his left hand, this did seem strange to Obend.

The stranger stood and watched as Charles Obend got closer. Obend glanced at his face: lumpy, with a mustache and huge brushy eyebrows.

Obend had to walk past him to get to the Camaro. As he approached the four-door, Charles Obend looked away from the stranger.

"Hey, Charlie," the man said, "I know that's you."

Obend didn't answer. He needed a second or two to sort this out.

The stranger said, "Charles C. Obend of Bruce Street, Lee's Summit, Missouri."

"What about it?" Obend said.

"Susie sent me," the stranger said.

The stranger thrust his gloved hand into the bag. He was holding a big glass bottle, a half-gallon orange juice jug full of some clear liquid.

He started walking quickly toward Obend, three or four rapid strides that brought them almost within spitting distance. Obend saw that the bottle was open. As he walked, the stranger brought his arm back and then forward again, a motion so swift and deft that Obend could only stand and watch as that pale liquid fountained out of the bottle, reaching through the air.

Obend smelled it before it hit him, a quick whiff. Then it was all over him, stinging his eyes, soaking his clothes. Charcoal lighter fluid. Tinged with the definite stink of gasoline.

Charles Obend turned half away from the stranger and brought a sleeve up to his eyes, try to wipe away the gasoline. But that didn't help. The sleeve was soaked too.

The stranger took one step back and threw the bottle at Obend's feet. It broke, and the rest of the fuel spread across the concrete floor of the garage.

He knew he ought to run. Do something. But he couldn't move. The phrase ran through his head, *paralyzed with fright,* and in the back of his mind he realized that it was not just words.

"Idiot," the stranger said.

Obend turned back toward the sound and looked at him through his tearing eyes. The stranger clicked a flame into a Bic lighter. He was holding a wadded ball of paper, paper must be soaked with something, Obend thought, because when the stranger touched it to the lighter, it caught right away, *whump,* it blazed in the stranger's hand.

He tossed it toward Obend, and the world exploded.

Flames, flames everywhere, covering him, burning Charles Obend's clothes, his hair, his skin. God, burning.

Now his legs were moving, trying to make way across the fuel flaming on the floor. But too late. The floor was slippery from the fluid. He stumbled, fell hard.

Through the flames Obend could see the stranger holding a

second glass jug, hefting it once and then flipping it, a high arc that was going to bring it to earth about two feet from where Charles Obend lay.

But this was just incidental, really. He watched the second jug cartwheeling toward him, but it didn't really matter, it hardly had anything to do with him. All he cared about was the pain he already felt, the indescribable searing that not only covered his body but leapt into his throat and down into his lungs when he drew his next breath.

The jug hit the concrete, and shattered.

And Charles Obend screamed, a scream straight out of his gut, a scream that he could not hear above the roar of the flames.

The camera was already recording. The killer stepped back and brought it to his face. The fire flared in the viewfinder, and he wondered how it would look on tape, what this would do to the exposure.

He kept shooting as he backed toward the stairwell, trying to keep the camera pointed at the flames.

By now Charles Obend had stopped screaming.

On the stairs the killer pulled off the fake mustache and eyebrows and the makeup putty that had altered his chin and cheekbones. He zipped them, along with the camera and gloves, into the nylon bag.

In the terminal he stopped in the men's room to check for traces of adhesive. None. Good. He bought a Coke from an all-night newsstand, and he walked straight to Concourse C, where the United flight to San Francisco was boarding. Nonstop service. He stepped aboard as they were announcing last call.

He had a window seat. As the airplane taxied, he looked over toward the terminal building, Concourse A. A fire truck was trundling out of the parking garage.

He put his head back against the seat, closed his eyes. Slept all the way to San Francisco, woke just before the plane touched down.

It was a couple of hours before daybreak. The killer went to his vehicle—it was a Dodge cargo van, tobacco-colored—and drove straight home.

22

Julia Chua was awake in the early hours of that Sunday morning, when her tenant came home to the two-story clapboard house on Tenth Avenue. Her husband was out of town on business for two weeks, and she always slept fitfully when he was gone.

Her bedroom window was above the entrance of the basement apartment. The window was open a few inches, so she could clearly hear his footsteps along the walkway at the side of the house, then his fumbling with the locks—both of them.

He first opened the padlock that secured the door to a hasp on the jamb, then turned the key on a deadbolt. Opening the door, he flipped on the light. Julia Chua heard him grunt. He was probably picking up the mail that she had seen the postman shove through the slot that morning.

It was the first piece of mail he'd received in the two months he'd been living there. And it was nothing special, just an advertising circular.

That bothered Julia Chua. He never got letters, he never had guests, she never even heard the sound of a TV. He came and left at strange, irregular hours, and the rare moments when they met, he seemed open and affable but revealed nothing. His geniality *was* false, she was sure of it. Julia Chua knew these things.

And why did he need that padlock he had installed in the door the day after he moved in, though the original door lock was strong? What was there to steal? The apartment was only one low-ceilinged room, furnished simply with her worn, plain castoffs. His most valuable possession was the computer that sat on her old Formica dining table.

He didn't need that padlock to keep out the world.

Just his landlords.

What was he trying to protect?

Or hide?

She wasn't afraid of him—he had never given her a reason to be afraid—but he had too many empty spaces, he suggested too many questions.

She didn't trust what she couldn't understand.

One of these days, she thought, she would start filling in some of the blanks that surrounded her mysterious tenant, Mr. Corwin Sturmer.

23

Early that same morning, a single page curled out of the fax machine that sat on a desk in the corner of the squad room in the homicide division of the SFPD, at the Hall of Justice on Bryant Street.

It remained there until a clerk reporting for duty noticed it and picked it up.

The clerk looked at it, then looked again, closer. He had never seen anything like this. For one thing, the ID line at the top of the page didn't show the number of the sending machine. No cover page, not even any "to" or "from" in the message.

It didn't look like official business.

He thought that maybe it was just a mistake. It happened sometimes, with all the faxes going back and forth these days. People dialed the wrong number, and ended up transmitting to the wrong machine.

Hell, hardly anybody actually *talked* anymore.

The message read:

MEATWARE Version 3
5–7
Taken: 17029 21067
Slain: 17029 21067

LAMERS
CLUELESS LAMERS

But on the off chance that the piece of paper was intended for someone in the squad, the clerk pinned it to the corkboard on the wall beside the coffeemaker.

PHILLIP FINCH

It stayed there for about an hour. Then Lee Wade came into the squad room. It was a Sunday morning, but whenever a case was going sour, he usually compensated with unpaid overtime.

He hung up his coat and went to get a cup of coffee.

He was stirring in sugar when he looked up at the corkboard. His eyes went to the fax message right away. The look of it—he had seen one like that before.

"Son of a bitch," he said with feeling.

24

The trip across Richardson Bay was just a few minutes. Jon put in at Ayala Cove, on the north side of Angel Island, in the narrow strait between the island and the Tiburon peninsula.

They rode a small Zodiac inflatable onto the sandy beach of the harbor. Directly ahead was the state park headquarters, a low white two-story structure that had once been the administration building of a turn-of-the-century quarantine station for immigrating Asians.

Dozens of people picnicked and played on the lawn in front of the building. The forested promontory rose up behind them.

Jon tied up the Zodiac, and she led him to a hiking trail that worked its way along the west side of the island. Jon walked beside her, the trail narrow enough that their shoulders sometimes bumped, their arms brushed.

A strange feeling. She had walked this trail dozens of times, but never with any man except Ellis. Having this near-stranger beside her almost made the island a different place.

She liked that. She felt renewed.

In a couple of minutes they had left behind the cove and the people. They were surrounded by trees. The smell of eucalyptus and madrona were heavy around them. Through breaks in the trees they could see Sausalito and the Golden Gate, and the Pacific beyond that, receding into a gray mist.

He reached for her hand, and she let him take it, and they kept walking.

The trail was taking them around the circumference of the high central hill, Mount Livermore. It dominated the island's 740 acres—a little more than one square mile. As they walked, the trees opened up, and the view now was San Francisco across the bay:

the wharves, Telegraph Hill and Coit Tower, the Marina, on west-ward to the neat layouts of the avenues that lapped out toward the ocean.

Directly below them the hill fell down toward a spur that ex-tended out into the water, pointing southeast down the bay.

At the base of the spur, on a slight bluff that dropped down to beaches on two sides, sat a broad, flat concrete pad. Angel Island had been the site of a series of military installations, from the mid-nineteenth century until the early sixties. Evidence of them—in-cluding barracks and roads and gun emplacements—dotted the island. This was the most recent: From 1954 to 1962 it had been the site of a missile battery.

Kate and Jon stood there for several minutes. The panorama was alive with the movement of boats, the intermittent glinting of sunlight off the water, the nearly imperceptible squirming of traffic on the bridges and in the city.

"Beautiful," he said. He put an arm around her waist, his eyes all the time on the view before them. He drew her closer, and she didn't resist.

He turned toward her.

"Beautiful," he said again.

But this time he was looking at her.

By late afternoon they were heading back across Richardson Bay under diesel power. Kate stood beside Jon as he guided the boat easily toward the dock, so easily, gently, that when she went to the side, she was surprised to find it snug against the rubber bumpers.

From the wheel he said, over the burble of the engine, "We ought to see each other again," he said. "We really should. It'd be crazy not to."

"Okay," she said.

"Lunch tomorrow. You want to pick me up?" Gesturing toward Gate Three.

"Eleven-thirty," she said. "You'll be there?"

"Where else?" he said.

Oh, that grin again.

She stepped onto the dock, waved, and watched him back the boat away. Then he turned it south, toward Gate Three. She watched him and the craft as they receded from view: almost dreamlike.

An exceptionally good dream.

The houseboat seemed empty and pointless when she went inside. She puttered for a while with housecleaning that the place really didn't need.

Within an hour she was wishing that she hadn't let him go. That had been her idea: Keep it short with him, keep this thing casual. This thing, whatever it was.

But now that seemed dumb.

She knew where she could find some companionship, after a fashion. It seemed awfully thin and unsatisfying after the past few hours, but with a live presence gone, it was the best she could do.

She went to her desktop computer, turned it on, and she dialed Verba.

After she logged on, the system greeted her as always.

Welcome, Ziggy

She typed:

visit WI

Three of the regulars—Nancy-T, Michiko, Aurora—greeted her as the system connected her with the group.

She hadn't been there for almost a week: She sat back to read for a while, catch up.

Salome arrived a couple of minutes later, and Michiko wrote:

Michiko> Another vagrant spirit wafts through the ether. Long time no see.

Salome> I have an impeccable excuse for my absence. The pool service sent over a ripe new repairman last week, and he arrived just bursting with the yen to spend a long week-end in Santa Cruz.

Nancy-T> Excuse accepted. Can Ziggy top that?

Ziggy> Work is my excuse. As ever.

Michiko> You'll never meet anyone that way.

Ziggy> You may be wrong about that.

Aurora> Ziggy strikes oil!

Salome> Is it a gusher?

Michiko> Come clean, Zig . . .

Ziggy> Quite a nice guy. Interesting. Certainly not cut from the standard pattern. He's a sailor.

Nancy-T> Returned from a long voyage, no doubt.

Salome> Single?

Ziggy> Yes.

Michiko> Good-looking? And please don't say something like, "It's all a matter of taste."

Ziggy> In this instance the verdict would be unanimous, I think. He's an attention-getter.

Nancy-T> This sounds serious.

Ziggy> I hardly know him, really.

Michiko> Don't waste time on the standard disclaimers, we are not interested.

Ziggy>   He's intriguing, I'll admit it.

Salome>   Silence, all. A respectful hush. Let us keep our hot little
            fingers off the keyboards so that the Zigster may take
            the floor. . . . That's better. . . . Now, Ziggy, you tell us all
            about the dear boy. And don't leave out a single deli-
            cious detail. . . .

25

That afternoon, Lee Wade visited 2600 Tesla.

Since the fax arrived, he had been thinking about the scruffy guy up there in the dark house on Telegraph Hill.

Whoever wrote that note was certainly bent in some unusual directions. That seemed to fit Ellis Hoile, for sure.

Records checks had already told Wade that Ellis Hoile had no apparent criminal record, that he owned the house on Tesla free and clear, and that for all the affluence that address implied, the only motor vehicle registered in his name was a 1974 Datsun 510 sedan.

After the fax showed up, Wade had asked his partner, whose name was Ronson, to interview Ellis Hoile's immediate neighbors. This was how he had learned of Ellis Hoile's marriage and divorce.

The neighbors were unanimous, Ronson reported. They thought he was a very nice man, friendly, though somewhat distant—and a little strange. Keeps to himself, more so since the divorce. But nice.

Lee Wade thought this was pretty funny. It sounded like what the neighbors always tell TV reporters upon the arrest of the mass murderer living next door.

And none of it meant anything. All Wade had, really, was an instinct, a feeling, about Ellis Hoile. The instinct told him that he needed to see Ellis Hoile again, talk to him, look him in the eye: examine him in those first few unguarded moments when he realized that he might actually be suspected of a crime.

Lee Wade believed that the reactions you got from suspects at that moment could tell you more than hours of interrogation. This was especially true of guilty people, who tended to be defensive and flustered when you ambushed them this way.

And now Ellis Hoile was opening the door on the third ring. He didn't look flustered or defensive though. Just tired and mildly curious, if that, as he opened the door and said, "SFPD homicide, uh, Wade is the name, right? Sergeant Lee Wade."

Wade could almost see his mind working, the name clicking into place.

"You remember," Wade said.

"I know who I know. As I mentioned the other day."

"You did say that."

"Don't tell me somebody else got killed."

Funny you should mention that, Wade thought. But he shook his head, saying, "No, I'm still hung up on the Donald Trask matter."

"I don't know what I can do for you," Ellis Hoile said.

Wade said, "I was thinking, you having such a good memory and all, you might remember something about him that didn't come to you last time."

"I told you what I know."

"You might remember that you met him once, it slipped your mind."

"No, I never met him," Ellis Hoile said, "I'm sure of that."

"So you told me," Wade said.

"You don't spend much time on line. Computers."

"Can't say that I do."

"If you tried it, you'd know what I mean. That's one of the interesting aspects of on-line culture, the whole question of identity, who somebody is and what they claim to be. In a way, who you *really* are is inconsequential. You can claim to be a Nobel-winning physicist, see, and it might be a lie, but if you fake it well enough, if you pull it off, nobody would know. And if you *could* fake it that well, if you somehow had acquired anything close to that level of knowledge, then you've earned some respect anyway."

Wade believed that Ellis Hoile was veering off the subject. Maybe on purpose. Thinking that he would get the conversation back on track, he said, "If you had met Mr. Trask, you wouldn't want to keep lying about it. That would be a bad deal. The more often you lied about it, the worse it would look for you if I found out."

Bringing it out in the open.

Wade was watching him closely now, tuned in to how Ellis Hoile reacted when he was pushed.

Like he was just figuring it out, Ellis Hoile said, "You think I killed him. That's what this is about."

Wade didn't deny it. He kept watching Ellis Hoile's face. What he saw was a very slight bemusement, but not panic, not anger. Nothing forced. Lee Wade had watched some excellent liars try to con him—it was enlightening, to let them keep trying when you already had proof that they were lying.

"Listen to me," Ellis Hoile was saying. His voice was calm and low, almost like a good parent talking to a kid, the little smile now leaving his face. "I did not kill Donald Trask. I have never killed anyone. I don't kill people. I don't even like to hurt people. It isn't in me."

"It's in everybody," Wade said.

"I can't prove a negative," Ellis Hoile continued, apparently unaware that he was on trial. "I don't think I can demonstrate with absolute logical certainty that I did not kill Donald Trask, that I did not even know Donald Trask, but I'm telling you, if that's what you think—"

This was going nowhere. Wade cut him off with a gesture, his hands raised slightly. Try something else.

"Look at this," he said.

In Wade's right hand was a folded piece of paper. It was a photocopy of the killer's two notes. With nothing to lose, he held it out to Ellis Hoile.

"This mean anything to you?" he said.

Ellis Hoile gave it a quick glance and said, "On what level?"

Jeez, this guy could drive you up the wall.

"Tell me what you think," said Lee Wade. "Pretend I don't know jack shit about it."

Which was pretty much the truth.

"Whoever wrote this has spent time on line," Ellis Hoile said. "But you probably already knew that."

This was news to Wade.

"Computers."

"Right."

"What makes you say that?" Wade was thinking, *Great, fucking computers, just what I need.*

"The language," said Ellis Hoile. "The version number is software nomenclature. A new program might be version one-point-oh. You make a few small changes, it becomes version one-point-one. Version two-point-oh would be a whole new update.

"Clueless lamer, you hear that all the time on line. Meaning somebody who has no idea what he's doing."

Wade thought that one hit way too close to home.

"And meatware?" he said.

"That's not nearly as common. You hear that mostly around hard-core hackers. Meatware, wetware, like that. Let's say some people were having trouble with a certain system. If you're the programmer, you might say the hardware is solid, the software has been debugged, but there's a problem with the meatware component."

"Meaning?"

"The users," said Ellis Hoile. "Human beings."

"Nice," said Wade.

"It doesn't really mean anything. It's just a term."

"It's not just a term to this asshole," Wade said. "How about the numbers, I don't suppose you recognize those?"

"Not offhand. They might be two-dimensional coordinates. Two sets each. But the second one, both sets are the same, that's intriguing."

"Intriguing," said Wade. "Right."

"I assume these are connected with the murder."

Wade, with the image in his mind of the assistant M.E. extracting the plastic capsule from the body of Donald Trask, just nodded.

"That's about all I can tell you," said Ellis Hoile. "He's been around computers. Maybe a lot. I'm quite certain of that."

"That's a help," said Wade, though he didn't really mean it.

Ellis Hoile started to return the paper, but Lee Wade, again on a whim, said, "No, that's a copy—you keep that. Maybe something'll come to you on those numbers."

"All right."

"It does, you give me a call."

"I will," said Ellis Hoile. He didn't seem to be finished though— as if he had something else that he wasn't sure he should mention.

"Spit it out," Lee Wade said.

"The man who wrote this is organized. He's methodical, you can tell. His whole approach. He's intense. He doesn't screw around. Don't ask me to show you where I get this, because I can't. It's how his words sound, the way he arranges things. Just an impression, okay? But you asked."

"Anything else?"

"This may be a formidable person."

A wry, self-conscious laugh.

"Am I anywhere close?" said Ellis Hoile.

"You have no idea," said Lee Wade.

26

A few minutes before midnight, Stephen Leviste was still at his computer. He had been playing TRY ME all day.

It was a great game: plenty of action, ingenious traps and tricks. He hadn't won yet, but he didn't consider the game unwinnable. He had been making steady progress through the maze.

The main obstacle was a faceless assassin who seemed to wander the concrete corridors at random. You could run away from him sometimes, but eventually he would find you. He always did.

And when he caught you he would kill you, no getting away from that. Stephen Leviste had died hundreds of times in the maze.

Now he pushed through a door in the sixth level and found the fiend standing on the other side. Waiting.

Stephen moved his mouse so that he could flee.

From out in the hall, he heard scuffling. Then came his mother's sleepy voice. "Stephen, for heaven's sake. What are you doing?"

Stephen pushed his mouse forward, hurrying his character back through the doors, around two corners.

"Stephen . . ." said his mother.

"Okay," he said.

He went over and turned off the bedroom lamp. Then he waited, still staring at the monitor, until he heard his mother padding back to bed.

When he reached again for the keyboard, the fiend reappeared. He was holding a chain saw, stepping closer. Pulling the starter cord. The chain saw's engine caught on the first try.

Brrrrrrap was the sound that rasped through the computer's speakers as the assassin stepped forward, revving the engine, pushing the saw so close, it filled the screen. . . .

"Stephen!" His mother was back at his door.

The screen went to blood red for a moment, then black, as it once more asked:

Try Me Again?

Stephen's mother did what he couldn't bring himself to do. She walked in and turned off the computer and the monitor. Then she kissed him on the cheek.

27

Lee Wade had picked up a pizza on his way home, to the half a duplex off Taraval Street where he lived with his wife and their two children. It was not far from Ocean Beach, one of the last neighborhoods in gentrified San Francisco that was even close to working-class.

They had gotten the kids off to bed early, for once. Then Wade had drawn a hot bath and lay in it to stew.

His wife had come in to where he lay, neck-deep in water that was near scalding. She'd brought him a beer, washed his hair, kneaded the muscles of his neck.

He'd luxuriated not only in the touch, but in being accepted, understood.

"One step slow, not quite smart enough," he'd said. His first words in nearly an hour. "It's the worst damn feeling I know. Being just smart enough to know that you're not real smart."

She had soaped his chest.

"You're plenty smart," she said.

He'd just shaken his head.

Before long they had walked together to the bed, and for a little while she had made him forget about it.

He had been asleep for hours when the phone rang. Usually he answered it, but she had ended up on his side of the bed.

She listened and said, "He's right here," and passed the handset to her husband.

"This is Ellis Hoile," said the voice in the earpiece.

Lee Wade tried to focus on the digital alarm clock beside the bed. Two forty-seven. Where was the guy's sense of time?

"I hope you don't mind. You asked me to call if anything else came to mind. I was considering our conversation, when something came to me, and since it may be time-critical, I wanted to reach you as soon as possible."

Wade just lay there, propped up on one elbow, trying not to nod off.

"Are you there?" asked Ellis Hoile.

"Yes."

"You should examine the contents of the hard drive of Donald Trask's computer. Also any diskettes. There's a reasonable probability that you'll find the name of his killer on his disk storage. Or at least some reference to his killer."

Suddenly Wade was wide awake again.

"It's been right in my face," Ellis Hoile said. "The victim used an on-line network, and I'm sure that the killer has on-line experience.

"Now, granted that could be a coincidence. A lot of people have gone on line in the past couple of years. It could be that the killer didn't select Donald Trask for reasons that have anything to do with computers. On the other hand, maybe he did.

"I've been thinking about this. In a purely theoretical way, of course, so don't start getting any ideas about me again. But I was thinking, an on-line network would be an ideal place to stalk a victim."

Ellis Hoile's words were rapid, slightly breathless. He seemed to be excited. Lee Wade had gotten a couple of glimmers of him this way before: totally focused, turned on by what was in his head. Almost incandescent.

"I mean, when cops investigate a murder, the first people they look at are the victim's family and friends. Most victims of murder are killed by someone they know—am I right? And in normal life those connections are easy to follow. You know where the victim lived, where he worked. You have an idea who he's been in contact with.

"On line, though, the connections vanish the second you log off. That doesn't mean the contact is any less real. When you meet somebody out there, you really are meeting them. It's like you're both in some neutral territory, and even though you'd never find it on a map, it's there, it's a real place, and you both know it.

"When you jack out, you disconnect, whatever you want to call it—then it's gone, and there's no trail. But that doesn't mean it was any less real while it lasted."

Silence on the line.

"I'm here," Wade said. "I'm trying to get this straight."

Grappling with an idea that Ellis Hoile had digested—no doubt with ease—long ago.

"You think he stored the killer's name?"

"Maybe. A lot of the on-line culture is e-mail and downloaded messages. That would be the only record of their contact, if he saved any of that. If you looked on his disks, you might find a lot of names, and there might not be anything to tell you that any one of them killed him. And maybe none of them did.

"It would be a ton of work, checking them out. But you might be better off trying that than what you're doing now. If you're really stuck."

He caught his breath. When he spoke again, Ellis Hoile sounded like a guy delivering bad news. He said:

"I don't mean to sound presumptuous. Really. But the world is changing. A lot of the old ways of doing things don't work as well as they used to."

Another pause. He seemed to be waiting for Lee Wade to say something.

"I appreciate this," said Wade.

"Sorry to disturb you at this hour," said Ellis Hoile. "But I thought you ought to know."

He hung up.

Lee Wade reached over his wife, and replaced the phone in its cradle.

He put his back flat against the mattress and looked up at the ceiling in his dark bedroom. He wasn't sleepy anymore. His shoulders were knotted again, and his head hurt.

He felt it again: the sensation that life was running away from him, becoming more distant all the time, getting so far beyond him that he would never catch up.

After he had hung up the phone, Ellis Hoile connected to Verba.

He did this by swiveling in his chair so that he faced a microphone that stood on his desktop.

In conversational tones, he said:

"Comm. Verba. Connect."

One of the computers on his desks responded by opening a communications program, selecting the entry for Verba, and executing a short script he had written to automate his log-in.

The modem connected. As always, Verba's system asked for a user ID, and Ellis Hoile's script supplied the handle by which he had been known for years, and then added his password.

Verba's computer responded:

Welcome Avatar
You have new mail.

"Check mail," he said, and by the time he was at his chair, the index was on the screen with a single entry.

Stoma@verba.org   21:18   A new game!

PART IV

Avatar

May 8–May 12

28

Alone in the apartment on Tesla Street, Ellis Hoile opened the message from Stoma:

Hi,

I need beta-testers for a new game. It's a twist on the old dungeon adventures, but heavy on graphics.

Being the game maven that you are, I thought you might like a peek at the beta version. Find it attached. Source included! Your comments are welcome.

Ellis Hoile enjoyed computer games—most hackers did. Whenever personal computers got faster and more capable—which happened about two or three times a year these days—the first applications to push the envelope of the new systems were usually graphics-heavy games.

You had to play games if you wanted to stay current on the state of the art.

Ellis Hoile's specialty was maze games. Many hackers liked them, though most preferred actual physical mazes when they could be found. For many hackers—Ellis Hoile among them—the chance to spend a week lost in the sewers of Paris would be a sublime delight.

He downloaded the attachment and copied it to a diskette that he immediately scanned with a virus-checker.

He would never boot an unknown executable directly after downloading it. A computer virus only a few lines long could erase key files, even damage a hard disk. And the knowledge of how to write those few lines was no longer arcane. It was within the grasp of many thousands, a large proportion of whom were adolescent boys.

The virus-checker found nothing: The game was free of known viruses.

Ellis Hoile still wasn't ready to boot the game though. He opened a text editor and began to examine the file.

It seemed to consist of two parts. The program was in machine code—unreadable. But the hacker had also included the original uncompiled code, in the programming language known as C++.

That Ellis Hoile could read.

He loaded it into an editor, and the software routines and processes that comprised the game began filling his monitor screen in chunks forty lines deep.

He intended just to glance at the listings, look at the first few hundred lines: one programmer inspecting the work of another.

But what he saw made him keep looking.

Because it was good. It was *real* good.

He continued to punch down through the listings, dense lines of words and shorthand that would seem gibberish to an outsider but which Ellis Hoile recognized as sheer art.

The program was clean, precise, economical in the way it would use a computer's resources. He himself would have been pleased to produce code like this.

This was no juvenile project. It was the work of an inspired expert.

Three hours later, Ellis Hoile still hadn't left his seat, except to pour coffee.

The source code of the game had kept him engrossed.

Instruction sets reveal the methods, the approaches, which underlie any computer software. Furthermore, he believed, they reveal something about the programmers who designed them.

That more than anything else was what kept Ellis Hoile in his chair. The program was a window into the mind of its creator. By that standard, Stoma was a real piece of work.

Any good program shows foresight, ingenuity, clarity of thought.

Whoever wrote this, Ellis Hoile thought, had all of that going for him. That and more.

You almost would have to say that he was cunning.

Maybe even scary, he was so clever.

That kept Ellis Hoile from doing what he would very much have liked to do: to actually run the program.

Something was happening here, and he wanted to find out what it was. He kept at it without a break, the blocks of code sliding up on the screen in front of him.

Then he found it.

An encrypted string, about three-quarters of the way through the program listing. This *was* gibberish, at least to the eye. But it was not random. Ellis Hoile was sure that it had to be some kind of virus or worm, hiding within the innards of a Trojan.

Ellis Hoile stripped out the encrypted lines. He quickly paged down through the rest of the list, hurrying along now, looking for a second parasite.

At three-forty A.M. he finally reached the end of the list. He had found nothing else that didn't belong. He then copied the disinfected version of the game onto a diskette that he set aside.

He still wanted to try it. But not just yet.

He got up from his chair and pulled a computer from one of the racks of shelves that stood against one wall. An old 286 with a 40-megabyte hard drive—he hadn't used it in more than a year.

The hard drive was a relic, disposable hardware that Ellis Hoile was ready to sacrifice out of his curiosity to see what the hacker had planned.

Ellis Hoile attached a monitor and a printer to the back of the computer, and plugged the power cord into an outlet. With a few keystrokes he set the system to print out every command issued through the processor.

He inserted the disk, copied the game to the hard drive, and booted it from there.

The hard disk clicked and churned. One of those clicks, he knew, would mark the parasite program's escape into the system.

The printer hummed and clattered.

One line. Carriage return.

A second line.

A third. And more. The parasite was already at work.

The printer fell silent.

Ellis Hoile read the printer's output. The parasite had identified the two serial ports that were the computer's principal data outlets. At each port it had searched for, but failed to find, an operating modem.

Regardless, it scanned the hard disk directories and found a communications program. It located the initializing file that fixed the start-up settings of that program and set the software to silence the modem speaker—if there had been a modem.

With that the parasite went dormant.

But Ellis Hoile could guess what this was all about. The parasite wanted to make a phone call, most likely to the man who had written the program. Stoma was trying to crack into Ellis Hoile's computer.

And Ellis was going to let him in.

He went back to the shelf, pulled out an older modem and a

set of cables, and connected them to one of the computer's serial ports and to the nearest phone jack.

For several minutes he sat at his machine, deleting any file that might possibly reveal who he was or where he lived.

Finally, because the battery had run down after a year on the shelf, he reset the computer's internal clock to show the correct time: four-twelve A.M.

With that, the parasite came alive.

It searched again for a live modem, found one this time, immediately booted the comm program, and began to silently dial a phone number.

Ellis Hoile read the number as the printer clattered it out. He waited for the call to connect—then reached for the modem button and turned off the power, breaking the connection.

The number was a local cellular call: He recognized the prefix right away.

His cellular test set was already at his elbow, on the desk in front of him. He switched it on, then turned on the modem again. Immediately the parasite found the modem again, initialized it, and began a call.

Another cellular call.

To a different number.

This put a whole new spin on things. It meant that Stoma might be even smarter—and more serious—than Ellis Hoile had believed.

Every cellular telephone is assigned a unique electronic serial number at manufacture, and is later assigned a calling number. These two numbers—known respectively as the ESN and NAM— identify the phone and its owner to cellular systems around the continent. Each time it is switched on to send or receive, a cell phone broadcasts its ESN and NAM to the local carrier, using special encrypted data channels. No call can be made until the local company recognizes and approves the phone's ESN and NAM. They are the basis for cellular billing—the basis for the entire cellular concept. Without them the system would cease to function.

Not long after cellular phones became popular, electronic pirates learned to receive and decrypt the ESNs and NAMs constantly streaming between phones and cellular systems.

Once the pirates had valid numbers, reprogramming a phone to match those pilfered numbers (thus passing charges onto the true subscriber) was relatively simple.

Computer crackers—those who illegally enter private computer systems—became some of the most enthusiastic users of clone phones. Not only were clones useful for evading calling charges to distant computers, they reduced the chances of a call being traced to a specific geographic address.

The only drawback was that as cellular operators became more sophisticated in detecting fraudulent calling patterns, the useful life of an ESN or a NAM dropped to as low as a few days, even a few hours.

For that reason, crackers sought a way to update a clone with a new valid ESN and NAM each time it was used.

A few succeeded: the very brightest and most technically adept. Their payoff was a device that guaranteed unlimited long-distance calls on demand, and was almost untraceable.

Almost.

The exception was that a clone call could still be traced to a certain cell location if someone with the right equipment could know which ESN and NAM pair the clone would use next.

Ellis Hoile now understood that Stoma must have written a list of phone numbers into the parasite—numbers that the clone on the receiving end would use, in sequence, if for some reason the first connection was broken.

It was what he himself would have done.

But Stoma could not have guessed that Ellis Hoile owned the equipment to track him down.

The test set was able to monitor conversations at random and pull out the ESN and NAM of the phone making that call—thus it would be ideal for pirating valid numbers to use in clones. But it could also work the other way: If given the ESN and NAM of a given phone, the set could monitor all calls made by, or to, that number. It could even follow that phone from cell to cell.

That was what Ellis Hoile intended to do now. He couldn't determine the phone's exact location, but he could place it within a cell.

The connection to Stoma's phone opened through the modem. As it did, Ellis Hoile sat at the test set's keyboard and entered the phone number that the parasite had just dialed.

The LED numerals on the test set stuttered, flickered, and then fastened. It displayed:

872.220

E17BG

And Ellis Hoile laughed out loud.

The cellular phone was using a channel reserved for the local non-wireline cellular operator, and was located within a cell identified as E17BG. Ellis Hoile owned a map that showed the names and locations of every cell in the Bay Area. But he didn't need it this time. He already knew E17BG: It was located right at the foot of Telegraph Hill, no more than a mile away.

For a few seconds Ellis Hoile watched the commands print out in front of him. The hacker was controlling his old computer now, copying directory lists, opening and then closing files.

Go right ahead, Ellis Hoile thought. He was enjoying this.

The idea that some super-cracker had picked him for a target—hacking the hacker—he *loved* it.

He hadn't had this much fun in months.

So far the phone hadn't switched cells, which meant that it probably wasn't moving. Ellis got up, went over to the window, and pulled the drapes back. From there he could see the entire area of cell E17BG. Most maps represent the cell system as a neat honeycomb shape, perfect hexagons surrounded by six identical hexagons, ad infinitum. But in reality the cells aren't nearly so regular. In a city of hills, valleys, and high buildings, cell coverage is tailored to fit the contours of the terrain.

E17BG was almost kidney-shaped. It was served by a low-power 320-degree transmitter on the side of Telegraph Hill, and its coverage extended roughly from the foot of the hill to the edge of the first high office buildings of the financial district, and from the waterfront to Hyde Street.

Fifteen, maybe twenty city blocks in all.

The antenna of the Van Eck scanner sat on its tripod, a few feet from where Ellis Hoile stood. At this hour, when most TVs and computer monitors were dark, it would be easy to pick out the few still operating.

Besides, he had made a few modifications to boost the scanner's range, and he hadn't had a chance to try them yet. If the changes worked, the scanner should be effective to the outer edges of cell E17BG.

With any luck, he would find the building where Stoma was operating.

Once he knew the building he could figure out Stoma's address, probably learn his name. After that? Maybe a little good-natured harassment, hack the guy who hacked the hacker.

It was just a game anyway.

He turned on the video scanner and the NEC monitor beside it, and he used the remote control to point the antenna toward the area of the cell.

Ellis Hoile knew that he ought to be tired. But he wasn't. He couldn't remember the last time he had been this interested in anything.

He was completely alert, invigorated.

Just a game, he thought.

But a *good* game.

29

"Don't let him worry you," Roberta Hudgins said. "He's a little standoffish, but he don't mean nothing by it. You're going there to run the machines anyway, that's all. I asked and he said fine. So don't you worry none."

Her fifteen-year-old grandson, David Hudgins, sat beside her in the taxi that left the TransBay Terminal, headed for Telegraph Hill. David said nothing, but he seemed a little dubious.

Roberta Hudgins also had some doubts, though she didn't want to let David see that. She wasn't sure whether Ellis Hoile would even remember that she was bringing the boy today. She had mentioned it to him last time, that she had a grandson who needed to practice on computers, and would he mind letting David use one next time she came?

Fine, fine, he had said.

But you never knew about him. You were never sure what he might remember from day to day, or—more important—what he really felt about things.

The taxi sliced easily through Saturday morning traffic. Before long they were climbing Telegraph Hill. Roberta Hudgins caught the boy picking loose skin around one thumbnail, and she slapped at his hand.

"Don't do that," she said. And, "Be polite, but don't go overboard. Answer if he asks you any questions. You don't have to be no chatterbox though."

He was a smart child, David. Good grades across the board. Very good grades in math and science. Only, he needed computer time. At McClymonds High the fast-track juniors got three hours a week in the computer lab. That was actually fifty minutes a session, and they sat two to a machine.

David needed more than the high school could give him. The counselors all admitted it. At most good colleges, so she had heard, freshmen drew a computer at the start of their first term, right along with their textbooks.

You needed those machines if you wanted to go anywhere. They were the express route to the future. And David was not going to miss the ride, not if she could do anything about it.

That was why she had approached Ellis Hoile.

All those computers sitting around, the man could use only one at a time, right? So she had asked him, I got a grandson that's crazy about those machines, would you mind if he sets and tries one out next time I work?

Not the easiest thing she had ever done. She hated to ask favors of the people who paid her.

He had said fine, no problem. As if it really weren't a big deal, and he didn't mind at all.

But with him, how could you be sure?

The taxi turned onto Tesla Street.

She held her grandson's hand.

You're going all the way, she thought. Right to the top.

"Sit up straight," was what she said.

Ellis Hoile had worked the video scanner through the night and well into the morning. It was a tedious job, moving the antenna by the slightest of increments, stopping to pull in a fringe signal, then continuing when he found that it wasn't what he wanted.

After a while the sun came up in his face. The job slowed even more as the signals started popping all over, CNN and kids' cartoons, mixed in with the occasional on-line junkie getting a fix of America Online or the Internet to start the day right. The city's video screens were lighting up again.

Still, he kept at it.

His relish for the job had driven him through the darkness. Now just force of habit kept him going. Programming had taught him that the successful end of any job usually requires the defeat of tedium. Even the most brilliant software usually represented not so much genius as the dogged willingness to apply effort, dully and incessantly.

You never got anything done if you stopped pounding away.

So he kept at it now, the sun in his eyes, the city fully alive below him. He kept clicking the remote control, glancing back and forth between the NEC monitor and the cityscape as the antenna crept along. The task was as mechanical as working an assembly line.

He became vaguely aware of the lock turning in the front door, up beyond the landing. He didn't turn to look.

Because the monitor beside him was resolving still another signal. Not a cartoon this time. Not CNN.

It showed a computer screen, a directory listing with seven items, in the typeface of an IBM-PC system font. Below it were the lines:

```
24 file(s) copied
DISCONNECT
DISCONNECT AT 04:26.42
CONNECT TIME 00:14.23
                copy c:\cap\*.* b:
```

The door opened.

Ellis Hoile walked swiftly to his old computer. It was still running.

The file listings on the screen matched those that his scanner was now reading, on a machine somewhere down below. They were followed by the lines:

```
24 file(s) copied
DISCONNECT
```

He walked back to the tripod. This was important.

He sighted straight down the shaft of the antenna. He saw that it was pointing toward a block of flats beyond North Beach, low on the flank of Russian Hill.

That would be Union Street, about two blocks up from Washington Square.

In that building sat the computer that now contained the files copied from his old 286.

Down there was Stoma.

David fidgeted nervously as his grandmother turned her key in the lock while calling out, "Hello?"

The room was huge. In the center stood a man with his back to them. He didn't notice they were there.

"Hello," Mrs. Hudgins said again, and this time he turned.

Standing in the sunlight, he was. She muttered, "Wonders never cease."

David wasn't listening. He was gaping at the four computers: a Power Mac 9500, a Pentium under Linux, another Pentium running NT—David had never even seen such machines before, except in magazines—plus an old 286.

Mr. Hardware, David started to call the goofy white guy in his own mind.

Now his grandmother led David to the bottom of the stairs.

"This is my grandson, David," she said.

"Sure," said Ellis Hoile. He was walking over to meet them, putting out his hand. And David took the hand and shook it.

"I told you about him, I mentioned would it be all right if he used your machines. . . ."

"Sure, you bet. Hey, David, we'll get you fixed right up."

Mr. Hardware looked awfully tired.

But pleased, somehow.

He dragged out a 486 laptop for David to use.

So he had *five* computers! And that didn't even include the boxes and other goodies up there on the shelves, stuff that David could hardly keep his eyes from—oh, Mr. Hardware, those goodies!—as the guy checked him out on the 486.

David's grandmother stood behind them, watching this. David didn't have to turn around: He already knew how pleased she was, seeing him treated this way.

Mr. Hardware saw that David had brought along a diskette, with a little music-cataloguing program that David had written in BASIC. The man looked bleary, but that didn't stop him from listing the program and going through it, showing David a couple of places where it could be tighter, then telling him: Not bad, you've got a clue.

David got the impression that this was high praise.

Then Mr. Hardware blinked his eyes twice, almost nodded off right there, and said, "I b'lieve I'll crash. Go to it."

He was ready to get up, but he stopped, reached for some diskettes on the table. He said, "I've got a couple of games here. You get bored, you might try jacking into them. I stripped a wicked little worm out of one of them, but it's clean now, and the code actually looked kinda spiffy—you might tell me what you think."

And then he was gone, headed straight for bed.

30

Kate Lavin had rescheduled the production meeting for the jaguar shoot—herself and three others, the core crew for the project—for ten on Monday morning.

Cynthia Frain, Kate's assistant, was going to be the field producer. It was a step up for her, and well deserved; besides, her presence in Belize would help Kate to control a location shoot that could become expensive and chaotic.

Sandy Weil, a freelance director, had done several other projects for Kate, and she knew how to work under a tight schedule.

Louis Markham would be the principal shooter and technician. He was on the studio staff. But Louis was late this morning. He finally rolled in around ten forty-five.

He was a tall man with long hair tied back in a ponytail.

"Sorry. Monday mornings, you know how it goes," he said, and he folded himself into the last empty chair at Kate's desk.

Kate tried to keep it short. The deadline was firm, she said: something close to a final cut in ninety days. They couldn't let costs get out of hand, but it had to be done right.

Cynthia and Sandy should be on a plane to Belize City within two days, to start arrangements; Kate had been given a list of contacts, including a guide who was supposed to be able to find a jaguar in the wild.

Louis would stay behind for a few days, until they decided how to tape the cat, at night, on his home ground.

Then she opened it up to the three of them, a free-for-all discussion about what the film should look like and how they would approach it.

Logistics permitting, they would do this several times before they began shooting, and several times more after that.

Kate had a rule for these meetings: Any new idea was allowed five minutes of life before someone spoke against it. It was a way to encourage fresh thinking.

But it sometimes slowed the meetings too. Now Kate was glancing at the clock on her desk.

Eleven twenty-two.

Eleven twenty-eight.

He was just a stranger, she thought. Nobody important: three days ago at this time she had been unaware of his existence. He would be gone soon anyway.

Eleven thirty-six.

Eleven forty—and Gate Three was another five minutes away, once she walked out to her car.

She stood and said, "You guys have this under control, right?"

They all looked surprised. Kate rarely bailed out of meetings.

"You're leaving?" Cynthia said. She knew that Kate had nothing else scheduled today.

"I'll be out for a while." No reason to be more specific, she thought; she was the boss, after all. "If you're gone when I get back, have a good trip. Get some rest tonight and tomorrow, I want you to dig in right away when you get down there. Anything you need, let me know."

Louis Markham said, "I thought I would call Ellis on this cat-in-the-night deal. See if he has any ideas."

Until a few days earlier, Kate Lavin would have said, right away, *Sure, go ahead and do that.* She would have liked the idea, seeing that Ellis had something useful to occupy him.

But now she reminded herself that she was trying to make a break—having Ellis around wouldn't help.

"Ellis doesn't work here anymore," she said.

"I know, that's why I'm checking."

"Why do you want to bring Ellis in on this? That's what you're getting paid for."

"Ellis is smarter than I am," said Louis Markham.

Can't argue with that, Kate Lavin thought. And she reminded herself that they were pushing the limits on this one: They could use help.

"All right, fine," she said, and she added, "Make sure that he gets a check, from now on he's like any other contractor."

And then she was gone, stopping just long enough to glance at a mirror before she walked out to her car.

She put the top down on the Miata. It was that kind of day.

She turned out of the parking lot, onto Bridgeway, the water-front drive.

Eleven forty-seven by her watch.

Traffic was heavy up Bridgeway. Tourists, damn tourists were everywhere.

Eleven fifty-one; she turned into the Gate Three parking lot.

And he was there, hunched against a post at the dock entrance, reading a paperback book, in jeans and a crew-neck sweater. She pulled up a few feet away and sat there with the engine idling.

He looked up from the book.

An easy smile. Fine white teeth, tousled hair, broad shoulders.

She couldn't help it—he looked *golden* out there in the sunlight.

He stood, unhurried, and ambled over to the car. She got a glimpse of the book before he tucked it into the pocket of his Wind-breaker.

Poetry. William Carlos Williams.

Lord, she thought: All this, and he reads too.

"I'm sorry," she said, "I couldn't get away, I know I'm late."

"Are you? I didn't wear my watch. It's stowed somewhere."

He slipped into the seat beside her.

No watch. How did anyone live without a watch?

Then she realized that a few minutes one way or the other wouldn't make a lot of difference when you were moving at five knots.

She herself was immersed in timekeeping. She could remember long, loud discussions in an editing suite about whether to include one more frame of videotape in a scene: an argument over one-thirtieth of a second.

No wonder this guy moves so easy, she thought.

He had something to teach her.

For the few days he would be around. This had been on her mind for the past morning and the evening before that.

She drove out onto Bridgeway again, headed back north. She was going to take him to a restaurant on the dock in Tiburon.

Brake lights flared on cars up ahead. She downshifted and braked, and the Miata lurched to a stop. A few seconds later, trying to sound casual, she said, "How's that generator?"

"I swapped it out for a rebuilt unit this morning. I'll bolt in the new one today or tomorrow."

"When are you planning to leave for Mexico?"

"It wasn't a plan," he said. "More like a general statement of principle."

She turned to look at him.

"What the hell does that mean?" she said.

He gave her a level look right back.

"It means I'm not going anywhere for a while."

Traffic was moving again. She just nodded once at his words, and dumped the clutch. The Miata shot up the road.

31

Roberta Hudgins was saying, "David boy, we got to be going."

Her grandson reluctantly pushed away from the desk and reached to turn off the laptop where he'd been sitting for the past four and a half hours.

Right then Ellis Hoile emerged from the bedroom, still a little bleary-eyed, but looking better than when they had arrived.

He walked straight to the laptop, snapped it shut, and handed it to David, tried to put it in his arms.

David took a step back and said, "What's that for?"

"For you."

David took another step back. As if the machine were toxic.

"No," he said. "No, sorry, I can't."

"Sure you can. You'll use it more than I can."

"No. Thank you. No."

"Didn't you like it?"

The machine, David loved it. At school he used an old XT and an Apple II, nothing wrong with them except that a 486 like this one would spoil you for anything else, the way it chewed through work. It felt about ten times faster than an XT.

He wanted that computer. But he could imagine his grandmother's reaction if he so much as hesitated to refuse.

"I was planning for you to take it," Ellis Hoile said. "I had it ready for you. I already loaded the software."

He was—what was he doing?—he was pulling a stack of manuals from where they'd been sitting on the desk, dropping them into a shopping bag. So he wasn't lying, he really had been planning it.

He was better organized than he looked, David thought.

"No," David said.

Behind him his grandmother shifted her weight. Losing patience, he thought.

She said, "You need it."

At first David figured that she was talking to Ellis Hoile. But it was a pretty silly thing to say, he thought, anybody could see that the last thing Mr. Hardware needed was another computer. . . .

Then David realized that she meant *him.*

"You can use it," she said again. And to Ellis Hoile—this time definitely to Ellis Hoile, David was watching her now—she said, "Could we make this a loan? A long-term loan?"

"Any way you want," said Ellis Hoile, and once more he tried to press the machine into David's hands.

David looked at his grandmother. She nodded once, firmly, and finally David grasped the handle.

"You'll get it back," she said.

"I know that," said Ellis Hoile. "But I won't be looking for it any time soon."

"That's fair enough."

He put the straps of the shopping bag into David's other hand, and he threw in a modem with cables, too, before David could take the bag away.

"Have fun," he said.

"I will," David said. "I will."

"David . . ." his grandmother said.

And David, taking the cue, said, "Thank you. Thank you very much."

Ellis Hoile gave a small shrug, showed the slightest smile.

He asked, "Hey, did you play a game?"

"Yeah. The one called Try Me," David said.

"That's it."

"I played it for a few minutes. It's a point-of-view game. I like that kind. It really gets you into the action. And the graphics are great. Texture mapping, ray-tracing. It scrolls real smooth. I don't know how it would work on a slower machine, but it runs fine on a 486. I think it might support a sound card too. It doesn't say so, but I got that idea. Just the way it was put together."

"So you liked it."

"Not really," he said.

"What's the problem?"

David bit his lower lip before he answered. He seemed to be weighing his words, almost reluctant to speak.

Finally he said, "Too creepy."

32

When he was alone again, Ellis Hoile checked the video eavesdropper. It was blank. He thought that Mrs. Hudgins might have jostled the antenna when she cleaned, but when he scanned the block of flats he found no computer screens. Stoma must have turned off his monitor some time during the last few hours.

Ellis Hoile remembered that Kate had once kept a pair of binoculars, to watch ships in the harbor. He rummaged now for a couple of minutes and found them hanging in a closet.

He brought them to the window and studied the apartment building down on Union Street. White stucco. Three floors, four windows per floor on the side that fronted the street.

He wanted to be able to find it again, from down in the street.

He walked up to the landing to the front door.

He felt the sun on his skin, the breeze in his face, as he stepped outside and began to walk down the street, down the hill.

He crossed Kearney Street, headed down Filbert. Past the big church—Saints Peter and Paul, it was called; and today somebody was having a wedding—past the pocket playground at the corner of Washington Square, where kids climbed bars and rolled in the sand.

He wished he could have used some route that he and Kate had not walked together. But he couldn't think of any block in North Beach that they hadn't walked many times.

They would amble down the hill and pick out a place for brunch, a bakery—that one there, across Columbus Avenue, they had been there more times than he could count.

They'd been together nearly half their lives: For Ellis Hoile, San

Francisco and Marin County were studded with poignant places where he and Kate had some history as a couple.

In the last year he had refashioned the house to his own tastes, so that he hardly recognized it as a site where they had lived and loved. But he couldn't change the world outside. He couldn't seem to stop the dull ache that he got within himself when he dwelled on her. . . .

He pushed the ache aside now. He had done that many times, get the hurt under control. It was persistent, but so was he.

He walked a block up Columbus, crossed it against the light, and found himself at the corner of Union Street.

Two more blocks up Union, climbing Russian Hill now. The white stucco building was easy to find.

Like most of the places in this neighborhood, it was built up to the sidewalk. Mailboxes and buzzers occupied a wall panel beside the glass front door. Twelve units, four to a floor.

A short driveway lay along one side of the building. Ellis Hoile followed it around and saw that it connected with an alley that ran nearly the length of the block, parallel to Union Street. Behind the building, under an overhang, was a row of parking spaces marked with apartment numbers.

There was also a recess where a big movable trash bin sat beneath a chute.

Ellis Hoile walked to the bin and looked over the top. A little more than half full. He thought that the chute stood at the end of the hallway on each floor: It was where all twelve tenants threw their trash.

Ellis Hoile was about to do something he had done often, but not for years. He grabbed the rim of the bin, pulled himself over the top, and rolled down into the trash.

When he was a teenage phreaker he had looted trash often. The refuse barrels behind phone company offices were especially rich—

technical manuals, printout lists of the newest test loops—handing you the keys to the entire phone system if you understood what to do with them.

He had learned to enjoy Dumpster diving very quickly, once he saw what people throw away.

He knelt in the bin now, careful to stay out from under the chute itself. He began pulling bags to the top, ripping them open and spreading out the contents in one corner. Mostly paper trash, some cans and bottles, an old folding chair.

The bin wasn't especially ripe—the kitchen sinks must have garbage disposals, he thought—but he still wished that he had brought gloves. When he was a kid, and doing this all the time, he never left home without a pair.

One green plastic bag felt heavy. When he tore it open he found a stack of magazines. The name on the labels was C. Hartmundt, of Apartment 1A.

C. Hartmundt subscribed to *Byte, Computer Shopper, PC Graphics & Video*. These were all mainstream magazines. In the same stack, though, Ellis Hoile found three specialty items that he himself read: *Dr. Dobb's Journal*, a **DOS** programmer's monthly; *Morph's Outpost*, for software developers; *IEEE Spectrum*, an electrical engineers' monthly.

But even these heavyweight journals didn't prove that C. Hartmundt was Stoma. These days San Francisco was to multimedia developers as Los Angeles was to screenwriters. Roll a bowling ball down a street in the right neighborhood, you were likely to mow down three or four of them.

Ellis Hoile put the magazines aside and kept going through the bag.

C. Hartmundt also received the newsletter of a multiple sclerosis support group.

And a catalogue of health aids, wheelchairs, and prosthetics.

And a telephone bill—no, *two* telephone bills—in the name of Christian Willem Hartmundt, showing only the charge for basic service, month of March, and a surcharge on each for an unlisted number.

The numbers were printed on the bills. Ellis Hoile stuck them into his pocket.

He stayed in the bin for about another twenty minutes. He was nearly out of sight there. He kept ripping open bags, but he found nothing else that seemed to matter.

He climbed out. Down at the end of the row of parking spaces, the stall for 1A was empty. On the wall in front of the space someone had fastened a handicapped sign.

Around to the front of the building again. C. Hartmundt was the name on the mailbox for 1A. Through the glass door Ellis Hoile could see that 1A was the first unit on the left.

When he went down to the corner of the building, he found that the bottom of 1A's front window was about six and a half feet above the sidewalk, a little too high for a casual glance inside.

Anyway, the shades were drawn. Somebody else seemed to think that sunlight was just glare on a monitor screen.

A few feet around the side of the building was a second window that had to belong to the same apartment. This one, too, was about a foot above eye level.

He went around to the bin, pulled out the folding chair, opened it, carried it back around to the side window, and stood on it.

Nobody saw him. Nobody shouted to stop him.

It was a bathroom window. The shades were down, venetian blinds, but the slats were open enough to let him peer through.

The bathroom door had been left half open, enough to give him a view into the front room.

There he saw two computers on a table, a Mac and a PC. The screens were dark.

But beside the PC, connected by a data cable, was a black hand-set with a stubby rubber antenna.

A cellular telephone.

Back home, in the house on Telegraph Hill, Ellis Hoile drew the drapes shut again.

He sat at one of his computers and picked up one of the disk-ettes that David Hudgins had left on the desk.

Creepy, huh?

He copied it to a hard disk and booted the program from there.

The screen flickered and dissolved to black.

He found himself standing on a steel catwalk. . . .

33

Stephen Leviste had Monday off from school. There was a teachers' conference. So he had another whole day to play TRY ME.

He had managed to make his way through seven levels of the maze, avoiding the homicidal stalker. Now he jumped through a hole in the floor and found himself landing on a steel catwalk.

This was the first time he had seen the catwalk. It did not come at the opening of the game that he had received, for this version was unique, modified solely for him.

This newest level was different, he saw right away. It was not a cramped maze, but a large, open room that the catwalk traversed. He had the feeling that the game was near a climax.

And he was right.

He moved down one end of the catwalk and found a steel mesh cage enclosing a concrete landing. The cage had a door, but it wouldn't open. So he walked down to the other end of the catwalk. It was open—no railing.

He jumped, and landed easily on his feet.

He moved out into the huge concrete room: empty, almost featureless, though across the broad floor he could make out a single door, painted red, at the bottom of one of the room's sheer high walls.

He tracked across to it. Here he paused. So often in TRY ME, the faceless killer waited behind an innocuous door like this one. But he didn't know where else to go.

He clicked on the door, and his virtual, in-the-game hand reached and turned the knob, and the door swung open.

A pastoral vista of trees and green grass and bright sunlight greeted him. He was out of the maze—he had won the game.

He shoved the mouse forward, and his virtual self stepped out into freedom.

And then the screen changed.

It showed a text message:

Greetings and congratulations, JOYBOY

You have completed the quest . . .

Thereby qualifying yourself to apply for membership in the most highly ultra elite hacker/cracker/phreaker bulletin board . . .
SHADOWMASTER'S ABYSS
No dorks, dweebs, lamers, or wannabes
You must be The Real Thing
Few are called
Even fewer are chosen
Your activities have caught the attention of our membership.
(Yes, we are out there! We know you! You have been noticed!)
Having gotten this far, you have proved that you are not a total and complete loser.
However, you haven't pulled the sword from the stone just yet.
The next step is much more difficult.
You can qualify now for full membership in SHADOWMASTER'S ABYSS by passing our on-line entrance exam (don't hold your breath though).
Twenty questions follow.
ARE YOU READY TO PROCEED?

The cursor blinked on Stephen Leviste's monitor screen as he digested this. Then the message vanished from the screen, replaced by these lines:

> If you have some reason to hesitate, maybe we should forget the whole thing.

> Time out in ten seconds. Do you want to proceed?

Stephen pressed the Y key. The machine responded:

> Great.

> Enter your handle and telephone number.

Stephen did that.

The program responded:

> Now, do you suppose you could connect the modem, O Clueless One?

Stephen switched power to his modem and plugged the cord into his phone jack.

He realized that someone must have seen his on-line posts, thought that he had potential, and mailed the game to him.

Try Me was actually a test to weed out lamers.

Otherwise known as a bozo filter.

Way cool, thought Stephen Leviste, as TRY ME automatically initialized the modem and began to dial out.

The call connected to Corwin Sturmer's computer in the basement apartment on Tenth Avenue.

The killer had discovered Joyboy's true name by reading his posts on various computer bulletin boards around the Bay Area—

many of them run by and for the cyberpunk underground and populated almost exclusively by boys and young men, adolescent to mid-twenties.

No telephone or address in the Bay Area was connected to that name; and Stephen Leviste did not appear in any of the student directories of local colleges and universities. This suggested that Joyboy might be living at home with his parents and using their telephone. So he had sent diskette copies of the game to every address in the area that showed the name Leviste.

He figured that only the proper Stephen Leviste would know what to do with the program. And on the assumption that his modem might not be plugged in at all times—which meant that the daemon inside the Trojan horse might not be able to do its work—the killer had slightly altered the game, and had rewritten the daemon to prod Joyboy, if necessary, into making the connection.

Now, as the call connected, the daemon triggered an automated script that the killer had written for this moment.

It sent the message:

Welcome, Joyboy. Are you ready to play Twenty Questions?

Stephen Leviste typed:

Y.

The first question came across his monitor:

Question 1. Define DTMF.

Stephen Leviste typed:

Are you joking? DTMF—is this the best you can do?

The computer demanded:

Define DTMF.

Stephen Leviste decided to stop fooling around. He answered:

>Dial Tone Multi-Frequency. Touch Tones on a telephone.
Correct. Question 2 . . .

As the next sixteen questions came across the monitor, Stephen Leviste's fingers danced on the keyboard of his computer. He was nailing every one of them as fast as the Shadowmaster could type them. Like he couldn't miss. He was getting cocky now. The Shadowmaster couldn't possibly keep him out.

Question 18. Specify frequency pair for keypad numeral "9."
>852 Hz + 1477 Hz

Question 19. You have dialed into an unknown system that displays the prompt: "ER!" What have you found?
>Mainframe or supermini running PRIMOS. Hard to crack without an account ID.

Question 20. Specify the UNIX process which generates the login prompt.
>getty
Congratulations. Most impressive. The one true Shadowmaster admits Joyboy to his Abyss. You are instructed to log onto the Verba Interchange tonight at 8 p.m. for further contact.
An adventure awaits you!

Then the call disconnected.
Stephen Leviste read the message twice, and a third time.
He was in.

34

Stephen Leviste told his parents that he would be busy in his room all evening.

Homework, he explained—he had piles of homework.

He logged into Verba at 7:45. After a minute or two a line flashed at the bottom of his display:

Shadowmaster offers a back-channel chat.

In a moment they were connected. Shadowmaster wrote:

You're eager.

Stephen answered:

>Why not? I have the goods.
What do you bring to The Abyss?

Shadowmaster wanted to know what the newcomer had to offer. Stephen answered:

>I have five virgin codez.

Shadowmaster's answer came quickly:

Codez are useful in their place. However, they are extraneous when one has been shadowing passwords at a CS terminal at Stanford.

The most direct way to crack a remote computer system is to steal legitimate passwords. A shadowing program captured passwords that users entered at a terminal, and wrote them to a file, to be retrieved, and used, later.

Any valid password was a step in the door. But accounts at a university's CS—computer science—machine might include some powerful privileges on a very interesting system.

Stephen typed:

>You can do that?

And the reply:

Do not doubt Shadowmaster.
If you must be convinced of his authenticity, however, you may accompany him to said terminal and try for yourself.

What a break, thought Stephen Leviste. A password into Stanford wouldn't give him just a chance to explore a great system. Once he was inside, he would be able to reach thousands of other machines linked via the Internet.

He wrote:

>Hackarama!

The Shadowmaster answered:

Indeed. Want to try?
>When?
Tonight. Midnight.

Joyboy was slow to answer. The cursor paused. It sat, blinking, until Shadowmaster typed:

Is there a problem?
>That's late.
Prime time for a true phreaker. Fewer prying eyes. But, hey, if you aren't sufficiently motivated . . .
>I'll be there.
Will pick you up. We'll bomb down together. You live near Serramonte shopping center, isn't that correct?
>How do you know that?
Shadowmaster knows all. Across from east side of Serramonte. In front of Denny's.
>12:30 would be better for me.
Later the better.
>How do I recognize you?
Fear not—Shadowmaster will know *you*.
>May I ask how?
I assume you'll be the only phreaker standing in front of Denny's at 12:30 answering to the name of "Joyboy." That's a polite way of telling you not to bring along any friends. Shadowmaster has no time for dweebs. If I see two, you'll never see me—understood?
>Yes.
Be there. You may never have a chance like this again.

35

Ellis Hoile was backed into a corner.

The big, shadowy bogeyman advanced toward him, holding—what was it this time?

Jesus, a baseball bat.

With nowhere to go, no way to defend himself, no weapon with which to retaliate, Ellis Hoile waited for the blows to fall.

Now here came the first one, delivered with two hands, not to the head but to what seemed to be Ellis Hoile's midsection.

Thwump was the sound that came from the speakers attached to the computer sound card. You could almost hear ribs cracking.

The faceless bogeyman raised the bat again. The next blow was straight to the head, and that did it—the screen went black.

It always ended the same.

Here came the message once more:

Try Me Again?

Unable to resist, Ellis Hoile typed:

Y

One more time he found himself alone on that damn steel catwalk.

He was playing the game at a computer that he set up near the view window in the living room. Periodically he would pick up the binoculars and glance toward the apartment house down on Russian Hill, watching for a disabled man to enter or leave the building.

Occasionally, too, he would adjust the antenna of the video

scanner, minute movements that he hoped would pick up an active computer monitor in the first-floor corner unit.

But he found nothing. The monitor displayed just an unvarying tweedy blank. If Christian Willem Hartmundt was at home, he was not using his computers.

When he tired of playing, Ellis Hoile fiddled with the program's source code, trying to find out a programming subroutine that led to a different outcome than automatic death for the player. There had to be a method—a subtle one—that allowed escape from the maze.

It had to have a brilliant angle, a worthy resolution.

No one, Ellis thought, would deliberately create a game with no escape hatch, a game that could not be won.

Nobody could be that twisted.

36

The killer believed that he could not be caught. He could not be touched. He operated in a realm that was beyond the reach of law or retribution.

Except for the actual moment of abduction and murder, his crimes existed wholly on a plane that—while it overlapped the physical world—was invisible, intangible, ephemeral. It was a place that police work did not comprehend, much less penetrate.

The killer understood cops' methods and took them into account. Because he knew that patterns in murders can yield psychological clues, he varied his manner of execution, adding deliberately bizarre touches, not from an inner craving but in order to mislead.

Peeling the skin from a victim's face—let them muddle over *that* one for a while, he thought.

Moreover, he didn't believe that he needed any such subterfuge. Not so long as he planned his crimes and stalked his victims in a world where location was meaningless and identity was fleeting.

Here he moved easily and without a trace. Here he was the master. He knew, as few others did, the rules, the methods, the techniques. For him the digital domain was simultaneously camouflage and weapon.

His arrangement to meet Joyboy was one example. The killer did not remember a Denny's restaurant east of the Serramonte shopping center. But he knew it was there.

It showed on the liquid-crystal screen of a second computer, a notebook portable, at his elbow.

The screen displayed a street map, the area around the shopping center. The map showed not only street names, but the location of every home and business with a listed telephone number. A small red dot blinked on a location just east of the mall. A box at the bottom of the screen displayed the address and phone number of the Denny's restaurant there.

With a few keystrokes the map shifted to show the street in Pacifica where Joyboy lived. The killer now knew Joyboy's name, his address, and where he had promised to be at half an hour past midnight that night.

It worked this way:

The daemon in Stephen Leviste's computer had transmitted the phone number that he entered. The killer, using the notebook computer, checked the number against a database of listed phones in the Bay Area. That database, stored on an optical disk connected to the notebook computer, had yielded the address where the phone was located.

The listings of phones and addresses were linked to a map display of the Bay Area, also stored on the disk. Besides finding locations from an address, the map database could work in reverse: Given a location—a certain block on a certain street, for example— it could immediately show all the names, street addresses, and telephones listed on that block.

Both of these resources, the digitized street maps and the telephone listings, were widely available on commercial software: The killer had merely combined them for his own use.

That had been a simple task.

Other, more-revealing databases were also publicly available: Public records of births and deaths, marriages and divorces, bankruptcy filings, license applications, real estate transactions, postal forwarding-address notices, could potentially be linked to the map-address display if the killer chose.

Unlisted phone numbers, credit card records, criminal and driving records, and motor vehicle registrations were theoretically closed to the public, yet knowledgeable computer users penetrated them at will. The same was true of the huge, fabulous databases maintained by credit reporting firms.

All that information could be correlated, so that an investigator working with just a name and address could immediately compile a dossier on a stranger, and on that target's family, coworkers, and neighbors.

The real riches in digital information, however, were stored in the computers of the state and federal governments: tax records, military service records, census forms, Social Security and public assistance files.

Methods to match these records, and the computing power to search and compile them, had existed for some years now.

They were tools of unimaginable, incredible power.

Using the data this way was illegal in theory. But the killer understood this to mean that—since human beings administered both the laws and the data—the means for monitoring all citizens and laying open their lives were at the whim of creatures whose instincts had not appreciably changed in the past ten thousand years.

The idea that those in power would not use such tools for their own benefit—sooner rather than later—struck him as ludicrous.

Humans always use the tools at their disposal, he thought. And they will inevitably use them in the service of their own irresistible impulses and cravings.

Just as he himself was doing.

The invasion of a life, the dissection of an individual this way, was as thrilling as the act of murder itself. Using the digital tools that he knew so well—with his own canniness and ingenuity—the killer had fatally insinuated himself into the existences of Dee-TeeDude, Portia, and Chaz; he had come to know them intimately.

Joyboy had been a litttle more of a challenge, but one that the killer had overcome with a little ingenuity.

Ziggy had been the easiest of all.

Then there was Avatar, who was unreachable so far. The killer had hints that Avatar might be someone whose grasp of this realm approached his own.

There was the handle, for one thing.

In Hindu belief, an avatar was the physical embodiment of a divine being.

On Unix-based computer systems, "avatar" sometimes denoted a user with root privileges—a super-user, a system god.

And the branch of computer science known as Virtual Reality had appropriated the term to describe the computer-generated representation of an actual person or object.

Which was to say that an avatar was something that seemed to be real, but was not. A stand-in, a false front.

The killer *liked* those concepts. The possibility that Avatar might also have some grasp of this world was tantalizing.

It would add some zest to the chase.

But it would not change the outcome.

37

Midnight.

Stephen Leviste climbed out of his bedroom window onto the redwood-shingled surface of the cupola below.

The time was a few minutes after midnight. The last lights in the house had gone out about fifteen minutes earlier, first in his sister's room, then in his parents' bedroom.

The cupola extended maybe six or seven feet, over the small deck along the side of the house. He stepped lightly, easily, across the sloping cupola—he was small, maybe, but agile, and unafraid of high places. Then he lowered himself down the corner post, using the wooden pegs where his mother sometimes hung plants.

His feet found the deck rail, and he hopped down to the ground. The noise started the neighbor's terrier barking.

Please shut up, he thought. He couldn't imagine the trouble he would be in if his parents learned that he had gone. In case they somehow did discover his bed empty, he had left a handwritten note on his pillow—

Went riding my bike, I'm OK, don't have a cow
Love, Stevie

—so that they wouldn't go completely berserk and start calling the police.

He pushed his bike around the side of the house. The dog yapped a few times more and quit barking. Then Stephen Leviste hopped onto the bicycle and began to ride, an impossibly frail figure lost in loose jeans and a Batman sweatshirt, his sneakers pumping the pedals as he propelled himself down the silent street.

By the time he reached Denny's, the clock behind the counter showed twelve twenty-four. He locked his bike to a power pole, stood at the curb, and waited. Traffic was light—the mall had been closed for two and a half hours—and he had time to watch each car, individually, as it approached the restaurant and then passed by without stopping.

After a while he checked the time inside again. Twelve forty-three.

He went back to the curb. By now he had stopped watching each vehicle as it passed: He kept his head down, studying the cracks in the sidewalk and scuffing his sneakers on the concrete.

The clock said twelve fifty-seven, the next time he pressed his face to the glass. He told himself that he would wait three more minutes. If Shadowmaster was more than half an hour late, he must not be coming at all.

Stephen thought that he had been taken for a fool.

At five past one he unlocked the chain and wound it under the seat. Somewhere, no doubt, Shadowmaster was having a good laugh. Only thing that didn't make sense was why somebody would have gone to the trouble—create the program, mail him the disks, administer the test—just to zing a twelve-year-old kid. It was crazy.

But the world was full of crazy people, he thought, and he started for home.

While Joyboy was heading up the hill, the killer was finishing a piece of lemon meringue pie in the restaurant. He watched as the kid pedaled out of sight, and he followed a lingering mouthful of the pie with a swallow of coffee.

He was in no hurry.

He had been at the restaurant since about a quarter past twelve, when he took a booth beside the front window. A set of half-curtains—café curtains, they were sometimes called—covered the bottom half of the glass, but from where he sat the killer could open the part in the curtains to check the sidewalk outside.

He ordered a full meal—he was not surprised to find himself famished as his task approached—and he sat and watched Joyboy arrive.

On a bicycle!

He hadn't considered that. It made the mechanics of the abduction just that much easier, certainly meant that he could do it where and how he pleased.

But Joyboy was so puny.

Just a child, he thought, watching the skinny little runt at the curb. Not what he expected. He could feel the great bubble of killing lust begin to collapse inside him.

He couldn't imagine any satisfaction in snuffing this smooth-cheeked schoolboy with matchstick limbs.

But Joyboy was supposed to go. There was an order to these things: Joyboy was part of a set that would be flawed and meaningless without every one of its members.

A little scrap of nothing. Crush him like a paper cup.

Then it came to him: a way to make this interesting.

Perfect.

That bubble swelled inside him again, pressing for release.

Joyboy's route from home to the shopping center was obvious from the map on his notebook computer. Two blocks up from his home was Skyline Boulevard, which ran along the top of the high ridge that separated the coast from the rest of the San Francisco peninsula. The shopping center was at the bottom of that ridge, a straight shot down to the bottom of the hillside, about a mile and a half in all.

Downhill he would have made good time on a bike. But the climb back up to Skyline would be a hard pull.

Between the shopping center and Skyline Boulevard the map display showed an overlapping patchwork of several large empty areas that had no markings at all.

These were cemeteries that spread across the hillside. The road down from Skyline passed between several of them, hundreds of acres as big as an Iowa cornfield, sprouting only grave markers.

Not inappropriate for the occasion, the killer thought. He left enough cash on the table to cover the bill and a generous tip, and he walked outside.

Not in a hurry, but very much with the definite look of a man with somewhere to go and a job to finish.

Stephen Leviste dismounted when the hill got steep. There was no sidewalk, just a strip of dirt and grass beside the road, so he pushed the bike uphill. It was not much slower than pedaling, and a lot easier.

He was three blocks from the shopping mall, out of sight from any house. He was in among the graveyards now.

He pushed. The squeak of his back wheel—it needed oil—was by far the loudest sound. He hadn't seen a car for the last four or five minutes.

No streetlights up here either. The local residents did not require them.

Dumb idea, he kept thinking, dumb idea, what am I doing, I could be home in bed right now.

The cemeteries were dark and completely still.

And now a car was coming up behind him, the engine surging as it climbed, revs kicking up as it dropped into a lower gear. It lit up the path in front of him; he threw a shadow that got shorter and more distinct as the car got closer.

It was slowing as it neared him. He turned to look, and blinked into the headlights, high-beams.

Not a car: a brown cargo van.

It was pulling up beside him. The window was down on the passenger side. From within the van a man's voice said, "Joyboy, right? Sorry I'm late."

Stephen couldn't see the face that belonged to the voice.

This could only be the Shadowmaster. But they were four blocks from Denny's. Shadowmaster couldn't possibly know him.

Something was way wrong here. . . .

"Go on, get in," the man said. "If you don't want to go to Palo Alto, no problem, we'll do it another time, I'll give you a ride home."

"No, thanks," Stephen Leviste said, a little surprised that he could actually force up the words through the tightness in his chest. He turned away and resumed pushing his bike up the hill.

The van began moving again, pulling even with him, staying at his side.

"Go on, get in," the man said.

Stephen kept his eyes straight ahead, trying to ignore him, pushing forward.

The van kept rolling beside him.

So he moved fast.

He pivoted the bike on its back wheel, swung a leg over, and headed downhill, pumping his knees, gathering speed.

Behind him—he could hear it happening—the van braked and the transmission chunked and the engine revved and the tires shrieked.

The van was in reverse, chasing him, racing backward down the hill as he picked up speed.

Maniac, Stephen Leviste thought.

And the maniac was gaining on him.

Stephen pumped faster, and the van roared after him. At the edge of his vision he could see it swerving and roaring, the rear wheels darting back and forth, barely in control.

It slewed toward him.

His eyes caught the swerve, and Stephen reacted, flinched, and then he, too, was out of control, skidding and braking hard and finally falling, tumbling, bouncing along the turf at the side of the road, coming to rest against a waist-high stone wall that bordered the cemetery.

The van fishtailed to a stop, not far down the hill, close enough that Stephen could plainly hear a door open and then slam shut.

Footsteps were thumping toward him, across the grass.

Stephen Leviste bolted to his feet, flung himself over the stone wall and into the cemetery, and dashed onto the path between two rows of graves. Behind him he could hear another set of feet thudding into the turf as the stranger vaulted that same stone fence and followed.

For a few moments they were in sync, Stephen's feet cutting across the short grass between the rows of graves, the stranger's feet pounding along at exactly the same rate.

Stephen cut to his right, across some rows of stones and markers, toward a section down the hill, where eight or ten sepulchers stood among monuments and larger upright tablets. He could find cover there. The stranger followed. But Stephen raced in among the slabs and blocks of marble, ducked in behind one of the big tombs, and halted.

The pounding footsteps slowed, then stopped.

Stephen waited.

He heard nothing for a minute or two. He worked his way

around the edge of the tomb so he could look back the way he came, up the hill.

He saw no one. The sepulchers gave him cover, but they would hide the maniac too.

The road was off to his left, out of sight just now, but he knew it couldn't be far. He started moving in that direction, putting distance between himself and where the maniac would have seen him last.

He left the cover of the tomb and crept behind a monument, a pedestal topped by a statue of a child in a robe, with an angel's halo.

No sign of the stranger.

Stephen left the pedestal and slid behind a broad tombstone tablet.

Up the hill, nothing moved.

To his left, across a gap of maybe twenty yards, was one more marble sepulcher. From there he could break for the road.

Still nothing up the hill. Stephen Leviste crouched on his haunches, ready to scramble over to the last sepulcher.

And then a hand grabbed his shoulder from behind.

The shock alone might have stopped him from running. But the grip of that hand was strong too. Then a second hand clamped around his mouth, tilting back his head. He was being pulled off balance, hauled backward to the ground while the maniac straddled him and shoved a knee into his stomach.

The maniac hauled him up and held him and started to carry him. A hand clutched his face, choking off any sound from his mouth.

Stephen Leviste tried, just once, to squirm free. But both arms tightened on him, one shutting off the air to his mouth and nose, the other forcing the breath out of his lungs.

Stephen realized that the maniac had the strength and the will to kill him right there.

He stopped wriggling and let his body go limp.

The death's grip relaxed. Stephen Leviste gratefully drew in breath once more, and he let his captor carry him across the dark cemetery.

38

At that moment, Ellis Hoile sat in his Datsun, parked along the breakwater near the Gate Seven entrance.

Louis Markham had asked him to come to the studio around dinnertime, talk about the jaguar-at-night shoot.

For a couple of hours they had discussed thermal imaging and remote sensing, all the ways a cameraman might record a wary black cat in a jungle at night, the kind of stuff Ellis Hoile could talk about all night.

He had found himself hoping that Kate would show up. But he still hadn't seen her when he left the studio a couple of hours before midnight.

He walked out and sat in his Datsun, a twenty-year-old car that suited him perfectly. He found himself turning, almost against his will, toward the breakwater across the parking lot.

From there he had sat and watched the houseboat, and thought of Kate.

He wanted to see her—it had been too long since he looked in her eyes and heard her voice. He had been jarred by the way she left the last time they were together. For the first time he had begun to feel truly estranged from her.

And he hated that, the separation: It was wrong, he thought, it should not be happening.

He knew that he should be saying this to her, telling her what was in him. He knew that if he had done this during their marriage, he would not be there alone—they would be together in the house on Telegraph Hill.

He didn't often pay attention to what was happening inside him; this was part of the problem. Feelings seemed to take care of themselves, perk along in the background, leaving him free to turn his attention elsewhere.

So he was often oblivious of feelings, and until Kate's departure, that had seemed to work fine, at no cost to him.

Even when he was aware of emotions—as he was now, in painful detail—he felt gagged when he tried to discuss them.

Words seemed not just weak, but irrelevant, when you applied them this way.

Like tonight, right now: He could not imagine putting into words what he felt, seeing that houseboat across the water, knowing that she was in it and that he did not belong there with her.

Walking up the dock, saying this to her face, seemed inconceivable. A fantasy. So he stayed where he was, watching the boat, and thinking of her, until he nodded and slept with his head against the window.

39

Stephen Leviste was trussed and blindfolded. His hands and feet were bound together by a cord, fastened behind his back: The maniac had tied them that way in the brown van.

Several hours had passed since the abduction—Stephen guessed that it was that long ago, but he couldn't be sure. The strips of duct tape were still stuck across his mouth, cutting off any possibility of his yelling, even grunting. The hood of black cloth that the maniac had slipped over his head and tied at the neck was still in place too.

He was hanging, suspended, in what seemed to be a net of nylon webbing. Maybe a cargo net. He didn't know where he was hanging, or how far above the ground he might be.

He'd had nothing to do with it. The maniac had tied him into the net with straps at his feet and waist, and closed the net with some kind of snap—the click had been audible—and then set him swinging out in space.

But first the maniac did something strange. He loosened the cords at Stephen Leviste's wrists.

An invitation to escape.

At least, to try.

So now, working his wrists, trying to find enough slack to pull his hands through, Stephen Leviste realized that he was probably doing exactly what the maniac wanted.

He wasn't going to stay there though—wherever that was.

With much effort he had managed to wriggle onto his side. That took the body weight off his wrists, and he could work the cords better. He flexed his wrists, pulled one arm, groped, and flexed some more and pulled his left hand . . .

Free.

The right hand was still tied to his ankles by a length of cord, but with one arm unbound there was more slack now, and he pulled the right wrist loose in half a minute.

He brought both arms out from behind his back, shook and flexed them until he got some feeling back.

He untied the hood, reached up, and pulled the cloth from his face.

He almost wished he hadn't.

He saw that it really was a net of webbing surrounding him. He was suspended in a shaft that was ten feet square, at least three stories deep: thirty feet or more.

Deep enough to hurt you bad, even kill you, if you landed wrong.

Below him was a concrete floor. The shaft was open on one side, near the bottom, and this admitted enough electric light—from a lamp out of sight—that he could see the floor directly beneath him.

He pulled the tape off his mouth. His immediate instinct was to yell, scream.

I give up was what he wanted to shout. *I'm finished, I've had it . . . do what you want.*

But one stubborn part of himself wouldn't allow that.

He opened the strap at his chest. Another strap still fastened his ankles to the net, but he couldn't reach that yet, hanging as he was.

The net was suspended from the ceiling, at the end of a rope. Two metal D-rings—a tool of mountaineers—attached the netting to a loop at the end of the rope and clasped the net shut.

To open the net he would have to release at least one of the D-rings.

He reached with his right hand, grabbed the loop of the rope.

This relieved the tension on one of the rings, and with his left hand he was able to open it, slip it out from around the webbing.

Half the net dropped away from the rope, fell away from his shoulders. This was no good, he thought, he had opened the wrong ring, he had wanted to free his legs first.

He tried to pull himself up the rope, get into a position where he could free his ankles from the net.

And then his right hand slipped, he lost his grip, and his torso fell toward the concrete floor . . .

. . . but jerked to a stop.

The straps at his ankles held him in the net. And half the net was still attached to the line from the ceiling, held there by the one last D-ring.

He hung, upside down.

And he felt his ankles slipping through the strap, gravity pulling them through, trying to claim him.

He thrashed for a moment, then calmed himself.

The straps at his ankles were the last thread that held him from the concrete below. In a few seconds he would plunge down there, face first.

He lunged, reached, and snagged the net that hung down beside him. His ankles were going, but he pulled the net toward him, grabbed it with both hands.

His ankles popped free. His legs swung down, his body flipping again, turning as he fell, but he willed his hands to hold as the webbing twisted in his grip.

And he held.

He was head up now, swinging on the net inside the shaft. His feet found holds in the webbing, and he climbed, his hands reaching and grabbing and pulling himself along.

As he ascended, he glimpsed the amazing sight at the top of the shaft.

The shaft was enclosed on three sides, but the fourth side opened onto a broad, wide concrete room, a huge room.

A concrete cavern with high, sheer walls.

A steel catwalk extended the length of the cavern, and ended abruptly—without a railing—at the edge of the shaft.

He was even with the catwalk now, both hands holding the rope just above the D-ring. He began to rock back and forth, setting the rope to swing, the arcs increasing, each swing carrying him closer to the lip where the catwalk ended and the open space of the shaft began.

He swung, he swung, and at the end of the last arc he let go, and he flew, and he crashed onto the steel honeycomb of the catwalk.

He was out of the shaft.

He sat up and looked around. A few feet along the catwalk lay an aluminum extension ladder, collapsed into five or six sections.

He tried to gather himself, collect his thoughts.

The concrete floor was dusty. The air smelled stale and earthy. He had noticed that already as he hung in the net, but the smell of things hadn't seemed very pressing then.

Put aside the dust and the smell, though, and this place looked familiar: the shaft, the huge concrete room.

He opened the ladder and began to feed it down into the shaft. This was actually easier than it looked, once he figured it out: The aluminum was light, and the hinged sections snapped into place as he lowered the ladder.

When it was fully extended, the ladder stood on the floor of the shaft and rested against the edge of the catwalk. It fit.

But he didn't go down the ladder right away. He headed to the other end of the catwalk. A muffled, thrumming sound became audible as he approached the end of the walk—he thought he knew what it was, what brought power to the overhead fixtures that lit the big room.

At the end of the catwalk was a wire mesh cage surrounding a concrete landing—just like in the game. Across the landing was a gray metal door and a stairwell that descended out of sight.

The cage had a door of steel mesh: He tried it, but it wouldn't open.

It didn't open in TRY ME, either.

The catwalk there was much higher, scarier, than it had been in the game. But everything else matched. He was convinced now: This was the last level in the game.

And if it was, he knew how to get out.

He stepped back along the catwalk, headed for the ladder at the other end. He was halfway across, when a sound stopped him: a slight squeak from back where he had just left. He turned in time to see the gray metal door close at the landing, inside the wire mesh cage.

He could make out a shape, a man, stepping out onto the landing.

"Hello, puppy," said the maniac.

The voice chilled Stephen Leviste, but it didn't shock him. By now he was beyond shock.

The maniac broke into a singsong chatter—"Here, pup-pup, here boy, c'mon here, puppy"—with a whistle and a little clap of the hands, just like calling a dog.

Stephen began to edge away from the voice, toward the other end of the catwalk. He tried to stay calm. Had to get to that ladder.

The maniac opened the mesh door of the cage and stepped out onto the catwalk. He began striding toward Stephen Leviste. Fast.

Stephen broke into a run. Their feet pounded the catwalk.

Stephen reached the end of the catwalk, the shaft where the

ladder stood. He grabbed the top of the ladder, dropped his legs over the side, and his feet touched a rung.

The maniac was sprinting toward him.

Stephen came down the ladder fast, half sliding, slowing his fall by gripping the ladder's uprights, his feet slapping the rungs.

The maniac's footsteps resounded on the catwalk.

Stephen's left ankle twisted when he hit the floor. But he stood, ducked under the ladder, grasped a rung, and began to push the ladder away from the edge, straining to get it upright.

One more push, and he let it fall backward, clattering against the back wall of the shaft.

The footsteps stopped on the catwalk.

With the ladder out of reach, the only way down was to jump.

The maniac was big and strong, but Stephen Leviste doubted that he could fly.

Stephen Leviste stepped out of the shaft into the big concrete cavern. From there he could see the maniac on the catwalk, looking down at him.

The maniac followed along the catwalk as Stephen Leviste ran across the endless concrete floor.

At the bottom of the far wall was a metal door, painted red, the color faded, not quite as bright as it had been in the game. But close enough.

He ran to the door.

Above him, the killer disappeared into the mesh cage at the end of the catwalk.

Stephen stood at the door.

A few hours earlier, in the game, he had opened it with a click of his mouse, and he had found freedom and escape.

Now he reached for the knob, twisted it, pulled . . .

It did not move.

He twisted the knob and shook it. The door did not budge.

In his mind Stephen kept seeing the red door in the game, and the sunlight and openness that had waited behind it. He shook the door in desperation, and once more twisted the knob.

It turned in his hand. The door swung toward him. Stephen flung the door open and stepped forward.

The maniac stood in his path.

Stephen recoiled backward.

The maniac, grinning, said, "It's not all the same, is it, puppy?"

Stephen didn't answer at first. He was looking behind the maniac, who stood at the bottom of a concrete staircase that obviously descended from the cage up top.

There was no opening to the outdoors. No escape.

"Is it?" the maniac yelled.

"No."

"You like games? Hey, I know the answer to that one. You didn't like games, you wouldn't be here, would you? You're eating this up, you love it, tell me the truth."

"No," said Stephen Leviste. "I'm scared."

"You've got reason to be."

The maniac continued:

"The lights go out in about eight hours. You can expect me anytime after that."

And then he stepped back, and the red door slammed shut behind him, and he was gone.

The killer locked the red door and ascended the stairs that rose behind it.

It was a triple flight of stairs that ended at the concrete landing at the end of the steel catwalk, thirty-five feet above the concrete floor.

He paused at the top of the stairs' long reach. To his right was a heavy steel-mesh barrier, with a mesh door. On the other side of the barrier was the catwalk.

At the other end of that catwalk was the shaft. The ladder in the shaft was the only way to the bottom except for these stairs.

And only he used the stairs. The mesh barrier up there and the red door down at the bottom sealed this part of the complex off from the rest.

Joyboy could run loose everywhere else.

The killer turned to his left and opened a heavy fire door. Behind this fire door was his exclusive domain. He entered a short passageway from which three rooms branched: two on one side of the passage, a third on the other.

Each of these three rooms had a function: He was an organized person who liked all things in their place.

The single room on the right side of the corridor—larger than the other two—was his supply room. A second room, across the passageway, held the generator that powered the lights. The noise of its gas engine was low but constant in there: Most of the time he wasn't even aware of it anymore.

The third room, beside the generator compartment, was his dirty room. The floors were bloodstained. Here Portia and DeeTee-Dude had died.

He now entered the short passageway and turned into the supply room.

It had a lived-in look, with an air mattress and several televisions, a cellular phone, a workbench of electrical and computer equipment, cartons of food, sealed plastic containers of water lined against a wall, a propane camp stove, and a couple of lanterns and several valved tanks of propane gas.

It was a place where you could ride out a bad storm; in fact, this was exactly how he thought of it.

He picked up a plastic jug of water, carried it out across the landing at the top of the stairs, through the wire mesh door.

He put it down on the catwalk. Joyboy would find it there.

He didn't want the kid to die of thirst. The idea was to preserve him for a while. Keep him alive for better uses.

The killer left the catwalk and returned to the supply room, to the workbench where several PCs and monitors—and more specialized equipment—waited for him.

The idea had come to him as he watched Joyboy from the restaurant. Physically the kid was a joke. But he was smart: If his body matched his brains Joyboy would be a real test. And he knew Try Me well enough to have escaped from the last level.

The killer had come up with a way to bring those smarts into play. It involved a minor tweak of the software and an ingenious use of basic electrical equipment.

Now, for about an hour, the killer worked at the bench, first rewriting segments of the software code and then adjusting the hardware.

Then he tested it.

The result made the lights dim momentarily as the generator bogged under a sudden overload.

Oh yes, the killer thought. This was going to do just fine.

He still lacked a few pieces, more specialized stuff, but he would pick them up later. For now he would let his appetites simmer and build for a few hours.

He knew how to stoke that fire. In the large room off the passageway, a video camera sat on a tripod. The killer entered the room, ejected a tape cassette from the camera, and carried the tape out with him as he left.

A few moments later he was leaving the concrete cavern, emerging into the open air, the stillness of the last hour before dawn.

Telling himself that Joyboy's time would come, and it would be soon.

40

The rising sun woke Ellis Hoile. From where he had parked, it rose over Angel Island to burn directly in his face.

He shaded his eyes and looked toward the houseboat. A light burned in the kitchen window. She must be awake, he thought.

He didn't want her to find him here. Not that.

He quickly started the car and drove away.

About half an hour later, he was walking through the front door at 2600 Tesla. The living room, with its array, looked shabby and pointless.

This was one of the reasons he didn't leave much anymore. After he had been out, even for just a few hours, he began to see his life from the world's perspective. It was not a flattering view.

He wasn't sure whether this meant that he should get out more, or stop going out altogether. This morning it seemed to be an open question.

His first act, reflexively, was to log onto Verba, so that he could check his overnight e-mail. He let his log-in script go to work while he went into the kitchen. He splashed cold water on his face, towelled it dry, poured a glass of orange juice.

He returned to his desk, to the computer that had logged into Verba. The screen showed:

```
STOMA>    Yo, Avatar.
STOMA>    Avatar, hello.
STOMA>    Earth to Avatar, anybody out there?
STOMA>    Yo, Avatar.
```

Ellis Hoile, still standing at the desk, pulled the keyboard in front of him. He bent and typed:

```
AVATAR>    Yes.
STOMA>     Try the game yet?
AVATAR>    Your game is an evil piece of excrement.
```

The response came:

```
STOMA>     That's an interesting response. Maybe we ought to talk
           about it. Why don't you give me your phone number?
AVATAR>    *You* are an evil piece of excrement.
```

The reply was immediate:

```
STOMA>     I'm always happy to get feedback. Give me your phone
           number, we'll discuss it.
```

Feedback? Ellis Hoile thought. *Feedback?*

This sounded all wrong. And he thought he knew why. He typed:

```
AVATAR>    Eat shit and die.
STOMA>     Hmm, I hadn't considered that. I'd like to discuss it fur-
           ther. What's your phone number?
AVATAR>    Roses are red, violets are blue.
STOMA>     That's interesting. Maybe we ought to talk about it. Why
           don't you give me your phone number?
AVATAR>    May you rot in hell.
```

The screen showed Stoma's answer:

```
STOMA>     I'm always happy to get feedback. Give me your phone
           number, we'll talk about it.
AVATAR>    Ever had the clap?
```

> STOMA> You ask an interesting question. I'd like to discuss it at greater length. Why don't you give me your phone number?

It was a bot—a software robot, operating from a set of canned responses. Bots were designed to mimic a human user; a good bot, cleverly scripted, could carry on a simple "conversation" for several minutes, so long as the exchange remained predictable.

But bots couldn't improvise: Faced with an unexpected statement or question, they could only fall back on their scripted responses. Then the illusion ended.

Ellis Hoile tried again, to be sure.

> AVATAR> The Owl and the Pussycat went to sea in a beautiful pea-green boat.
> STOMA> I'm not sure I understand. Give me your phone number, we'll talk about it.
> AVATAR> They took some honey, and plenty of money, wrapped up in a five-pound note.
> STOMA> I'm sure we could discuss this more effectively if we spoke by telephone. Give me your number, I'll call.

Definitely a bot. It had been looking for him when he logged in. Stoma had designed it to wait for Avatar's appearance, in order to chat him up and tease out his phone number.

A lot of trouble, for just a phone number.

Who is this guy? Ellis Hoile wondered.

He logged off, turned from the desk, and drew the drapes away from the big picture window. He found himself looking down at the apartment house on Union Street.

He powered up the video scanner and monitor, then checked

the alignment of the long antenna on the tripod. It was still pointed down into C. W. Hartmundt's apartment.

The monitor faded in from black. A distorted image came to life as he watched: It slid in and out of the screen, and dissolved to running vertical lines.

Ellis Hoile used the remote control to shift the tripod's power head almost imperceptibly to the left.

He lost the image. The scanner had been designed to seize the strongest signal within a given range of wavelengths, to fix on that signal and reject all others. The strongest signal was usually the one most closely aligned with the highly directional antenna, so that shifting the axis of the antenna, even by a fraction of a degree, would change the signal that the scanner received.

He tapped another button. The screen stayed blank.

Another tap. Still blank. He had lost it.

A tap upward this time.

Another tap up, then back down again, and this time the running lines parted and the picture aligned.

It showed a nude woman stretched out on a floor. He couldn't make out many details: The video quality from the scanner was grainy, only marginal, and the lighting in the video itself was hot and harsh.

But he could see blood on the woman's face and more blood smeared on her arms.

It was dark against her skin—the bright lights made her skin seem almost white.

He didn't like this. But the thought that this was coming from C. W. Hartmundt's apartment kept him from turning away.

Then a man entered the frame from behind the camera. The shot didn't waver, but the focus moved in and out until the man stopped and stood over the woman.

The image was from an autofocus videocam, Ellis Hoile

thought. The camera was on a tripod, unattended. The man had set it recording and then walked out into the shot.

He seemed to be a tall, somewhat slim man. His back was to the camera—his face wasn't visible. The woman's eyes had revived, and they followed him as he crossed the floor.

He looked down at her, and kept looking.

Ellis Hoile watched too.

The man on-screen shifted his feet, his body seemed to tense, and he went into a half-crouch, and raised his right arm. The arm was long . . . it seemed to have an extension. . . .

He was holding a machete.

He swung it down toward the woman's head. She flinched slightly and made a reflex move to stop him, but it was too slow, a gesture much too weak.

The machete crashed down into her neck. Her body shook—blood flew—the man withdrew the bloody blade and looked down at what he had done.

Her limbs shook. An artery spurted black blood.

Ellis Hoile knew for sure that nobody was holding the camera. No photographer on earth could have held that shot without flinching.

The thin thread of life that had been in the woman's eyes was gone now. Her neck was bent at a deep, meaty notch.

And the man tensed and swung the machete again, into the notch, hard.

Ellis Hoile closed his eyes when the head rolled free.

When he looked up again, the scene was reversing. It was a tape, he thought, and someone was rewinding it.

Going back, stopping at the moment before the first machete blow.

Now forward again. The machete rose again and fell once more into the woman's white neck.

Again the tape stopped and reversed, and then went forward again.

The woman again made that same small, pitiful move to stop the machete as it fell. Again the blow landed.

And the tape stopped, then reversed, then moved forward once more.

The thought came to Ellis Hoile: C. W. Hartmundt was not just watching this. He was eating it up.

And then Ellis Hoile thought *he* should be taping this too.

He had built a second video jack into the scanner so that he could copy the output, but he had never bothered to attach a VCR.

He went to the rack in the living room. On the monitor the machete was falling again.

Up on the top shelf of the rack was a VCR, a professional recording deck. He reached high and brought it down.

When he carried the VCR over to the scanner, the scene on the monitor had changed somewhat. Same room, same man, same woman—or body, it was now. But the tape had finally run on, past the first two blows; now the man on the tape was crouching at the corpse, chopping with the machete, not in fury, but with careful, calculated swings.

He was dismembering the body.

Ellis Hoile stopped for a moment to watch. The man in the tape had already separated the right arm at the elbow. He was at the other elbow now.

Ellis Hoile looked away and began to screw in the cable. It took longer than it should have: His hands were shaking.

He tried the VCR—it needed a tape.

Over to the rack again. He grabbed a cassette from a stack. The video on the screen was quick and jerky now. C. W. Hartmundt was fast-forwarding through action that showed the man tossing limbs into a ghastly pile beside the body.

Ellis Hoile inserted the cassette and began to record.

Almost simultaneously, the ghastly scene ended on the monitor, and was replaced by the tweedy look of blank tape.

This lasted for several seconds. Then more video.

Different scene this time, different lighting, another setting altogether.

A parking garage at night. Long zoom down a row of cars, to a plump man in his thirties walking toward the camera.

This was clearly handheld. The zoom pulled back as the man got closer.

Then the shot jounced and swung crazily. The photographer was moving the camera in a big way, without bothering to turn it off. The frame briefly showed the floor of the parking garage, the wheel and fender of a car.

Then an orange glow bloomed across the scene. Almost as if someone had lit a sudden fire somewhere at the edge of the shot. The glow bloomed a second time, brighter now, as though the fire had been turned up higher.

The camera swung up—the shooter bringing it to his face, looking into the eyepiece again—and the shot fastened on a conflagration where the man had stood. Flames rose and spread across the ceiling.

And then Ellis Hoile saw that the man was still there, but on his knees now, in the middle of the fireball. The shot tightened, framing the man's face, a silent howl as his skin crinkled and darkened in the fire.

The shot held there for five or six seconds, full on the contorted face. Then it widened. The camera swung once more, and Ellis Hoile could see that the shooter was climbing into a car, the camera bumping and bouncing, photographing an interior door panel and the driver's legs and feet before he shut it off.

The signal vanished on the scanner.

It was over.

Ellis Hoile sat on the floor, where he had placed the VCR.

He realized that he wasn't sure exactly what he had witnessed. His mind seemed dull that morning. He felt dangerously frayed.

There was one way to know, he thought.

He rewound the cassette for a few seconds and then began to play it.

He expected a few moments of blank tape before the scanner recording appeared. What he saw, though, was Kate blowing out the candles on a birthday cake.

Her birthday, her twenty-fifth birthday party, God, he remembered it, they had rented a house at Lake Tahoe that week, he had bought the cake and surprised her, he had shot this tape.

The stack where he had picked up this cassette was not blanks, it was home movies.

Now she was at the lake shore, wearing shorts and a T-shirt, up to her calves in the clear water, looking across the huge lake at the mountains on the other side, then turning to show him a smile.

Oh, hell, a loving smile.

She had been happy. *They* had been happy.

Abruptly the scanner recording kicked in, cutting off Kate and Lake Tahoe: the moment now lost forever, replaced by a plump man about to die, walking through a parking garage.

Ellis Hoile forced himself to watch, pay attention.

The cars in the garage were late model—he noticed it this time—so the scene had been shot within the last year or two.

The license plates were dark, not like California's blue lettering on white. He couldn't read the plates, but he thought that this scene hadn't been shot around here.

He watched the man's face, the moment when he noticed that he was being photographed. What showed there was mild bafflement, a muted surprise. Nothing like recognition.

The victim did not know his killer.

Technical quality, he thought, was poor. Camcorders had improved greatly in the past few years, but they were still a noticeable notch down from professional equipment.

This had not been shot with a pro camera.

Contrast was poor, lighting was bad: The only lights were what you'd expect to find in a parking garage.

And that fire: In the frame it became just a searing white blob. It lost all detail, the brightness overwhelming the range of camera and tape. A professional photographer, in a staged situation, would have found a way around that.

Amateur stuff.

The look on the dying man's face . . .

This was not staged. This was real.

Now Ellis Hoile watched again the jiggling camera, the jerky movements as the shooter lowered it from his eye and lifted it into the car, the car's interior and the floorboard as the driver's right foot stomped the gas.

Snapping back to Kate in Tahoe. Her face was drawing into a moue as the lens zoomed in tight on her—Ellis could now remember taking this shot—and then she laughed and grinned and finally let her features relax into an expression that Ellis Hoile recognized as pure unfettered love.

The tape kept playing as Ellis Hoile reached for the telephone and dialed Lee Wade's home number.

"This is Ellis Hoile," he said when Lee Wade answered. "I want you to come by this morning, can you do that?"

"Is it important?" Lee Wade said.

"I think so," Ellis Hoile said. "Yeah, it is. Yes."

Fine, Lee Wade told him—it would be an hour or two.

"I appreciate that," Ellis Hoile said, and he hung up the phone.

Meanwhile the tape kept running. Kate's presence filled the

screen; she was coming alive in a long-gone afternoon, so distant that it seemed like another life. In its own way this was as hard to watch as the horrible death of a stranger.

Ellis Hoile's eyes were liquid. Filling. Full.

He let it happen, the tears falling. It was too much, the inexpressible sadness of it all: Kate and her Lake Tahoe birthday, and their lost happiness, and the shabby look of his home and his life, and his weariness, and the horror on the video scanner . . . he couldn't separate them.

He allowed himself to weep.

No reason to hold it back, he thought. It couldn't hurt. Nobody would know.

He was, after all, alone.

41

Stephen Leviste knelt on the concrete floor.

Directly in front of him, notched into the floor, was a steel grate. He leaned forward and tried to peer through the slit openings of the grate.

He had been roaming the big concrete cavern for several hours now.

Big as it was, Stephen Leviste thought, the huge room was really just a jail cell, featureless and confining and offering no hint of escape or reason to hope.

At least, this was true of the part that was open to him. The red steel door at the bottom level and the heavy wire mesh at the end of the catwalk shut him off from all the rest.

Stephen Leviste couldn't imagine why the huge room had been built. It seemed to have had a purpose at one time. Half a dozen steel disks were set into the ceiling high above the floor—they must have been there for a reason, he thought.

On the floor, in a straight drop below these disks, lay six massive steel plates that were extensively tapped and drilled, as if they had once held heavy machinery of some kind. But the machinery, whatever it had been, was now gone. To Stephen Leviste the bare concrete cavern seemed a place that the maniac had discovered long after the rest of the world had forgotten it.

Since the maniac's last appearance, Stephen had been over the place a dozen times or more, across the broad floor and into the shaft that fell away beyond the catwalk, even back up onto the catwalk. He had catalogued its features—what few there were.

That shaft was actually a deep stairwell. Somebody had cut

away the steel steps that once stood there; they were in a jumbled pile near the bottom of the shaft.

Along one wall was a large warehouse-style sliding door, welded shut.

A galvanized air duct ran up one wall and along the ceiling, parallel to the catwalk, far above the floor.

And he had found this grate.

The grate lay in a steel frame in the floor. The grate seemed to have been designed to lift out of the frame, but now four neat drops of welded steel—one at each corner—held it in place.

Stephen rose from his knees and crossed the floor to the jumble of steel stair parts. Most of it was too big to move, whole sections of stairs and steel support columns, but with some effort he pulled out a piece of handrail, about eight feet long.

He dragged it over to the grate.

Through the narrow slits in the grate Stephen could see nothing. The grate seemed to cover blankness, a void.

Stephen stood the steel rail on end, resting it at one corner of the grate. Then he raised the rail above the corner of the grate— ten, twelve inches, as high as he could manage while keeping it balanced.

Dark emptiness wasn't much, he thought. Still, it held more promise than the bleak vista of concrete that surrounded him.

With all the force he could manage, Stephen drove the butt end of the steel rail down into the grate, down onto one of the four weld tacks that held the grate in place. The rail clanged and rang. He raised it again, and smashed it once more into the corner of the grate.

Ten, fifteen, twenty times he raised the pole and smashed it against the corner of the grate.

Whatever lay down in the darkness, he thought, it had to be better than waiting here to die.

He raised the pole again, and once more smashed it down. This time one of the four beads of weld cracked beneath the force of the blow.

He didn't know what was down there, in the darkness beneath the grate. But he intended to find out.

42

Ellis Hoile looked awful. Beat and bedraggled, Lee Wade thought.

Had he been *crying*?

He didn't seem the weepy type. But those eyes . . .

Right away Ellis Hoile said, "I want to show you this."

It was the tape that he had scanned from C. W. Hartmundt's apartment. Ellis Hoile put it into a VCR, but before he played it he had to explain the video scanner, the idea, how it worked.

Wade had two comments when he heard about the scanner.

He asked, "Is that legal?"

And he said, "Civilians have all the great toys. Civilians and the feds. I could put that little hummer to some good use, no question about it."

And then Ellis Hoile played the tape. When it was finished, he reversed it and played it again.

"Realistic," Wade said when it was finished.

"Not realistic. *Real.*"

"You have no way of knowing that."

"Come on. You saw it."

"The things people put on tape. It could've been anything. One minute I see a guy walking toward the camera. Then the camera looks at the floor for a while. Then, the next thing, the camera looks up again, something's on fire. Could've been anything. It could've been a setup, you have no way of knowing. Soon as the camera was off him, the guy might've run off, and he got a dummy and lit that. It could've happened that way."

"Why go to all that trouble?"

"People do some kinky shit for no good reason," said Wade. "Believe me, I know."

"This one was real," Ellis Hoile said. "That's as kinky as it gets."

Lee Wade said, "The problem is, I'm not investigating any murder where somebody got burned to death in a parking garage. I never even *heard* of a case where somebody got burned up in a parking garage."

"It ties in," Ellis Hoile said. "Donald Trask used Verba. This asshole uses Verba, too, and he's using it to pull some very strange moves."

Then Ellis Hoile started telling him about the game, about Stoma and Christian Willem Hartmundt, and about the Trojan Horse, and the daemon.

This was where Lee Wade started to glaze over. Trojan Horses and daemons, it was all beyond him.

"He tried to hack into your computer," Lee Wade said. "Is this what you're telling me?"

"I'm guessing that I'm not the first. Most people wouldn't have caught him—his method's too slick."

"I don't know if that's a crime," Lee Wade said. "Hacking into other people's computers. But if it is, it's not a homicide. And that's what I get paid for."

Ellis Hoile made an effort to be patient: Lee Wade could tell.

"Something is going on here, and it's all wrong," Ellis Hoile said. "This and the tape. It smells. It stinks."

"You want me to check him out," Lee Wade said.

"Yes."

"Go down and talk to him, is that the idea?"

"You're the cop. But I would say that's a start."

They were standing near the big picture window. Lee Wade looked down at the apartment house on Union Street, and at Ellis Hoile's face—earnest, almost desperate—and at the video tape in his hand. Then back down to the apartment house.

Right at the bottom of Telegraph, wouldn't take more than a few minutes. And Ellis Hoile seemed so sure.

"Better give me that name and address again," Lee Wade said.

A few minutes later Lee Wade was checking the names on the mailboxes at the apartment house on Union Street. Hartmundt, there it was. He took out his foldover ID wallet, opened to the ID and the shield. Then he went to 1-A, knocked on the door.

After a few moments he heard someone—or maybe it was some*thing*—come to answer the knock. A kind of clanking noise inside: kunk ka-*chunk* kunk ka-*chunk* getting louder as it approached.

The door swung open and right away Lee Wade understood the noise. Because the man across the threshold wore a metal leg brace. Lee Wade gave his name and said, "Are you Christian Hartmundt?"

"I am."

"You live here alone?"

"I do."

Lee Wade couldn't take his eyes off the brace. It was a big, heavy-looking device of steel and leather that extended from the ankle to mid-thigh of Christian Hartmundt's left leg.

Christian Hartmundt said, "Is there a problem?"

"You wear that all the time?"

"Except on those rare occasions when I want to fall on my face." He sounded amused and irked at the same time.

Lee Wade tried to imagine wearing that brace while killing someone. Having to chase, catch, fight, subdue an unwilling victim while wearing that monster.

No way.

Christian Hartmundt added: "It's multiple sclerosis, if you were wondering. I was diagnosed with it ten years ago."

Lee Wade slipped the foldover into his jacket.

"There's been a mistake," he said. For sure. "It has nothing to do with you, sorry to disturb you."

"You don't need me? I've got breakfast on the stove . . ."

Lee Wade shook his head and turned away. Behind him the door shut, and when Lee Wade paused he heard the sound again—kunk ka-*chunk*, kunk ka-*chunk*—now receding as Christian Hartmundt labored away from the door.

Angry as he was, Lee Wade didn't want to see Ellis Hoile again. So he called, instead.

Ellis Hoile picked up on the first ring. Right away Lee Wade said, "You can forget your theory. The guy down the hill may have funny taste in videos, but he's no killer."

"Did you see him?"

"I saw him, all right."

"Did he know Donald Trask?"

"I didn't ask. No way he could be a killer. He's disabled."

"I thought so."

"You knew that?"

"I had an idea he might be. It's MS, I think."

"You *knew* that? Let me get this straight, you knew he was crippled, and you still yank my chain, telling me he's a killer?"

Ellis Hoile didn't say anything.

Lee Wade said, "Well, damn. Damn. God damn, I don't believe this."

He realized that he was starting to sputter. He tried to calm himself down, take a breath, and then he said, "Would you please enlighten me. Would you do that? Would you tell me what the *fuck* you're thinking about, to make you say a crip killed at least two people?"

"I know what I know," said Ellis Hoile.

"Thank you," Wade said. He was trying hard to keep his voice under control. "No, really, I mean it, thank you. Thanks for the little demonstration, thanks for all the pointers, all your concern. We depend on the support of our citizens."

He knew he should let it go at that. But after a moment, when Ellis Hoile didn't speak, Lee Wade said, "You knew? You fucking knew that he was a crip? And you didn't tell me?"

He said, "You're a very intelligent person. I know you are. A real brain, no question about it. But I wouldn't trade an ounce of real smarts for a ton of what you've got up there."

And then he hung up. Thinking, *To hell with this crap, I've got work to do.*

43

Down on Union Street, Christian Hartmundt sat motionless in the silence of his apartment.

A cop at the door.

The cop had seemed surprised. That much was obvious, the cop's surprise at seeing him.

Asking no questions, almost in a hurry to get away. That was good.

So it could be true, that the cop had showed up by mistake.

No, he reminded himself, it *had* to be true. Because Christian Willem Hartmundt had done nothing to attract attention. Christian Willem Hartmundt had done nothing to cause anyone, even the police—especially the police—to notice him.

In the strictest sense, Christian Willem Hartmundt had broken no laws. He was impeccable. He had nothing to fear from the police.

So gradually the tension eased out of him.

It still scared him, though, the idea of a cop at the door, within an arm's length of the most revealing, the most destructive possible evidence.

The videotape was in a plastic case, on a table beside the door. He had to get it out of there.

He dropped it into a plastic shopping bag, and he carried the bag with him as he left the apartment and clomped down the hall as quickly as the creaking mechanism on his leg would allow.

44

In the house on Tesla Street, Ellis Hoile was playing the tape. He was watching it on a monitor, waiting for the right few seconds . . . the moment the camera swung up from the floor to reveal a man engulfed in flame . . . *there*.

He froze the tape, and now connected a line from the tape deck to the input jack of a video capture card, in one of his computers.

He played the tape for a couple of seconds, and now the computer's hard drive clicked, entering millions of bits of data, the horrifying onscreen image reduced to binary form that was no more potent than the file of a digitized scribble or shopping list.

He stopped the tape, ejected it, and put it aside.

Now he turned to the computer. He entered a video editing program, and he called up the brief clip captured from the tape.

He began to examine the file, frame by frame. He wanted to find a frame that was especially horrifying, that was unmistakable.

Just about all of them fit that description.

He chose one, from the moment when the camera began to tighten on the burning man inside the inferno: You could see details of his face, yet the nearby cars and the garage itself were still distinct.

There would be no question of what this was, where it had come from.

He saved the single frame and deleted the rest. The editor allowed him to enter three words at the bottom of the frame, and then to encode the file into a form that could be sent as e-mail.

While he worked, Ellis Hoile kept hearing Lee Wade. *Would you enlighten me? Would you tell me what the* fuck *you're thinking about?*

The answer was pretty simple, Ellis Hoile thought. Sometimes you just embrace what you know, without drawing conclusions, making judgments.

Let the truth be true and the rest will work itself out.

Stoma—who had to be C. W. Hartmundt—had wanted Avatar's phone number enough that he had written an autobot to get it.

This was not a minor task. A conversational bot required algorithms, a set of software rules that analyzed speech and chose an appropriate response from a set of prewritten answers.

Ellis Hoile realized that he had tripped the bot accidentally, with sudden profanity that the algorithm did not expect. Then, once he guessed what was happening, he had hung up the bot with nonsense phrases that the software could not possibly recognize.

But it could have worked, he thought. Except for one lucky break, he might never have known.

The bot might have worked already, with other users.

What had Stoma wanted from *them*?

Ellis Hoile believed that Stoma must have had a purpose, a reason for devoting this kind of effort. From what he knew of Stoma, the glimpses into his mind and his soul, Ellis Hoile thought that the purposes could not be good.

He did not dismiss the idea that Christian Willem Hartmundt, whom he suspected of murder, was a physical cripple.

He just chose not to deal with it for a while.

He logged onto Verba now, and uploaded the image file, the single frame from the tape. The address read:

To: stoma@verba.

And the message at the bottom said:

CWH: I know.

45

The killer returned to the concrete cavern in the late afternoon of that day, bringing with him the last of the equipment that he needed to complete the special project that he had begun that morning—his little surprise for Joyboy.

Playtime.

He dropped in the way he had left, down iron rungs along the side of a concrete well that descended from the surface.

He used a flashlight: The generator would be out of fuel.

The generator room was to his right as he entered the short passageway off the well. He went in, filled the tank from one of the jerrycans in the room, started the engine with the punch of a button.

For about the next half hour he bent over the workbench in the supply room. These were final touches on the equipment that he had begun to assemble that morning. When he was finished he began to carry it—several armloads—into the killing room, the abattoir, across the passage.

Then back into the supply room once more for a length of rope. For a moment he wondered whether he might need some sap or bludgeon, in case Joyboy proved difficult.

No, he thought. Joyboy was going to come easy.

He carried the rope with him, down to the end of the passageway, out onto the landing. He quickly checked the catwalk and found it empty. Joyboy had taken the water.

The killer turned down the long staircase off the landing, down to the red door at the floor level, and he stepped out into the cavern.

Joyboy was nowhere in sight.

Trying to hide, the killer thought. But the cavern afforded few hiding places. Joyboy must be crouching in the shaft below the edge of the catwalk.

The killer began crossing the floor.

"C'mon, puppy," he called, "time to come out and play."

He stepped into the shaft, ready to grab Joyboy if the kid tried to spring past him.

But the shaft was empty.

Quickly the killer double-checked the jumble of hardware from the dismantled staircase. Skinny as he was, he might have squirreled himself away in among all the junk.

But Joyboy wasn't there, either.

He couldn't have gotten out, the killer thought—it wasn't possible.

Then his eyes found the steel grate in the floor. He strode over there, crouched, and looked close at the corners where he had welded the grate in place.

The beads were broken.

Little bastard, he thought. *How did he manage that?*

Below the grate was a service corridor that allowed access to pipes and electrical conduit that had originally run under the main floor.

It was cramped, little more than a crawl space. The killer disliked it: In all ways, at all times, he craved mobility and freedom of movement.

Joyboy had to be down there. At his size, he would find the space a little less confining. But it would still be unpleasant. No lights down there, it would be absolutely dark.

And by now, smart as he was, he would have found that it was a dead end. This hole in the floor, which the grate covered, was the only way in.

Now the killer had to get him out.

He braced himself at the grate and yelled:

"You want it to go hard on you, just stay right where you are. You want it to go easy, come on out. I mean now. Got that? Come out right away, you've got no problem."

But even as he said it, the killer guessed this wouldn't fly. Joyboy had a big problem, and they both knew it.

From the other side of the grate, the killer heard only silence.

"Fine," the killer said. He stood, brushed the dust off his pants. He would have to dig Joyboy out. "You want a problem, want to make things harder on you, this is the way you want it, you've got it."

He needed a light. Several were upstairs, including the flashlight he had brought in.

He crossed the floor again, opened the red door with a key that he kept at a ring, as he retraced his steps back up to the landing and the supply room.

He grabbed a three-cell flashlight and hurried back down, across the broad floor again.

He lifted the grate, grunting. The thought came to him that Joyboy must be stronger than he looked, to move the grate aside, then pull it back behind him.

We'll see, he thought. He flicked on the flashlight, sat at the edge of the opening—feet dangling—and he began to lower himself down into the hole.

His head and shoulders were still above the opening when his feet touched the floor of the crawl space.

And at that instant pain roared up his legs, jolting him, his vision blooming white hot and red.

Something, somebody, had cracked him across the shins. Hard. This thought was still registering when it happened again, and after the second time the killer didn't think anymore: He pulled his body and his searing legs out of the opening in the floor, and he roared with pain and anger.

Down in the crawl space, almost directly beneath the grate opening, Stephen Leviste heard the bellow from above. A shadow at the opening showed him that the maniac had stretched out on the floor, where he groaned and softly cursed.

Stephen gripped the length of stair rail with which he had broken the weld on the grate, and which he had carried down here with him. This subterranean passage was cramped—even in the darkness he had discerned that—but here, just below the opening, it opened up slightly. Just enough that he could swing the rail.

He gripped it now and waited. The maniac could only come down one way, lowering himself from the floor above. In those few moments, the maniac's body was exposed, completely vulnerable. He could be hurt. Stephen had hurt him once, now, and would hurt him again when he got the chance.

A minute or two passed. Stephen waited. The maniac had dropped his flashlight; it shone now on the floor of the crawl space, but Stephen didn't pick it up. He gripped the rail and waited.

Gradually the muttered curses became inaudible. A shift of the shadows from above told Stephen that the maniac was rising to his feet.

Coming again, Stephen thought, and he readied the rail once more.

But the maniac was leaving. You could hear it from his footsteps. He was walking away.

This disappointed Stephen. He had hoped to break some bones, maybe cripple the maniac. But the maniac was not crippled.

Next time, Stephen thought.

He heard the red metal door slam shut across the cavern.

Then there was quiet.

Stephen put down the rail and retrieved the flashlight, which he turned off and laid beside the jug of water that he had carried down with him.

He waited. Before long the red door opened—in this silence Stephen could hear it plainly—and the maniac shuffled across the floor, toward the opening once more.

There was the shuffling, and something else: a periodic chirp, every second or so. To Stephen it almost sounded like a squeaky wheel.

It was coming closer. Stephen picked up the rail and held it ready again.

Up above, the maniac stood at the edge of the opening. Then bent and lifted the grate and dropped it into place in the floor, a clang that surprised Stephen. He had been expecting the killer to come for him again.

Now, from above, Stephen heard a soft *whump*. He thought that it sounded like a burner on a gas stove, when it catches fire a little late.

This was followed at once by another sound that puzzled him at first: a low, throaty hiss and crackle.

A jet of blue flame smeared through the seam where the steel grate rested in its frame in the floor. Yellow molten sparks sprayed down into the passage, just a few at first and then a blinding cascade that made Stephen turn his face away.

Up above, the maniac was welding shut the grate.

This time, the killer thought, he was going to do the job right. No puny spot-welds at the corners: This time he was burning a heavy molten bead around the entire grate where it met the frame.

Nobody, much less skinny Joyboy, was going to knock it loose this time. You would need a cutting torch, or a bomb, to move the grate now. And as resourceful as Joyboy might be, he wasn't going to muster either of those down there in the crawl space.

The killer closed the gas supply knob on the welding valve and flipped up the faceplate on the protective mask. He inspected his work.

Uh-huh. Let Joyboy pound on it all he wanted. That grate was going *nowhere.*

The killer stood—slowly, uncomfortably—and began to walk stiffly away from the grate, bringing with him the welding outfit on a squeaking handcart.

In a few days, the killer told himself, he would cut away the grate. Let the little twerp's water run out first. Let him beg to be released.

That was an idea. Joyboy had a thick streak of pride, the killer could discern that now, but when the water ran out, he would beg.

Yeah. The killer could see himself passing a few relaxing evenings this way. Sit up on the catwalk, pop a beer or two, listen to the moans and the begging and the cries for help, until it finally got tiresome, or the cries turned into gasps.

Then he would cut away the grate, let Joyboy crawl out.

Or maybe not. The way the killer felt now, the pain in his shins only now beginning to subside, he might just keep the grate where it was. Let Joyboy die slowly down there.

That would mean postponing playtime, delaying his chance to use the apparatus he had built today.

But Ziggy and Avatar still waited. Their time was coming. And the apparatus would suit them too.

It meant a delay, nothing more. He could still have playtime, and the satisfaction of having Joyboy molder down there in the crawl space, die slowly and remain forever in the hole where he had gone to ground.

Now *there* was an idea.

46

That evening Ellis Hoile parked his Datsun in the same space where he had awakened twelve hours earlier. He rolled down his window: The night air was clear. The city lights were crisp across the bay.

Unfinished business had brought him there once more. Something that had to be done before life could continue.

For a while he sat as he had sat the night before, watching. He could easily make out Kate's houseboat, the kitchen lights bright. He stood watching, knowing that she must be there.

The houseboat brought on a poignant ache. It represented her life apart from him. Every day he and Kate hurtled farther apart, their paths diverging, the shared times and memories becoming less important, less binding.

The outcome was inevitable if this continued: At some point they would look at the distance that had grown between them and know that they were strangers.

He was going to lose her.

Tonight, he told himself, he wasn't going to just watch and wait.

The kitchen lights went out. And Ellis Hoile began to walk toward the dock, then up the wooden pier toward the houseboat.

Kate Lavin brought in the last dishes from supper, set them in the sink, and turned the lights out on them.

She walked out into the living room, lit only by the flames of a couple of logs in the Swedish fireplace that sat off to one side of the room.

Jon Wreggett came up from behind her as she stepped out into the room.

He held her by the waist and turned her around to face him, and he kissed her.

For quite a long time.

She held him, his solid body against her, his arms moving up along her sides, then down her back, now under her shirt to find bare skin, claiming her.

A bottle and a half of wine at dinner, she was feeling a little loose, and probably so was he, she thought.

He pulled back a few inches, enough that she could get his face in focus: It had an expression that looked like the-time-has-come.

Well, she thought, I guess it has.

He bent to kiss her again. His hands began to move along the bare skin of her back. Big hands, warm and strong.

She kissed him again. It was good, she thought, she wanted this, she was ready for it.

She broke off the kiss and was about to lead him to the bedroom, when she remembered the sliding front door, which she had left open a foot to catch the evening breeze.

She turned and started for the door. That was when she saw Ellis.

He stood out on the dock, looking in, through the gap that the open door left. He could see her and Jon, could see the kiss—she wondered how long he had been out there.

She let go of Jon, pushed away from him, and began to walk toward the door, feeling angry and abashed and concerned, the emotions blooming and immediately fading, one after another, until she reached the door and got a good look at him.

His lips moved tightly but made no sound. His body was rigid, slightly trembling, his hands made hard fists down by his sides.

As if something powerful were inside, and he was fighting to keep it in.

Then she watched his face, and she saw that, no, he wasn't trying to contain it, he just didn't know how to let it out.

Only his eyes expressed it. They were anguished, they were full of pain.

"I can't stand this," he said, "I can't take it, it has to stop."

She thought at first that he was talking about what he must have seen, the kiss, her and Jon. And maybe that was part of it, but she saw that it went deeper than that.

"Please," he was saying. "Please."

"You shouldn't be here," she said. It sounded harsher than she wanted: The words hit him hard; he almost flinched.

She had never seen him that way, at the limit of control.

And he had never looked at her that way. She could almost feel his anguished gaze reaching down inside her.

At the other end of the room Jon Wreggett said, "You want me to handle this?"

"It's okay," she said without looking back—she couldn't take her eyes off Ellis.

"If he's bothering you . . ."

"No."

"Who is this asshole?" Ellis said, looking over her shoulder, seeming to notice Jon for the first time.

"*I'm* an asshole? Who invited you to the party?"

That's it, she thought, and she slipped through the open door and stepped up to Ellis, put her hands on his chest and gently backed him down the dock a few steps, saying, *Please, no scenes, please don't embarrass me, E.*

She didn't know Jon that well, had no idea how he would react.

But Ellis, unbelievably, looked ready to fight.

Now she was talking fast, telling Ellis, *Come with me, we'll talk down here,* as she led him down the dock; then turning and saying, *Wait, please wait right here, okay?* to Jon, who had stepped up to the door.

Ellis followed her down to the end of the dock.

"Ellis," she said, "what are you doing?"

"I couldn't let it happen." He looked, sounded, forlorn. "The end, it can't happen."

"It already did, Ellis. It's over."

He shook his head, adamant.

"Can't be."

"E, please . . ."

"Can't be over," he said, "because I still feel it."

She could feel the night descend, draw in tight around them.

"What are you saying?"

"The two of us together, the way it's supposed to be."

"Ellis . . ."

"I'm worthless like this, I need you, I never understood it, you know we were never apart, so I had no idea. But I need you."

She touched his face.

Just one gesture, her hand on his cheek, but he seemed to relax. The tension drained away. He wasn't anguished anymore.

Just forlorn.

"I love you," he said.

Footsteps behind her, coming down the dock. That had to be Jon.

"Oh, hell," she said.

"I do," Ellis said. "I love you, I need you."

"You had so many chances to tell me that when it would've meant something."

She wished she hadn't said it. True as it was, she wished that she had kept it to herself.

The look that came over him, shocked and sad, as if she had slapped him.

Jon was coming up behind her now.

"You need to go now," she said to Ellis.

He nodded once, glanced once at Jon, and walked away, defeated.

Jon Wreggett stood beside her. She watched Ellis trudge to his car. He started the Datsun, backed out of the space, and then—when she thought for sure he was just going to disappear—he pulled up a few feet from her.

He stared at her: his face first hurt, discouraged, then defeated as he drove away.

Jon Wreggett was beside her again. He slipped an arm around her shoulders.

And, funny, suddenly it seemed foreign there.

"Don't tell me," he said. "That has to be the ex. Ellis, right?"

She had mentioned him a few times to Jon, a little bit about the marriage, their life.

"That's him," she said.

"A little overwrought."

That made her smile: a private smile in the darkness that Jon couldn't see.

"Only when he's at his best," she said.

"Who or what is an avatar?"

The plates, she realized.

"That's him, that's Ellis, his computer alias," she said.

"Vanity plates," he said, "I love it, how precious."

"No, he's not the type. I bought those for him, he never would have done it on his own."

For some reason she felt the need to defend him: She did not want him misunderstood.

"He's a brilliant man," she said.

"If you say so."

The smile on Jon's face was snide—almost a sneer, she thought. He tried to lead her back up the dock, toward the houseboat.

"No," she said.

"Why?"

"Maybe another time."

"You're not going to let this put you off your feed, are you?" He sounded almost flippant.

"I want to be alone," she said, without warmth now.

It was unpleasant, finding this in him. If he didn't leave soon— right away—she would quickly stop liking him. Quickly and completely.

He seemed to sense this too.

"Sure, I get it," he said, "that's the way it is, you don't have to draw me any pictures."

He was walking away, back up the waterfront toward Gate Three and his boat.

Before he got too far away, he yelled back: "I'll be in touch."

But she didn't see him. She was watching the Datsun's lights melt into the traffic at the freeway interchange.

She didn't go back to the houseboat right away: just stood on the dock and let the events of the past few minutes settle within her. When she finally did go back to the houseboat and flip on the lights, it was like walking into a wall: the sensation that something had changed and might never be the same.

She cleaned the dishes, disposing of the last evidence of the meal and the evening. Then she climbed into bed, still clothed. She lay awake, trying to get past the feeling that she was in somebody else's home, someone else's life.

She thought: Now what?

A few minutes past midnight she got up from the bed. She grabbed her purse and keys, threw on a jacket, and hurried out.

47

Julia Chua kept thinking about her tenant downstairs. Corwin Sturmer had been in and out of the place for a minute and a half that morning, another hit-and-run visit to the room where he supposedly lived.

That had been twelve hours ago. She was still aware of him, not his physical presence, but the questions he provoked.

The answers were right below her, she was sure.

She told herself that she would be down there now if she knew a way. But there was that padlock on the door.

She then remembered. There was a way. . . .

She found the screwdriver on a shelf down in the basement, above the clothes dryer. Her husband was not the fix-it type—and neither was she, for sure—but they had put away this tool for a good reason.

She turned to face the partition of plywood and two-by-four lumber that walled off the downstairs apartment from the rest of the basement. This was the back side of the wall, so what she saw was unpainted wood, the water pipes for the apartment's bathroom and small kitchen, and the electrical wiring.

The apartment claimed more than half the basement: They had set aside just enough room for the washer and dryer and a couple of storage shelves.

She brought the screwdriver with her as she walked along the partition . . . there.

A single panel of plywood that was not nailed down. Unlike all the others, it was held in place by four brackets, each one fastened by a single screw.

It was the back of the apartment's bedroom closet.

Her mother-in-law, when she lived there, had insisted on bolting the front door at night. This had left them no way to get into the apartment. And they worried about her health, whether sometime she might need help during the night.

On the pretense of making repairs, they had brought in a carpenter to pull out the panel in the bedroom closet and replace it with this one that could be pulled away by loosening four screws. Then they had put the screwdriver nearby, on the shelf, so that it would be there when they needed it.

They never did: Albert's mother had collapsed and died while walking down Clement Street.

That was more than five years before. They had never changed the panel.

She began to remove the screws. When the last one was out, the panel tilted back gently. She moved it out of the way, then stepped into the opening she had created.

She was in the closet now. A couple of shirts and a scruffy leather jacket hung there. She pushed them aside and stepped into the bedroom.

She flipped on the light. The furnishings were cheap, simple, neat. The bed was made, the top of the dresser was empty—clean too, she noted when she ran a finger along the wood.

He was a tidy man, she had to give him that. Except for a pair of running shoes placed side by side at the foot of the bed, the place looked like a motel room after the maid had been through.

The same was true of the adjacent bathroom. The porcelain had been wiped, the chrome fixtures glistened.

She was beginning to form a certain respect for Corwin Sturmer. He cared about details—you had to admire that in a man.

She walked into the main room, which the computer on the table dominated like a Ferrari at a taxi stand. Otherwise the furnishings were spare and plain, garage-sale stuff. The kitchenette at the back side of the room was tidy. The refrigerator contained a carton of orange juice, some sliced ham in a plastic bag, a few apples. Several rows of canned soup were lined up in the cabinet.

Corwin Sturmer was neat, she thought, but boring.

She didn't understand why anyone would bother to double the locks on a place like this. The computer on the table in the main room couldn't be that valuable, she thought.

She returned to the bedroom. Here was where people kept their secrets.

Top drawer of the dresser was underwear and socks, laid out as if in a boot-camp locker.

Second drawer was shirts, folded.

Third drawer, a couple of sweaters.

And, stuck near the back, a videotape cassette. It stood on its side, against the back of the drawer, nearly hidden.

She pulled it out, then slipped it from its plastic case. It had no label.

Corwin Sturmer had no videotape player. He didn't even have a TV. But he had a single unlabeled tape that he kept hidden in a dresser drawer.

The tape begged to be watched.

She brought it upstairs, stuck it in her VCR, and began to play it.

The scene that popped up on the screen showed a man. A young fellow . . .

. . . a *naked* man . . .

. . . lying on the floor, stretched out full-length, faceup. His arms were pulled back behind his head, his legs were extended.

A sex tape, she thought, I don't want to watch this.

But at that moment a second person entered the picture, and she kept watching.

Because the second man—and this one wore clothes—was Corwin Sturmer.

She couldn't see the face clearly. The way he was positioned, she saw mostly the back of his head, but she recognized his walk and his build.

This was her tenant. She was sure of it.

He stepped over the naked man, straddling him.

The naked man writhed. Apparently he couldn't get up. His wrists and ankles were out of the picture, but from the way he struggled, she guessed that he was tied down somehow.

Corwin Sturmer sat on the stomach of the naked man.

Who looked terrified.

Then Corwin Sturmer put a hand on the man's chest. The man who lived in her downstairs apartment was holding a spike—a slim, shining spike, like a very long nail, maybe eight or nine inches long—and he was placing the tip of the spike against the chest of the naked man, his left breast, right above the heart.

In his right hand Corwin Sturmer held a mallet.

The naked man writhed, tried to throw off Corwin Sturmer, but he was helpless.

Corwin Sturmer held the spike in place, and he raised the mallet.

Julia Chua didn't wait to see it fall. She quickly reached for her telephone and punched the three digits of the emergency number.

A woman answered on the first ring.

Julia Chua said, "Send the police. There has been a murder."

48

About twenty minutes after she left the houseboat, Kate wedged the Miata into a space across the street from 2600 Tesla, and then she walked up to the house.

She felt like an interloper when she used the key to let herself in. But she could not see herself ringing the bell as though she were a stranger, either.

She entered, crossed over to the stairs at the top of the landing.

Three monitors glowed in the gloom, including the one that belonged to the video scanner. But Ellis wasn't looking at any of them. He stood at the big window, staring out, motionless at the glass.

She wondered whether he was ignoring her.

Softly she said, "Hey, E."

The quick way he turned, she knew that she had startled him—he hadn't known that she was there.

"Kate."

She came down the stairs and stopped a few feet away, the desks between them, looking at him across the equipment and the clutter.

"I'm sorry," he said, "I was way, way out of line. It won't happen again."

"No apologies."

"I blew it big-time, huh?" he said.

"No," she said. "You did good."

This seemed to surprise him.

"I thought you came here to give me hell."

"I could've done that over the phone."

"Then why?" He sounded tentative.

She walked over to him, covering the last few feet between them, close enough that she could see his eyes.

She said, "I want to hear some more. About how miserable you are without me."

"There aren't enough hours. I couldn't do it justice."

She reached both arms and held his neck.

"Let's try," she said.

He said, "My life's been a wreck. I never realized how much of what I did was for you, all the reasons you gave me for going on, day to day. Since you left, I've been living by habit, but it hasn't meant anything, it's just been worthless—"

She touched his lips with her fingertips.

"Later," she said, and she kissed him.

And then the pager rattled in her purse.

The killer, at the wheel of the brown van, reached for his pager to check the message. The pager was a clone of Ziggy's—the concept was similar to cloning a cell phone, but simpler—and it received her messages at the moment she did.

The readout showed:

PLEASE CHECK VOICE MAIL

A computer maintained all the voice mail accounts at the studio. In essence, it was a digital answering service. Callers could enter a code that instructed the machine to notify Kate by pager of an urgent message.

The machine was connected to the studio's local area network. And by now the killer had the run of that system.

Quickly he picked up his cell phone, dialed into the account, and entered her password.

The system played her message. A woman's voice:

"Kate, this is Sandy Weil. You're not going to believe this . . . "

Kate hung up the phone.

"What?" he said.

"It's nothing."

"C'mon, I know that look."

"They're having some problems in Belize. Cynthia just checked into the hospital with the roaring trots, Sandy said the guide is a drunk who couldn't find a tabby cat much less a jaguar; they're in advanced panic."

"You've got to go down there," he said. "Right away."

He walked away from her and sat at a computer.

"I could send somebody else," she said.

"No," he said. "You're overextended on this one already. It's going to get totally out of hand, you've got half a million dollars on this, you can't let it get away from you."

He spoke without looking up from the screen. His fingers were rattling the keyboard.

"I'm sorry, E, I really am," she said. "Of all the times for something to come up . . . "

He looked at her.

"Are you coming back?" he said.

"You know it. As soon as I can."

He showed a cautious smile.

"Back here?"

"Straight here, E, I promise."

"All I need to know," he said.

He went back to riffing the keyboard, staring at the monitor. She walked over and put her arms around him in the chair.

He said, "Booked solid."

Typed some more and peered at the screen and said, "Booked solid."

Typed some more and said, "There, gotcha. Last seat to Belize City for tomorrow. Quarter to two tomorrow with a connection out of L.A., can you handle it?"

"That's perfect," she said. "The afternoon flight is better anyway."

"Why is that?" he asked.

He was in a swivel chair. She tugged his shoulders to swivel him around, facing her.

"It will let us sleep in," she said.

She left a series of voice messages on the office system: her flight plans, instructions in her absence.

She was leaving tomorrow.

She expected to be gone at least a week.

But a week was too long, the killer thought.

There was too much happening, too many complications.

Her time was now.

49

"Drove a spike right through his heart," said one of the two patrol officers.

He was young, no more than twenty-five. His partner looked even younger. It had been a few hours since they had answered the call at Julia Chua's house. They were in her living room, while she stood to the side.

"You didn't watch it, did you?" said Lee Wade.

"No," said the older patrolman. "But she said so, and I believe her."

"That's right," said Julia Chua. She was holding the tape. "See for yourself, I'll play it."

"No!" said Lee Wade. "I don't want to see it. That was not a legal search."

"What I do in my house is my business," she said.

The younger patrolman said to her, "That tape may be evidence of a murder. If we take possession of the evidence without a warrant, we lose the evidence in court. And anything that we derive from it could be construed as the fruit of a poisoned tree."

This phrase cropped up more than once in Fourth Amendment tutorials at the police academy. No doubt he had heard the lectures within the past few months.

The patrol officer got full marks for his grasp of search-and-seizure guidelines, Lee Wade thought.

And once they had heard Julia Chua's description of what she saw, they earned extra points for having called homicide to ask whether anybody there knew about a white male victim with a spike through his heart.

That was how Lee Wade had been sent to the scene, at nearly four A.M.

He told Julia Chua that he would like to wait there in her living room if she didn't mind. He wanted to be there in case Corwin Sturmer happened to show up.

He sat on the blue velour sofa in the living room and picked up the telephone to call the squad room. He talked to his partner, Ronson.

They needed to run a background on Corwin Sturmer.

They needed a search warrant.

They needed the user records for Corwin Sturmer's phone in the apartment: Shake PacBell's tree real hard, they couldn't wait two weeks this time.

"I've still got the tape," Julia Chua said. "What do you want me to do with it?"

"You would make me a very happy man if you put it back where you found it. Don't even tell me where. We'll shake the place down good when we get the warrant."

"When does that happen?" she asked.

"We'll get started on it right away. Got to get a judge out of bed. It may take a few hours."

"What if he comes home first?"

"Then I'll have a nice heart-to-heart with him."

"He's a killer," she said.

Lee Wade believed that. The man who owned that tape was a killer or an accessory to murder.

"We'll see" was all he said.

50

The man who sometimes called himself Corwin Sturmer drove the brown van down Clement Street, which at this hour was empty of traffic but, as usual, full of parked cars.

He motored down Clement and paused at the intersection of Tenth. He glanced down the block.

Two SFPD patrol cars were double-parked in the street.

The lights were on upstairs in the Chua house.

He didn't make the turn, but continued straight down Clement for another block, then over to Geary. As he drove he used the cell phone again.

He dialed the number of his apartment. The computer picked up the call, silently, and Corwin Sturmer punched in a six-digit code on the keypad.

The code activated a short program that began to destroy the data on the machine's hard disk, overwriting the files so that anyone who might examine the drive later would find it filled with random bytes.

He continued up Geary, clicking through the blocks. He was not in a panic, not even in a hurry any longer.

When Geary ended, he had reached the ocean. Now he headed south down the Great Highway, with the beach and the surf to his right. To his left was a parking island that filled up on weekends with beachgoers. But there were no houses nearby, so tonight, as most nights, it was almost empty. He kept headed south, down the oceanfront esplanade, within the speed limit.

A couple of miles down the Great Highway, a car sat alone in the parking island. A white Chevy Cavalier. He parked a few spaces away from it, and stopped the engine.

The surf pounded. The beach was empty, and so was the highway.

From the glove compartment of the van he removed the registration and insurance papers, and a small tool kit.

He tore the papers into small pieces and scattered them in the wind that blew in off the ocean. When police accessed the database of the Department of Motor Vehicles for the digitized license photo of Corwin Sturmer, they would find that the image had been erased from the electronic files. They would also learn that the information in his records was a complete fiction, that the records themselves had been placed there by unknown means several months earlier.

The killer had been preparing for this moment for months. He had expected to shed Corwin Sturmer the way a snake peels out of its skin—though not quite so soon, or so abruptly.

Identities were temporary sanitary barriers—like surgical gloves, disposable.

He unlocked the door of the white Cavalier, threw in the license plates and the tool kit, and pulled out the aluminum brace from between the seats. He fitted it around his right leg, then swung the leg inside and shut the door.

He started the engine of the Cavalier, turned on the headlights, and drove away using the special hand-operated throttle control.

Being C. W. Hartmundt was inconvenient, but for the moment it had one great advantage.

C. W. Hartmundt was invisible.

Nobody suspected him of murder.

He lowered the window on his side and breathed in the raw marine air. It felt good—bracing—as it entered his lungs. It had the tang of freedom.

51

In the house on Tesla Street, Kate and Ellis shared the bed for the first time in more than a year.

Ellis was drifting around the edges of sleep, happily fuzzed, truly relaxed and unburdened for the first time since they had parted.

Kate had burrowed against him. His right arm was around her shoulder, holding her as if he wanted her to stay for a long time.

She liked that.

At that moment, several blocks away at the foot of Russian Hill, C. W. Hartmundt entered the Union Street apartment.

Three of Ellis Hoile's monitors still burned in the darkness of the big workroom, beyond the sight of Kate and Ellis in the bedroom of the house on Tesla Street.

Then the picture changed on one of them: This was the monitor connected to the video scanner, which was pointed down at Stoma's Russian Hill apartment. Grainy gray static surged, shifted.

C. W. Hartmundt had turned on his machine, and the video scanner was reading the display.

In the bedroom of the big house, Ellis Hoile was aware only of Kate's warmth beside him.

The scanner monitor—unwatched, unwitnessed—continued to display Christian Hartmundt's work.

He was logging into an airline reservation system, entering an authorization code, then searching for the record of Kate Lavin's reservations to Belize City.

He found it within a minute, then canceled the reservations. Automatically the system filled the empty slot with one of three passengers who had entered the standby list for the flight from Los Angeles to Belize City.

He logged off the airline computer, and brought up his data-linked map.

He entered the name:

Hoile, Ellis

In the bedroom, Ellis Hoile opened his eyes as Kate gently shook him awake.

"Hey, E, listen up," she said, "I've got a great idea, are you listening?"

He nodded.

"Why don't you come down to Belize? Grab a flight in the next few days, we can be together down there. You can help me if you want, I can use you on this one. But it won't be all work. Anyway, we'll be together, that's the point."

She shifted, slid a leg over his midsection until she was on her knees, straddling him, her hands on his shoulders.

"Like it used to be," she said, "what do you think about that?"

He didn't speak, but pulled her close and kissed her, drinking her in.

Out in the living room the scanner's monitor showed that the map had shifted to show San Francisco, the Telegraph Hill area.

The red dot blinked just below the symbol for Coit Tower.

A box at the bottom of the display showed:

Hoile, Ellis
2600 Tesla St
San Francisco

Christian Hartmundt's last task before he slept was to log on to
Verba to check his e-mail. He tried to do this once a day, but he
had missed it the night before.

The system wrote:

Welcome, Stoma
You have new mail.

His mail directory showed one new message, from the day before.

It was from Avatar.

He began to download it. His mail program automatically decoded and began to display the contents of the file.

He saw that it was a photograph.

It appeared line by line, starting from the top, so the effect was
that of a curtain slowly dropping, falling away, to reveal the picture
behind it.

The killer felt a rage rising within him as the image appeared,
as he recognized what it was.

A parking garage.

The dying Chaz with his mouth opened in a scream.

Avatar had sent him a frame from one of his own home movies.

His hands gripped the edge of the table in front of him. His
heart was tripping. He realized that this wasn't just fury building
inside him.

It was panic too.

The picture kept unrolling, down to the brief message that Avatar had added at the bottom of the image:

CWH: I know

PHILLIP FINCH

Quickly he shut off the machine. But he continued to stare at the empty screen, trying to force himself past the rage and the panic, to careful thought.

This was not supposed to be possible.

C. W. Hartmundt was above reproach.

C. W. Hartmundt was invisible.

First the cop at his door; now this.

He considered the possibility that he had been totally compromised. But how?

He rose from his chair, crossed the room, and opened the curtains of the front window. From there he had a clear line of sight up to Telegraph Hill, with Coit Tower at the top of the hill—and just below that, the home of the man who sometimes called himself Avatar.

I know too, he thought.

PART V

Sanctuary

May 12

52

David Hudgins heard the music all the way from the front walk as he followed his grandmother up to Ellis Hoile's house that morning.

Classical music—he was pretty sure that it was Bach, bright and real loud—was coming from inside the house.

"Uh-oh, what now?" Roberta Hudgins said.

Inside, they found sunlight blazing through the windows, and the music even louder, of course. They were at the bottom of the black iron stairs before they heard the woman's voice from inside the kitchen, softly laughing.

David could see them through the wide entrance of the kitchen, Ellis Hoile and a pretty lady, the two of them so wrapped up in watching each other eat breakfast that at first they didn't even notice they weren't alone anymore. David's grandmother had to stand in the kitchen entrance and wait a few seconds before they saw her.

David didn't know the woman, but his grandmother seemed to: went over and shook her hand. David decided that this must be the woman who had hired his grandmother, the ex-wife of Ellis Hoile.

Not looking much like an ex this morning.

While David watched, she gave Ellis Hoile a big kiss, then got up from the table, wearing a man's shirt and nothing else that David could see. She gave David a quick smile and a little wave, then hurried off to the bedroom.

David knew his grandmother, and he could tell that she liked the idea of finding the place this way, bright and alive after so many weeks of dead gloom. But David also knew that she was a little worried, that this development might put her out of a pretty good job.

He knew this was on her mind by the half-joking way she said to Ellis Hoile, "Maybe this means you won't be needing me no more."

And Ellis Hoile answered: "Maybe we'll both be needing you."

53

Lee Wade was still waiting for the warrant when PacBell released Corwin Sturmer's user records, a little before ten. Julia Chua's husband had a fax machine for business, so Ronson faxed over the several pages covering the past two months' activity on the number in the basement apartment.

He also sent along a copy of Donald Trask's phone records from the files.

Ronson had already caught the highlights, had underlined them by hand. On three different occasions Donald Trask and Corwin Sturmer had been on the phone to the Verba Interchange at the same time.

Including once on the night of the murder.

Lee Wade thought of Ellis Hoile and his speculations about killer and victims meeting on line, invisibly, through a computer connection.

Corwin Sturmer had spent plenty of time on Verba: sometimes hours a day, to judge by the length of his calls.

Score one for the genius, Lee Wade told himself: Ellis Hoile had the wrong suspect, but he may have had the right idea.

Take away the calls to Verba, Corwin Sturmer hadn't spent much time on the phone. He had called maybe fifteen, twenty different numbers, most of them local. He had received calls from maybe a dozen others.

Lee Wade had a cellular phone, and he began to call the people who had been on the end of the line with a killer, outgoing calls first. PacBell had attached a second sheet that showed the subscriber name of each number, and most were routine: small local businesses who had never heard of him.

Here were two outbound calls to a number in Mendocino County, town of Point Arena, in the name of a Jane Regalia. When Lee Wade tried the number it returned only a screech—a fax machine or a computer, Lee Wade thought.

And two long-distance calls to a number in Missouri; Corwin Sturmer had been called three times from the same number.

Lee Wade tried the number. It rang five, six times, and Lee Wade was about to hang up when he heard the answering click on the other end.

A man's voice said, "Hello?"

Lee Wade identified himself, and he said, "Is this Charles Obend?"

The pause in Missouri drew out so long that Lee Wade wondered whether the guy had put the phone down.

Finally the man said, "Charles Obend was my brother. His funeral is tomorrow, I'm clearing out his place."

Lee Wade found himself sitting straight up on the blue sofa.

He asked, "How did it happen?"

Charles Obend's brother went into it, the murder in the parking garage. The way he talked about it, he seemed to have trouble believing that it was for real, that somebody had treated his brother that way.

But Lee Wade believed. *And I saw it,* he kept thinking as the brother talked. He had seen it on a tape that Ellis Hoile scanned from the apartment on Union Street.

This meant . . . what? That Corwin Sturmer had given a copy of the tape to Christian Hartmundt?

Charles Obend's brother told him that the murder had been late Saturday night. Lee Wade remembered that the anonymous fax to the homicide squad room had showed up within a few hours of that time, on Sunday morning.

Charles Obend was Meatware3.

Lee Wade had just one more question.

"Your brother had a computer, am I right?" Lee Wade said. "The kind that plugs into a phone line."

"Yes. It's right in front of me."

The search warrant came through a few minutes later. Lee Wade's partner brought it over.

Julia Chua brought Lee Wade and Ronson down to the basement and showed them how to unscrew the panel. They seized the tape from the dresser drawer, where Julia Chua had replaced it.

They brought the tape upstairs to Julia Chua's VCR and began to watch it. Julia Chua stayed in another room: She had seen it once already, she said, and once was more than enough.

It opened with a body on a concrete floor, the body of a young man with a slick dark stain spreading on his left breast, right where the heart would be. Someone—a man whose face was out of the frame—sat on the chest of the dead man and reached into the spreading stain and extracted a long spike from the body, working it out, pulling hard.

Lee Wade realized that this must've been where Julia Chua had turned off the tape. He stopped it and rewound it and started it from the beginning.

As the tape began to play, Lee Wade told himself that this was a very strange experience. He had never before witnessed a murder that he was investigating.

It had to be Donald Trask who was bound hand and foot on the floor. This had to be his murder.

Lee Wade felt a growing letdown as he watched the tape from beginning to end. He kept waiting to get a clear shot of Corwin Sturmer's face, but it never happened. The guy kept his back to the camera the whole time. Lee Wade didn't know how Julia Chua could be so sure about who this was.

He realized that the tape alone wouldn't be enough for a conviction. The shadows, the way the killer stood in relation to the lights and the camera, would make it impossible to identify anybody.

Having watched the tape, he still wouldn't recognize Corwin Sturmer if they met on the sidewalk.

He watched it until it ended, almost ten minutes, then rewound it and watched it again until the signal ended and he was looking at the grainy electronic noise of blank videotape.

He was about to stop the tape, eject it, and take it away with him. But after a few seconds the blank part ended and he was watching a recording again.

This looked like the same concrete room as the first part of the tape. But this time a woman lay on the floor. She was alive: just barely, if you could judge from the tape. A man came out from behind the camera, carrying a machete.

He raised the machete, turning slightly toward the camera, showing his face as he did.

That was when Lee Wade sat up straight and reached for the remote control so that he could back the tape up.

He *knew* this guy. They had met less than twenty-four hours ago.

This was Christian Willem Hartmundt, but he wasn't wearing a leg brace, and he was getting around fine without it.

The machete fell just as Lee Wade reached for the phone. He told his lieutenant to arrange backup for the arrest of the killer of Donald Trask.

He removed the tape cassette and told Julia Chua that he was leaving. He said that if Corwin Sturmer showed up, she should leave the house right away and call the police from the nearest pay phone.

But he didn't expect it to happen. Not anymore.

Corwin Sturmer had another place to lay his head, Lee Wade thought. An apartment on Union Street.

But not for much longer.

54

Down in the crawl space that was meant to be his tomb, Stephen Leviste awoke in utter darkness. He had been asleep since within five minutes after the maniac welded shut the grate.

At that point he had been awake for a day and a half, forcing himself to keep his eyes open while he waited down in the crawl space, because he had to be alert and ready to defend himself whenever the maniac finally returned.

Once the grate was sealed, however, all the urgency was gone, and he had deflated. His head slumped, and sleep overtook him.

He had slept through that evening, and the entire night.

Now he woke.

He swallowed a surge of panic, remembered where he was and how he had gotten here, and remembered what he had intended to do before he fell asleep.

He reached out a hand, found the flashlight that the killer had dropped, and he turned it on. After a swallow of water from the jug, he began to explore the crawl space, which he had been unable to do in the darkness the day before.

Now he pointed the beam first one way down the tunnel, then the other direction. From what he could see, it was an unvarying narrow corridor that ran below the concrete floor.

It seemed to offer no hope. He doubted that there was an exit—why would the maniac have bothered to weld the grate if there was another way out?—but with nothing better to do, he rose now and hunched his back and began to make his way down the tunnel.

He guessed that he was headed toward the red door in the back wall, in the same direction as the catwalk. The crawl space remained seamless and unbroken; then he arrived at the wall where it ended, and he turned and went back the way he had come, until he was back under the grate again.

From here the crawl space continued in the opposite direction. Back to the far wall of the cavern, he guessed. He wondered whether there was any point in exploring down that way: From here it looked like more of the same.

He decided that he would look around down there. Better than sitting around.

For much of its length, he found, this end of the crawl space was like all the rest. He was about to turn around and head back when the flashlight beam found the end of the tunnel.

And he saw that this was *not* like all the rest.

He hurried forward. As he got closer, he saw that while the tunnel had terminated at the other end in a blank wall, this halted at a box of galvanized steel.

Not just a box, he saw: It was an air vent. With a screen. The box was part of a ventilation duct.

A ventilation duct, he thought—he remembered one now, running along the ceiling, above the catwalk. He hadn't paid much attention to it. But this had to be the same one, where it descended along the back wall of the cavern and then through the floor.

Through the floor . . .

He kicked the vent's screen until it was loose, then tore it away with his hands. It left an opening that was about a foot wide, maybe eight inches high.

Lying on his back, turning his head to one side, he was able to slip his head through that opening. But it was dark up there, he could see nothing. So he stuck the flashlight inside, rested it on its base so that it pointed up the vent duct, left it there, and then slipped his head in again.

Now, in the flashlight's beam, he could see up the interior of the duct. It rose straight, farther than the light could reach, full of cobwebs that shimmered slightly in the air.

The rail section with which he had defended himself the day before was back up the tunnel, near the grate. His first thought was to use the rail as a kind of battering ram. Beat the duct pipe where it came through the floor, loosen it or deform it enough that he could squeeze past it, up out of the crawl space and back into the cavern.

But he stopped.

He asked himself what that would gain him, to escape into the cavern.

He had been in the cavern already, and had found no way out. The maniac *wanted* him out there.

Up there he would be easy to catch, and to kill. Here, at least, he was out of reach.

As much as he wanted to get out from under this cramped space, an escape into the cavern was no escape at all.

He sat at the vent opening, and his shoulders slumped. The duct had turned out to be no better than a blank wall after all. Discouragement welled in him, and he could feel tears coming, and though he tried to hold them back, a couple escaped and streaked his cheek anyway.

Stop that, he told himself—crying was no help at all.

He wiped his face. The moisture felt cool on his cheeks. It felt very cool—the tears were drying fast.

He realized why. He couldn't believe that he had missed it. The shimmering cobwebs, the tears drying so quickly on his skin.

Air was moving out of the duct, a slight but perceptible breeze.

The vent duct was supposed to carry air. Of course. Move stale air out, move fresh air in. At one time a big fan had probably circulated the air, but this was just the natural current of air being pushed and pulled by changes of pressure.

But the pressure wouldn't change in a closed vent system, he thought.

And then he could feel it. He could *smell* it: the air. This wasn't a closed vent system at all. The air that fell down the ductwork and into his face now had a scent, a richness, that could only come from one source.

That air was coming from outside.

55

Kate left the house after breakfast: She had to pack for the trip, and she needed to spend some time at the studio before she left.

Ellis held her and looked into her eyes and kissed her before he let her go.

After she was gone he took a look at a program that David Hudgins had written during the past week. Then he made his own reservation to Belize City, leaving in three days.

Mrs. Hudgins was still busy—she would be there most of the day—and David was absorbed at a computer.

Ellis Hoile began to watch the tape that he had scanned from Christian Hartmundt's apartment, the fireball in the parking garage.

He had done this for several minutes the night before, while he was still alone in the house. He had been searching for details that he might have overlooked the first few times.

The search had been depressing and dreary—he *hated* that damn tape—but he thought that it might be more bearable in the morning, in the sunlight, with so much else having changed during the past twelve hours.

He began playing the tape in slow motion, reversing it, playing it through again and again.

He decided that he needed to see it frame by frame.

The sunlight was bright too. He kept getting glare off the screen.

Mrs. Hudgins and her grandson seemed to like it though. Everybody liked warm sun, he thought: He really had no aversion to it. It was just a hindrance sometimes.

Upstairs, at the top of the landing, was a room that had once been a garage, attached to the house. When he and Kate bought the house, he had hired a contractor to convert it to an office, and that had been his workplace.

He had used it for years, even after she left. Not until the divorce was final did he begin to spread out downstairs, not so much to find more space as to make the house more bearable, a little less empty.

He unplugged a computer—the Pentium had a video-editing board—and carried it upstairs.

He hadn't been there in weeks. The room was empty except for a single desk and a chair. That was enough. He put the computer on the desk and went down for the videotape deck and the cassette, and then he made a third trip for a color monitor.

He told Mrs. Hudgins that he would be up there for a while. He was at the top of the stairs, about to walk out the front door, when David Hudgins yelled up, asked him about Verba, how to get on, what he should do.

Ellis Hoile didn't like to be sidetracked once he had set himself in motion. And he was already thinking about the tape, what he was going to do with it.

He went to the landing above the big room, still lugging the monitor.

David was at the right machine, the one Ellis Hoile usually used when he was on line. There was an easy way to do this.

He spoke clearly, loudly, from across the room:

"Comm. Verba. Connect."

Down below, the modem beeped tones.

"That's my script, it's all automatic," Ellis Hoile said from the landing.

The number answered on the first ring. Modem squeal.

The squeal ceased after a moment. The system read the automatic password and greeted Avatar.

"You're in," Ellis Hoile said, "you're Avatar for a day, make me look good, don't do anything I wouldn't do. Any questions, just knock," and he went into the room.

Depositing the monitor on the desk, he connected the cables that would feed the videotape clip, the fiery death in a parking garage, into his computer.

Then he closed the door and turned off the lights. He could see well enough by the monitor's glow.

The quiet and dark felt good. This was how work got done. This was how things happened.

He began to play the videocassette. Once more he watched the awful scene, the approach of the unsuspecting victim as he walked through the parking garage, the fireball. The editing board read the signal, converted it into digital form, and stored it on the computer's hard disk.

Now Ellis Hoile played it again, not the tape this time, but the digital copy from the hard disk. He set the rate at a frame per second. At this speed the sensation was not of watching a movie, but of sitting at a slide show, with a series of near-identical photographs dropping onto the screen, pausing, then giving way to the next.

The entire clip consisted of 1,372 frames. Each frame was a frozen moment, stolen from time and preserved as points of light and color—pixels—arranged in precise rows and lines.

At normal speed, thirty frames per second, the clip played for about forty-six seconds.

At one frame per second, Ellis Hoile needed about twenty-three minutes to watch them all.

He leaned forward in his chair and studied the screen as the frames flopped onto it, one second apart.

Seven minutes. He stopped the flood of images and rubbed his eyes. Nothing new so far.

Another five or six minutes. Nothing.

He was getting close to the end of the clip. *Wait* . . .

He leaned forward, peered closer, and with keystrokes he first stopped the progression of the frames, then reversed.

One frame back. There . . .

A fleshy splash in a mirror.

The shooter had lowered his videocam and stepped beside a parked car. He had recorded his own face in a side mirror, a chance alignment of camera lens and reflection.

Ellis Hoile leaned close to study the frame. The face in the mirror was too small to make out.

With a few keystrokes he isolated the portion of the frame that contained the mirror and the image reflected in it.

That image was the face of a killer. And Ellis Hoile knew how to capture it.

56

Christian Hartmundt's computer emitted a low, protracted bleat.

The sound was an alert. He hurried over to the desk where the machine sat, and he saw that Avatar had logged in to Verba.

The killer finally was learning about Avatar. Not a great deal, but at that moment only three facts mattered.

Avatar lived alone; he was a solitary man.

Avatar lived his solitary life in a house less than a mile from this spot.

And he was now at his keyboard.

Minutes later the killer was walking up Tesla Street.

He wore navy-blue coveralls, and a blue ball cap, and he carried a canvas zip bag. With his brisk, purposeful stride, he gave the impression of a worker on his way to do a job: a repairman, maybe, come to solve an urgent problem in the home.

In a way, this was exactly true.

The problem was Avatar. Although the killer had planned to take him with much more drama and ceremony, Avatar had hastened his own end by leaving that photo in Stoma's mail drop.

Avatar had to be dispatched.

Because of the cul-de-sac a block away, Tesla Street got little traffic except for the local residents coming and going. And since this was an expensive neighborhood, it was a place where nearly everybody went to work during the day, to keep up the payments on those expensive houses.

The killer felt no eyes on him as he came up the sidewalk. No cars passed him.

The house clung to the steep side of Telegraph Hill, and was built straight down, with most of the living area below the level of Tesla Street. There was a gap between 2600 and the house next door, an opening just wide enough for him to slip through, vault over a fence and down the rocky incline of the hill.

It was even steeper than he had expected; he stopped his slide by grabbing a utility pipe that ran up the side of the house.

He had nearly reached the main living level. A few feet down the hill was a small window. He worked his way there and looked inside.

It was a bedroom. The door was open, and through it he could see part of the living room.

Nobody in sight.

He stopped to draw a breath. No hurry; in this spot he could not be seen from the street or from the house. From down the hill, if anyone happened to notice, he would appear to be a workman at his job.

He opened the duffel.

It was near full: plastic bags for bloody clothes, a spare pair of shoes, a container of Handi Wipes, a set of hand tools and lock picks, a roll of duct tape, a crowbar, and more that was out of sight: a kit for a burglar and a bloodletter.

He pulled on gloves and a ski mask. The window, he saw, was latched. He withdrew a large rubber suction cup, stuck it to a pane in the upper frame of the window, and used a glass cutter to scribe a circle around the edge of the cup.

One quick bump of the suction cup, the circle of glass popped free, and he reached into the hole to unfasten the latch.

He dropped the suction cup and the circle of glass into the bag.

From the bottom of the bag, where it lay covered, he withdrew a machete.

Not stainless steel, but it was spotless anyway, the blade burnished, with a fine gleaming edge.

He laid it down for a moment, and used both hands to pull the window up.

Then, machete in hand, he pushed through the open window and silently dropped into the bedroom.

He heard a tapping of keyboard strokes as he crossed the room and stood in the door, at the entrance of the living area.

He briefly took the place in. It seemed even bigger from inside—the ceiling two stories high seemed to add to the effect.

And the desks, the racks of equipment, the computers.

Avatar was a wizard, no question about it.

The tapping came from the killer's left, near the big window.

The killer held the machete ready, slightly raised, his right arm bent at the elbow as he stepped out of the doorway and turned left toward the sound.

Thirty feet away, a figure hunched at a keyboard with his back to the killer, facing the window.

The killer stepped forward, silently crossing the floor. His path took him past another, wider entranceway. A kitchen, it seemed to be, what he caught in the periphery of his vision, but he was watching the person at the keyboard, concentrating on a spot at the collar line where his neck curved into his shoulders, and he raised the machete.

He was thinking that this didn't seem right, Avatar didn't look like *this*.

When the phone rang.

·　　·　　·

f2f

It rang behind David Hudgins.

He looked away from the monitor, glanced back toward it, and saw the masked man, the machete shoulder-high, coming toward him, stepping faster.

Not Avatar, the killer realized as the figure at the keyboard turned to face him.

The surprise slowed him for a moment, and he hesitated and slightly dropped the blade. Then he told himself that he couldn't back out now, this had to be finished, so he raised the blade again and stepped forward.

Then, to his left, in the kitchen he had ignored . . .

. . . something happened.

57

Roberta Hudgins was in the kitchen.

She was standing near the entranceway beside a counter over which a rack of copper pots and pans hung, expensive stuff that gathered dust since the lady of the house left.

She glanced toward the phone when it rang the first time.

The pots and pans were stacked on the counter beside her, and she was wiping them, buffing them, placing them back on the rack one by one, when she looked toward the phone and saw the man with the masked face and that blade—*that blade, my Lord*—moving past her.

But he didn't see her.

David turned in his chair.

The masked man with the blade hesitated, but the blade went up and he stepped forward . . .

. . . and suddenly life was playing itself out with painful, agonizing slowness, every instant drawn out . . .

. . . without looking, she reached for a pan, a frying pan was right there by her hand, but her moving arm jostled a stack of the pots and sent them teetering and crashing to the floor, banging, clattering.

"YOU STOP YOU," she said, the sound starting from deep within her, a shout at first but rising to a bellow, a shriek, that came from her gut and carried all the force of her love for her grandson.

The phone rang a second time.

The shout and the clatter slowed the man with the blade, made him pull up short and turn toward her, away from David.

Facing her, his eyes uncertain through the holes in the mask.

As David rolled out of the chair, away from her and the man in the mask and that blade.

Good boy.

She reached for the pan and found it this time, the long, stout handle filling her hand.

He glanced at David, but David was scrambling out of reach.

The phone rang a third time.

The man was facing her directly, seeming to make up his mind, she could read it in his eyes, and he brandished the big blade and came toward her.

But not quite so sure of himself now.

He stepped toward her and she moved back, putting a corner of the counter between them, and she raised the big copper frying pan . . .

. . . the phone ringing a fourth time at the edge of her awareness . . .

. . . as he lunged across the counter.

And the blade came down.

She moved to block it. The blade struck the curved side of the pan, clanged, and glanced off.

She backed away.

He lunged again and swung, she moved the pan and it struck the blade, square.

And now the pan was a bell, pealing with the blow, and the machete was out of his hand, in the air, wobbling as it flew free.

It banged against a cabinet and fell to the floor by her feet.

Time was back to normal speed now.

She bent and picked up the machete.

In the living room, David had the phone and was hitting three digits, three sweet little numbers, 911.

She heard it and the man in the mask heard it too. He looked at David with the phone and her with the machete.

He turned and ran.

Ellis Hoile was barely aware of the clatter of pots and the shriek from Roberta Hudgins. He heard the telephone ring and wondered why she didn't answer. There were jacks up where he sat, but he hadn't brought up a phone.

He pushed the distractions aside: He was concentrating on the work in front of him.

He was enlarging the video frame, the section that showed the face of the killer reflected in a car's side mirror.

Enlarged to full-screen size this way, the face was indistinct. Zooming in again would just blur it more.

He had one more chance.

But he couldn't do it there.

Now more noise downstairs. Shouting: The voice was Mrs. Hudgins's grandson, and he was calling for help.

And then Ellis Hoile got up and hurried out.

He came out on the landing and saw Mrs. Hudgins down below, seated, an arm around her grandson.

She looked up at him.

"A tall man in blue," she said. "Tried to hurt David. He went in the bedroom, be careful. Cops are on the way."

The bedroom window was open downstairs.

Ellis Hoile looked out and saw nothing.

He ran upstairs and out the front door.

The sidewalks were empty.

     •   •   •

The killer scrambled down the hill below Tesla Street.

He had come out the bedroom window and then down the rocky incline below the house, into the next block, bringing the canvas bag with him and stripping off the mask and gloves.

Nobody stopped him. Nobody seemed to notice.

Nearby was the Cavalier, and he unlocked it and threw in the bag, got in, and started the car, and he drove away.

The first cops he saw were in a black-and-white patrol car at the bottom of Telegraph Hill. He was about to turn onto the Embarcadero, when the car approached from his right, moving fast, two uniformed patrolmen inside.

He stopped and let them cut across his path. The flashing emergency lights beat in his face for a moment, then the black-and-white was gone, headed up the hill.

He was becoming calm again. He felt safe. He was putting distance between himself and the fiasco up on the hill, and they still did not know him, they could not touch him.

As he swung out across the intersection he could see the Golden Gate Bridge above the roofs of the shops and restaurants at Fisherman's Wharf.

The bridge was where he wanted to be.

The bridge, Marin, Sausalito, the waterfront.

Enough of the sideshow, he thought.

Time for the real thing.

58

Kate Lavin had let the phone ring four times at 2600 Tesla; then she hung up her cell phone and stuck it into her handbag.

Ellis must be out, she thought. When he was at his desk he always picked up on the first or second ring.

She was at a ticket counter at the airport. She wanted to get her reservation number from Ellis; he would be able to find it.

"Please check again," she told the ticket agent. He made a slight gesture of exasperation: The line behind Kate was long.

"I'm looking at the list," the agent said. "I am examining the entire list, your name is not here. Nothing *like* your name is here."

"Look," Kate said, "I've got to get down there right away. What's the first opening you have?"

"I can get you to Los Angeles, no problem," the ticket agent told her. "But the standby list is long, and I would not say that your chances are good. Or, I can book this connection tomorrow."

She did not see the point of spending the night alone in L.A. The alternative was another night with Ellis.

She tossed her AmEx card on the ticket counter.

"Tomorrow," she said.

You could not get from the airport to the Golden Gate Bridge without using city streets, fighting city traffic. She didn't try to call Ellis again: She thought she'd invite him to spend the night on the houseboat, but she wanted to relax, have a long bath, before she saw him.

She was in the car for nearly an hour before she crossed the bridge. Several minutes later she was turning off the freeway, onto Bridgeway and into the Gate Seven parking lot.

She carried her bag up the dock, to the sliding door of the

houseboat. She opened the door and stepped inside, put the bag down, and locked the door behind her.

A cool breeze hit her as she walked into her bedroom.

That didn't seem right. She followed the breeze into the bathroom, where she found the window open.

She went in to close it, telling herself that she must have missed it this morning.

She pulled the window shut.

Then *he* stepped out from behind the shower curtain.

59

Roberta Hudgins and her grandson were giving statements to a patrolman when Lee Wade drove up, joining three patrol cars wedged in front of the house.

Wade had missed the emergency call to 2600 Tesla: He had driven up there to apologize to Ellis Hoile, who had been right all along about C. W. Hartmundt.

He spoke for a few moments to one of the patrol officers, a sergeant, then he took Ellis Hoile aside.

He said, "What the hell is this about?"

"Somebody came in and tried to kill them. But I'm sure it was me he wanted."

"Why you?"

"Why does he kill anybody?" Ellis Hoile said, but he added, "He knows I've got the tape."

Lee Wade said, "Oh, yeah, that tape was for real. Early Saturday morning, one of Corwin Sturmer's phone contacts got fire-bombed in the parking garage at Kansas City International. Has to be what you saw."

He explained about Corwin Sturmer, and his phone records, his calls to Verba and to Charles Obend, and about the videotape in his apartment, the death of Donald Trask.

Then he described how he had gone to the Union Street apartment with Ronson and a couple of uniforms to arrest the man who had been known as Sturmer and Hartmundt.

The two patrolmen had stood at the windows while Wade and Ronson buzzed at the front door. Buzzed and knocked and yelled, and got no answer.

When the building manager opened the apartment for them, they found nobody inside. The killer was gone.

"I think Sturmer is his real name," Lee Wade said. "Christian Hartmundt is a fake, obviously. The whole business about being a crip. Anyway, we'll find out as soon as we arrest him. Shouldn't be long now."

"How's that?"

"Hey, yesterday morning the guy had two safe addresses. Now he's been burned at both places. How many more can he have? He's running, got to be. He's not out in your network either, he's in the real world, and that's my turf."

He seemed sure of himself, Ellis Hoile thought, happy and confident.

No point in trying to tell him that he was wrong.

60

Kate Lavin was bound, gagged, and tied.

She couldn't move. She could see nothing but blue nylon: the side of a bag into which *he* had zipped her.

It was a very large bag, shroudlike. A sail bag was how most people on the waterfront would know it.

He was lifting her, laying the bag over his shoulder, and stepping out of the houseboat. He would look like one more sailor toting a bag of gear, you saw it all the time here in Sausalito.

He rocked slightly as he walked, toting her down the dock.

He was taking her away.

The vent duct seemed to rise forever.

Stephen Leviste guessed that the distance to the top of the duct, where it bent and began its horizontal run, was at least fifty feet.

To him, standing with his neck craned inside the duct, it looked endless.

He had managed to squeeze his body through the opening at the base of the vent. He went in arms and shoulders first, and pulled the rest in afterward. It was a very tight fit. To make it work he had to hold his arms up over his head.

Once he stood inside, with his hips and shoulders turned at an angle in the vent, he knew that ascending the duct might be possible.

It was also terrifying.

He stood at the bottom of the duct, holding the flashlight above his head, staring upward at the straight sides of the duct. The rectangle of sheet metal converged to a point as it reached up, up into the darkness, straight as a lance that skewered him through the heart.

He had to go, he told himself. He couldn't stay here in the pipe for long. He doubted that he could even manage to slide himself out the way he had come.

Besides, he had every other reason to want to go up, rather than back.

He released the flashlight—he would need his hands for other things. The light fell, struck him in the chest, and came to rest there. He shifted his body, and the light slid down, past his hips, and thunked against the floor of the pipe.

Now just darkness faced him overhead. Better that way, he thought.

He lowered his arms, twisting his torso to make room for them. One after the other he scissored his arms at the elbow and crossed them at his chest. He extended them a few inches—this pressed the opposing palms against the sides of the duct.

A short hop upward, and his feet were off the ground. He twisted his shoulders, pushing them against the vent. He crammed the toes of his sneakers into the corners of the pipe.

He stuck there, several inches off the floor of the pipe, jammed in place. Now he wriggled his body, shifted his shoulders, thrust upward with his legs.

That way he gained a few more inches.

Inches behind, and a long, long way to go.

He climbed.

61

Mrs. Hudgins and David had gone home in a taxi.

Lee Wade had stationed a patrolman in front of the house in case Sturmer appeared again.

Ellis Hoile was examining the broken window in the bedroom, thinking that he needed to get a handyman out to fix it.

But something else was working in his mind.

He was thinking about the killer, a man of varied names and places, of many levels. His methods and his acts revealed him. And he had displayed himself—however unknowingly—in the game and its program code.

But you had to know where to look, what to look for. Getting to the truth about him was like peeling away the layers of an onion: There was always another layer.

He was careful: exquisitely cautious.

According to Lee Wade, Corwin Sturmer had used a standard telephone to contact at least one of his victims, creating a trail from them to him.

He would have known that would happen, that it would compromise him at some point.

This meant his name was not Corwin Sturmer. That name, that existence, were throwaways. Losing them had cost him nothing that he could not replace.

And what did it gain?

Ellis Hoile thought he understood. He could still see the face of Lee Wade from a few minutes earlier, his brash eagerness and confidence.

That was exactly the desired effect. The killer had thrown his pursuers a few scraps, some bait for the hounds, something to keep their interest up.

He wanted to be chased. He liked games.

But he would always have a fallback position, some safehold, an identity within which he felt untouchable.

In such a sanctuary he might relax his guard. There, maybe— maybe—he would be vulnerable.

Ellis Hoile reached for the photocopy that Lee Wade had given him a few days earlier. He pulled it off the side of the monitor, where he had stuck it.

```
MEATWARE Version 1
4–16
Taken: 17424        05071
Slain: 17441        05086


MEATWARE Version 3
5–7
Taken: 17029        21067
Slain: 17029        21067


LAMERS
CLUELESS LAMERS
```

The killer was teasing his pursuers, Ellis Hoile thought.

He was demonstrating just how dumb they were; he was thumbing his nose at them.

Which probably meant that the answer was very simple.

Ellis Hoile believed that the numbers were map coordinates. But they weren't any system that he could recognize. He thought that maybe the killer had laid out his own arbitrary grid.

There was a way around that. With two known points you could reconstruct the entire grid, correlate it to a known map grid: the standard Mercator system. It was a math problem, really.

One of the murders had occurred at the international airport, Kansas City.

On the killer's grid it was 17029 21067.

Ellis Hoile brought an electronic atlas up on the screen and located the spot. It displayed the standard coordinates: 39.21 north, 94.70 west.

He had nailed down one of the two spots.

Donald Trask had lived in the Marina District. Assume that he had been kidnapped near his home.

The killer had it as 17424   05071.

The atlas showed 37.81 N, 122.42 W.

Ellis Hoile immediately sat at the keyboard and began to work. He was writing several dozen lines of a simple program.

He compiled it, and the program prompted him to input a coordinate.

He typed:

17441   05086

This was where Donald Trask had been killed—if the message was accurate.

And the machine responded:

37.85N 122.41W

Ellis Hoile knew, looking at it, that it was somewhere around the bay. But he couldn't place it exactly.

He entered it on the atlas program.

The map moved in on the bay. Ellis Hoile zoomed in closer to see where Donald Trask had died.

Then he sat staring at the screen, what it showed. He saw that 37.85 N, 122.41 W, was the location of his favorite spot in all the world, a place of trees and grassy hillsides and rocky shores. If he were forced to live without dark rooms and keyboards and computers, this was the place where he would choose to spend such an exile.

Angel Island.

Donald Trask had been killed at Angel Island.

And now Ellis Hoile remembered what he had been doing when the clamor downstairs interrupted him.

He took the stairs three at a time, up to the spare room where he had been working.

The indistinct face of the killer, caught in a fleeting reflection, still filled the monitor screen. He saved that image to a diskette, put the diskette in his pocket, and hurried out.

He nearly bumped into the patrolman standing by the door outside.

"You coming back?" the cop asked.

Ellis Hoile shrugged and kept walking.

For Stephen Leviste, the ascent inside the vent duct was a purgatory of pain and fear.

His body ached fiercely. First one and then the other of his calves had cramped from the exertion. Cobwebs clung to his face. He couldn't brush them away—he needed his hands for support—so his breathing sucked the webs into his nose and mouth.

He could not judge how long he had been wriggling up the vent. But it seemed a lifetime.

In the darkness, he could not see how much duct still lay above him. But he knew that if he relaxed, the sliding descent would be fast enough to maim or kill him at the bottom.

He willed himself forward. Pressed palms against the sides of the duct, pushed up with his legs, jammed hips and shoulders into the corners to hold himself in place. Then repeated the sequence. Again. Again. Again. Two, three inches at a time—maybe not even that much, he thought.

Hands. Feet. Hips and shoulders.

Hands. Feet. Hips and shoulders.

Hands. Feet. Hips and shoulders.

Hands . . .

His hands pressed for the duct and found nothing.

His heart skipped in panic.

Feet thrashed against the duct.

Hands flailed.

And found a ledge. Actual purchase for his fingers. He gripped the ledge, pushed once more with his legs, hoisted himself up.

He sprawled in the duct. The horizontal duct.

He was over the top.

The killer had carried her to a boat.

For fifteen or twenty minutes, Kate—still in the sail bag—had heard the thrum of the engine and felt its vibrations and the pitch of the hull as it plowed across the water.

Now the engine cut, and he was lifting her again, onto a bobbing, curved floor. Close to her ear she heard the ragged snarl of an outboard engine. They were in a dinghy, she thought.

Less than a minute later the dinghy grounded in sand and surf. He lifted her once more, carried her again.

Then he unzipped the bag. She looked around and saw where he had brought her.

"Ain't it a bitch?" he said. He was grinning. Loving it.

"Or maybe you're not in the mood for irony," he said.

Then he lowered her into the opening of what seemed to be a concrete well sunk into the earth.

Down into darkness.

Out of the daylight, out of the fresh air, she was going *down* . . .

62

As soon as he reached the studio, Ellis Hoile noticed the red Miata parked near the dock.

Had to be Kate's, he thought. He wondered if she had missed the plane.

The receptionist was leaving for home, coming out the front door, when Ellis Hoile met him and said, "Where's the boss?"

"Haven't seen her," the receptionist said. "She should be somewhere at thirty thousand feet."

So she hadn't called, hadn't been in to work.

Ellis Hoile went into her office, took a seat in front of her computer.

He called the houseboat but got no answer. Tried the cell phone: It shunted him off to her voice mail.

Gone kayaking, he thought, maybe jogging. After he was finished there he would go to the houseboat and wait for her.

He powered up her computer and began to search the files. Kate's computer was wired into the studio's internal network, and he had access to all the directories on the big file server that was the heart of the system. He himself had set up the network.

He was looking for a program: one of his own, that he had written and loaded there. That was nearly three years earlier, and he had forgotten the name.

But he recognized it now as it scrolled past him in a miscellaneous directory.

He booted the program, then loaded in the file—the blurred reflection of the killer's face—that he had carried over on the diskette.

The picture appeared once more on the screen in front of him, exactly as he had taken it from the scanned tape.

"Sharper" was the name he had given the program: a photo-enhancement utility. He had written it as an exercise, something to try. The copy at the studio was the only one he had ever circulated.

The program used fractal mathematics to sharpen blurred edges. It faked higher resolution, guessing at boundaries, interpolating crisp edges where none had existed before.

Sometimes it guessed wrong, and the image actually lost detail.

Most of the time it worked, though, if the image wasn't too badly blurred.

He pressed a key now to set it working.

The program made four passes over an image, beginning with the topmost line of pixels and flowing downward. The effect was of a wave slowly rolling down the screen, sculpting the image as it progressed.

The first pass showed little improvement.

On the second pass the image became more distinct.

The third pass was even better. He was beginning to see something now—something that made his heart begin to trip, that brought him to within inches of the monitor, staring at it, trying to make it out.

On the fourth pass the image seemed to crawl into focus, sharp and real. It was a real face.

Ellis Hoile gripped the edge of the desk.

He had seen that face.

When he got no answer on the phone, Ellis Hoile ran outside, across the parking lot and down the dock to the houseboat.

The sliding door was unlocked. He went in, began to call for her, then stopped. Because he saw at once that she was gone, she had been taken. The bathroom had been trashed—the shower door shattered, a dressing table overturned—and the struggle seemed to have carried out into the kitchen, too, before it ended.

Then Ellis Hoile did speak his wife's name after all, but it was a low, mournful groan of pain. Kate was gone.

He looked across the water toward Angel Island, about a mile distant, and he tried to imagine it as a place where a madman would bring his victims to be killed.

It was quiet and secluded. Though millions of people saw it every day, out in the bay, the island was actually remote, cut off from roads, beyond reach except by boat or air.

The killer would like that. A hidden place in plain sight: That would appeal to him.

But the island was also a place of open air and grand vistas, panoramas of earth and wind and water's edge.

He would not feel comfortable there. Too many uncertainties, too much randomness. The killer craved control: When he killed someone, he would want to be the master of the moment.

He would want to do it apart from the world, sealed off in a place that belonged to him alone—the antithesis of Angel Island's great wild openness.

Ellis peered across the water at the green-humped island, seeing it not only at that moment, from that spot, but recalling all the days and hours he had passed there, all he knew about it.

At the same time, he thought of a concrete maze that must be completely invisible, wholly unexpected.

And something moved in the mind of Ellis Hoile, memories and impressions falling into place.

·   ·   ·

"I need to speak to Lee Wade. He knows who I am, he knows what this is about," said Ellis Hoile.

The detective who had taken the call in the homicide squad room said that Lee Wade wasn't in, but he could be reached by pager if it was important. Was this important?

"Yes," said Ellis Hoile. "It's important."

"What's the message?"

"Check your fax machine in two minutes, it'll be there," said Ellis Hoile.

He hung up the phone and went to Kate's computer. Quickly he logged in to the studio's network, retrieved the map file of Angel Island, and overlaid it with five lines of text:

HARTMUNDT/STURMER HERE—HIS HIDING PLACE

HE HAS MY WIFE

WILL MEET YOU

HURRY

ELLIS HOILE

He added a pointer to a spot on the map, and sent this down the wire. At once it began to inch out of the fax machine in the homicide squad room.

He left the machine, and went around to the stern of the houseboat, where the kayak was. He lowered it into the water, eased himself down into it, and he pushed off and began to paddle out into Richardson Bay.

To his right was the Sausalito shoreline, the town climbing into the coastal hills. At the hilltops, fog was pushing over the crest, seeming to pause at the top and then rolling, cascading down.

He glimpsed the Golden Gate. A solid bank of gray fog had

pushed in from the ocean, swallowing all but the tops of the bridge uprights.

And he kept paddling, south toward the shaggy green island directly in front of him.

63

"What do you want?" Kate asked the killer.

He had carried her to the supply room, sat her up against the wall while he worked at a PC on the workbench.

She was still bound, immobile.

"Doesn't matter," he said without looking up. "It's beside the point. Because I'm going to get what I want, no matter what. It's out of your hands. You can't change a thing."

He looked up from his work.

"You can count the minutes that you've got left. You can count the heartbeats. It's all over, you're finished."

He left his work and walked over to her.

"And the way it's going to happen . . . " he said. "Well, you've got to see this for yourself."

Stephen Leviste lay motionless, recovering. His shoulders ached, the joints of his arms and fingers were numb, his legs throbbed from muscle cramps.

He was now in the horizontal duct that ran along the ceiling of the concrete cavern. Somewhere nearby, he thought, the duct vented to the outside. And he would find the way out, as soon as his strength returned.

He didn't have to move right away. Up here the duct was much larger than the vertical pipe he had just climbed. So he wasn't as cramped as he had been during his ascent.

He breathed deep and felt life return to his limbs.

Ready to move on.

He rolled over onto his stomach and began to crawl along the duct, feeling his way in the darkness. Soon he reached a junction, where the duct branched off into two directions.

To his left, he believed, was a long stretch of ductwork that ran parallel to the catwalk, along the ceiling.

To his right, if he guessed correctly, the duct pushed through the back wall and eventually made its way to the surface.

That was the way to go, he thought. And he was about to turn in that direction when he heard noise coming from down the other way, carrying down the duct.

The maniac, he thought.

But not only the maniac.

There were two voices. One of them was a woman's. She sounded unstable and a little shrill. From here he couldn't make out the words, but the tone carried down the vent.

He had always been a curious kid who craved knowing how things worked, who poked into the innards of life for the answers.

Now he hesitated only a moment. Something was happening here, and he had to know.

He turned left, toward the voices.

Ellis Hoile stroked, pushing on. His arms were tired, but he kept going, remembering afternoons on the water with Kate, how he had taught himself to push through the discomfort so that he could keep up with her.

Fog was pouring through Sausalito now, advancing past the waterfront, headed his way.

The island had grown much larger in front of him. Now he could see where he wanted to be, a rocky beach at the south end

f2f

of the island where the waves broke white about fifty yards offshore.

A boat was anchored outside that surf line: a big ketch-rigged sailboat, maybe a forty-five-footer.

The sailboat seemed empty when Ellis Hoile circled it in the kayak. So he continued on toward shore.

The fog was marching in fast. It overtook him as he crossed through the surf, but he kept paddling, stroking, and then the bottom of the kayak crunched gravel.

He was on the island.

64

The killer picked her up and carried her out, across to the killing room. The door was open a crack. He pushed it aside with his foot.

"Check this out," he said.

The room was dark at first, but she could make out some shapes.

The first object that caught her eye was a video camera on a tripod, pointed toward a straight-backed wooden chair. A computer, with keyboard and monitor, sat on a small desk along the back wall of the room.

Something was different about the chair, she thought.

He put her down on the floor, flipped a light switch, and she could see better.

The chair . . .

The voices resounded in the sheet metal as Stephen Leviste crawled down the long stretch of duct pipe that ran along the ceiling of the concrete cavern.

The man's voice belonged to the maniac, no question.

And the woman was in trouble. No question about that, either.

After a long straight run the duct pipe bent ninety degrees to the left. Stephen followed the bend. The voices were clearer now, and close. Slits of light showed through the darkness up ahead: As Stephen got nearer he saw that these were louvres on the cover of an air vent, on the wall of a room.

He was creeping now, careful, silent.

Where the ductwork ended, he peeked through the slits.

He looked down into a concrete room. Directly below him was the maniac, nearly at arm's length but unaware of Stephen's presence. The maniac stood almost directly below the louvres of the vent opening.

Beside the maniac was a woman in a chair. Her back was to the vent, so Stephen couldn't see her face. But there was despair in the slump of her shoulders. She turned her head away from the maniac, as if trying to avoid his eyes.

Stephen knew that feeling.

Stephen pressed his face against the vent cover, to get a better line of sight through the slits.

At this angle he could see not only the woman but the chair where she sat, and the floor at her feet.

The chair was fitted with nylon straps on the armrests and at the legs, with larger straps at chest height on the backrest.

And now Stephen drew in a sharp, involuntary breath that lodged in his chest.

A pair of heavy electrical cables, sheathed in black insulation, ran out of one wall.

The electrical wires coiled on the floor beside the chair and ended in flat terminals.

The maniac held up a hooded headset—Stephen recognized it as a Virtual Reality visor.

"Playtime," the maniac said.

Lee Wade was on Upper Market Street, Diamond Heights, when the message came through on his pager.

He wasn't in a radio car—he needed three or four minutes to find a pay phone and call in.

Then a clerk in the homicide squad room read him the fax from Ellis Hoile. Right away Lee Wade said they needed backup, a canine unit if they could find one, and a quick way across the bay.

He flew through with flashing lights and siren. Nine minutes later he was there. Ronson had pulled a dog and handler out of roll call. But the department's helicopter was busy on another call. They had to request assistance from the Highway Patrol.

For more than ten minutes they stood on the roof of the Hall of Justice, beside the helipad, cradling the pump shotguns that Ronson had brought from downstairs, until the CHP's Jet Ranger materialized over the South of Market skyline and set down.

They scrambled into the chopper, Wade last of all and taking the open seat up front, beside the pilot.

By now nearly twenty-five minutes had passed since Ellis Hoile's fax appeared.

The chopper lifted off while Wade was still buckling his safety belt. Quickly it rose away from the roof and picked up speed.

The water wasn't visible right away: Nob Hill blocked the view.

Then they skimmed over the hill and the bay hove into sight.

Lee Wade's eyes moved across the water. He looked for Sausalito, Richardson Bay, the island.

What he found was a low, thick blanket of fog that swallowed all landmarks as it pushed down the bay.

Lee Wade started to ask the pilot if they couldn't try anyway. The island was down there somewhere.

But he didn't get a chance to speak. The pilot was shoving the stick to one side, kicking the aircraft over and banking it back toward Bryant Street.

"Not a chance," he said.

.   .   .

Ellis Hoile walked up from the rocky beach.

He ascended a hump of ground and found himself atop the base of the grassy spit that the island threw off into the bay, like the tail of a comma.

The hump was maybe two hundred yards wide here, straddled by beaches on each flank. He couldn't actually see the water anymore: The fog was way too thick for that. But he had been here many times. His mind was filling in blanks that the fog created.

And then he walked out onto the broad, flat expanse of the rectangular concrete pad that marked the top side of the old missile installation.

She was here.

65

The killer had a pair of scissors. He was clipping her hair, cropping it close to the skull, working fast and rough.

"Why me?" she said.

"I told you, don't worry about it."

"You're going to kill me, at least I deserve to know why."

He leaned in close and hissed in her ear.

"You ought to know," he said. He was intense, contemptuous. "You're so clever."

The scissors were at her face now, not more than an inch from her cheeks, her eyes.

"All of you," he said. "Oh-so-clever, you think you've got it all figured out. But you don't have a clue."

He moved in even closer. His breath was hot.

"You mess with things you don't understand. You have this force at your fingertips, it's unimaginable, so powerful. And what do you do? You trivialize it. You waste it. Chat lines and flame wars and on-line porn. You turn on the switch, you log in, it's all for your amusement."

Computers, she realized: He was talking about computers.

"Like spoiled children with a tame tiger for a pet," he was saying. "This magnificent animal. And you want it to do tricks. You make it roll over, sit up and beg, oh, yeah, you think you're really doing something."

Swiftly he grabbed a handful of what remained of her hair. He yanked it, slamming her against the back of the chair.

"But the tiger has teeth," he said.

He was pulling her hair, hurting her, making her groan.

"You play with a tiger, sometimes the tiger bites."

He released the handful of hair, pulled his face away from hers. His tone became almost casual.

"You're out of your depth," he said. "All of you."

He went back to work without a word now, quickly chopping the rest of her hair. Then with a plastic razor he scraped bare two spots on her scalp, one on each side of her skull.

He stepped away from the chair for a moment, uncoiled the two black cables, straightening them out on the floor, then crossed the room to stand at the keyboard.

"You play games?" he said. "The computer kind?"

"No."

"Too bad. This was supposed to be for somebody who played games. But it'll do for you too. You're smart, you'll pick it up quick."

He tapped at the keyboard, and the monitor brought up what she recognized as a texture-mapped image: Ellis had used the technique often in his work. This one showed a bare concrete corridor not much different from the one outside this room.

The VR headset visor—like an oversized pair of wraparound sunglasses—was in her lap. He came over to her, slipped on the headset so that it rested against her brow.

Now she could see the same image as the one on the monitor. But the one on the visor screen was more vivid and immediate.

Smoothly, after he had put the headset on her, he bent down and picked up the electrical cables and slipped one into each of her hands.

"The story line," he said, "is that you're in a creepy abandoned property. Does this sound familiar? You're being hunted by a fiend. You want to stay away from him as long as you can. If he finds you . . . "

On the headset screen, a door opened, a figure stepped out from behind the door. Brandishing a knife. Coming toward her.

The on-screen killer raised his knife, thrust it down.

The screen became a livid blood red.

The metal terminals tingled in her hands—she yelped and released the cables and they dropped to the floor.

"C'mon now," he said, "that wasn't so bad. Two-percent capacity is what it shows. I know that didn't hurt."

He lifted the headset from her face and pointed to the computer monitor, a yellow rectangle at the bottom left of the screen. She had noticed it on her own display.

"A bar graph," he said. "Two percent of full charge. That was nothing."

He pulled the cables together and arranged them on the concrete floor so that the flat metal terminals lay an inch apart.

A few taps at the keyboard extended the yellow rectangle almost completely across the bottom of the screen.

"Ninety-percent capacity," he said. "That's a nominal ten thousand eight hundred volts—watch this."

The monitor view returned to the hallway she had seen a few moments earlier.

In a few seconds, as before, a door on the corridor opened and a figure stepped out. This time with a club.

The yellow bar at the bottom of the screen throbbed yellow.

He stepped closer, raised the club, swung it downward.

Again the monitor screen washed blood red.

Down on the floor, the cables writhed as a blinding blue clot of sparks arced between the metal terminals.

The lights in the room dimmed for a moment.

Then the yellow rectangle disappeared as the killer tapped once more at the keyboard.

"The computer controls a switching device," he said. "Open the switch, it passes power to these lines."

He was holding a big roll of duct tape. He picked up one of the terminals from the floor, pressed it against the left side of her skull, onto the bare patch that he had shaved. The flat tab was warm—no, hot—where the spark had jumped.

He taped the terminal in place.

66

Almost directly above her, on the other side of a thick ceiling of reinforced concrete, Ellis Hoile stood in the raw air of the bay.

The cops would come soon, he thought—they *had* to come soon, and he wanted to be able to show them the way in.

He had found what he believed was the entrance, a metal hatch cover with an empty hasp for a padlock.

But when he pulled the hatch cover he found it fastened from the inside.

When the installation was active, the missiles had been brought in through a loading door that was cut into the side of the slope—he had already found it. But that entrance was now blocked by fill dirt.

He decided to walk the perimeter of the place again, searching for some feature that he had missed the first time around.

The fog masked his footsteps and shut out the world. The late afternoon sun was a dim, amorphous glow in the west.

He walked, trying to keep the edge of the pad in sight. This place was remote at any time; in fog the universe seemed to contract to within a few feet. He could believe that he was alone in the world.

But he was not alone: Kate was here, somewhere close, and so was her captor.

He kept walking.

Then a wide standpipe loomed up out of the fog, directly in his path. The pipe was nearly two feet across and nearly as high, and was open at the top, the opening protected by a screen and a raised metal cap.

An air vent, he thought.

From inside the pipe a voice yelled, "Get me out of here."

·   ·   ·

When both cables were taped to her skull, the killer slipped the VR visor over her face again.

On one arm of the chair, under the fingers of her right hand, he placed a trackball mouse.

"You want to stay away from the bad guy," he said. "Every time you die in the game, you're going to get juiced.

"At first it'll be a tickle, no big deal. You're just learning, after all. But before long it gets *real* serious."

He crossed over to the camcorder on the tripod. Turned it on, looked through the viewfinder, adjusted it so that it pointed straight at her.

"Screw up then," he said, "and that's it, the end, you join the video hall of shame with all the other lamers."

He was standing over her, murmuring in one ear.

"I'll be jacked in on another machine," he said. "I'll be watching. Give me a good game, that's all I ask. You do, I'll keep you around. Like Scheherazade—you want to save your ass, you have to amuse me. Play the game right, you get to live."

He walked out and shut the door.

A few seconds later, the virtual corridor reappeared in the view screen of the visor.

A slim yellow rectangle popped up on the bottom of the view.

She pushed the trackball under her fingers. This moved the visor view; she was walking down the VR corridor.

But not fast enough.

A door opened in her path . . . out stepped the fiend. Carrying a chain saw.

He lunged.

The screen filled with red. Under the metal terminals she felt needle pricks as the power came on.

She stiffened. It was more than a tickle.

The corridor view came up again inside her visor. The yellow rectangle seemed to have grown.

This time she ran . . .

The killer watched her run.

He sat in the storeroom, wearing an identical visor. His computer was linked to hers by an Ethernet connector.

They were playing the same game. But they were not playing by the same rules.

In front of him he had not only a trackball, but a keyboard. He commanded the game. It would proceed automatically, but he could intervene at any time.

If he chose, for the thrill of the chase, he could control the movements of the on-screen killer.

He could also follow her movements: track her through the maze, even see the view that she was seeing. Get inside her head for a real visceral thrill.

The difference was that he was not wired for 12,000 volts.

He could set the level of the charge anytime, as high as he wished.

It was a lie, the notion that she could save herself by learning the game quickly and playing it well. A necessary fiction, he thought: Otherwise she might just give up.

But she could not save herself. No matter how quickly she learned, no matter how well she played. He was going to have his fun. And then she was going to die.

He bumped the charge level up to seven percent. A hard jolt, but brief.

In his visor, he had chosen the view of the on-screen killer. He stepped out in front of her as she tried to run, and he brought his hatchet down onto the head of the virtual figure that represented his quarry.

The lights blinked.

67

Up on the surface, Ellis Hoile smashed at the peaked metal cap that covered the vent standpipe.

He had found a large stone that he held in two hands as he battered it against the lip of the cap.

The cap was made of sheet metal. It was old, and had been corroding out here in the marine air. The force of the blows was bending it back, steadily but slowly.

Ellis Hoile's knuckles were bleeding from where he had scraped them against the sharp lip of the cap. He pounded without a pause.

Now the cap crumpled under a hard blow. Ellis Hoile threw down the stone, put his weight against the cap, and pushed up and out.

Inside the pipe, Stephen Leviste pushed upward at the same time. Together they shoved the cap aside. Ellis Hoile reached an arm down. Stephen grabbed it and thrust himself upward and sprawled out over the lip of the pipe, down onto the ground.

Ellis Hoile helped him to his feet and said, "Did you see a woman in there?"

Stephen nodded.

"Is she all right?"

"She's alive. But I don't know for how long."

"Can I get to her this way?" Ellis Hoile was gesturing at the vent pipe.

"Yes. But he's down there too," Stephen said.

Ellis Hoile looked around. The fog was thick. He heard no boat. He saw no help on the way.

A woman's scream carried up from the vent pipe.

Without another word Ellis Hoile swung one leg over the edge of the standpipe, then another, and he dropped down into the duct.

Unconfined for the first time in two days, Stephen Leviste sucked in fresh air and drank in the openness.

For a few seconds he did.

Then he, too, climbed into the pipe.

He knew the layout. He also knew the maniac—had looked into his eyes and heard his voice.

Anybody brave enough to take him on was going to need help.

Kate was running from the killer.

The VR display had become physical reality for her. She panted, her heart tripped, just as if her own legs were carrying her across actual concrete.

The yellow bar at the bottom of the view had extended yet another increment—the last charge had been agonizing, and the next one would be worse, when it came.

She stood on a concrete landing. Beyond the landing was a steel catwalk. She hadn't seen this before.

She ran out onto the catwalk.

Too late, she saw that it extended into open air, and ended there. The floor was far below.

The killer followed her out onto the catwalk. Holding a knife, coming closer.

She looked down at the floor, then leapt down into the abyss, wondering whether the fall could be survived.

The screen washed crimson.

Current seared her skull.

When she could see again, the view was reset. The yellow bar was a fraction longer. She thought that she might have blacked out briefly, she wasn't sure.

She ran.

Totally immersed now in the virtual scene, she was slow to become aware of movement behind her chair. Softly spoken words.

Hands were reaching around her head. Grasping the visor. Lifting it away.

Don't do that, she thought, *I need that*.

Her hand on the trackball was being pushed aside. Replaced.

The intruding hand went to work with speed and sureness. Somebody knew what he was doing.

Numbly she watched the hand, then followed it with her eyes, up the arm, to a shoulder.

She turned to look at the face.

Ellis.

68

From behind the duct opening in the wall, Ellis had taken in the scene at a glance—chair, computer, cables—and grasped what was happening.

He recognized the game, Try Me. He had examined its software code, he had played it for many hours.

He knew that game.

Kate was so absorbed that she didn't hear him kick away the vent cover. She remained unaware as he dropped down into the room, with Stephen Leviste following.

The computer monitor let him follow what was happening. He slid his hand beneath hers and took over.

He was in the game.

The killer, too, was absorbed.

In his visor, he followed his quarry down a stairwell, into a hallway with five doors on each side. Nine of the ten doors opened into identical empty rooms that had no exit. Dead ends. The fourth door on the right opened onto yet another stairway—the only choice for survival.

He hefted a machete and prepared for the kill.

Without hesitation, his on-screen quarry ran to the fourth door on the right and disappeared down the stairwell.

A lucky guess, he thought.

The stairwell dropped into another level, a foyer that was the entry point for a complex labyrinth with a single escape.

From here, seven corridors radiated like spokes on a wheel.

Only one of the seven offered a chance of reaching the outlet of the labyrinth; to select any of the others was to doom yourself to a frustrating demise in the maze.

Unerringly, the on-screen quarry ran into the correct corridor.

Awfully lucky, the killer thought.

She was keeping distance between them. Once more, at the end of the corridor, she made the perfect turn. Then another.

She was getting way too cocky, he thought. She needed something to worry about.

He typed a command, and instantly the yellow bar leapt. It now stretched end to end across the bottom of the display.

One hundred percent.

The next charge would be full power, twelve thousand volts.

The next time she died would be for real.

"Cut 'em, pull 'em, do whatever you have to do," Ellis Hoile said.

He had taken her place in the chair, and had put on the VR visor. But the cables were still attached to her head. Stephen was tearing at the tape, pulling it away, one layer of tape exposing the next.

Ellis saw the bar graph jump to one hundred percent.

Her life was now literally at his fingertips, if that graph meant what he thought it did.

He raced through the labyrinth.

Behind him, Stephen Leviste said, "That's one," and a cable dropped to the floor.

Out of the labyrinth, down a long vertical cylinder that deposited him in a concrete hallway.

Four doors. Three led into dead-end rooms. The fourth opened onto a concrete landing, and beyond that landing was a steel catwalk.

Oh, man, he knew this place.

"Two," said Stephen.

With his eyes locked on the visor display, Ellis Hoile said, "One more thing I want you to do."

Stephen Leviste listened, and grinned.

"That might work," he said.

Escaping from the labyrinth required sixteen correct choices without a mistake. Any one wrong turn foreclosed the possibility of escape.

Sixteen chances for a fatal error—the killer had counted them when he programmed the game.

Sixteen chances to die.

From behind her, the killer watched her race through every one. Fourteen, fifteen, sixteen.

Nobody was that lucky.

You could not even say that she was learning fast. She had never even seen the labyrinth before.

Something was wrong.

The killer tore off the visor and rose. In the visor, the virtual killer continued his fruitless pursuit, automatically controlled now by the computer.

The flesh-and-blood killer picked up a double-sided axe from where it rested against the workbench, and he stalked out into the passageway.

Kate Lavin reached down from the duct and helped Stephen Leviste scramble up, into the opening at the top of the wall.

Ellis Hoile had told them to get as far away as they could. He remained in the straight-backed wooden chair, wearing the VR visor, still playing the game.

In his visor view, he was standing at the edge of the concrete landing, where the steel catwalk began. To his right was a long flight of stairs. He knew that this was an easy choice: The catwalk was an absolute dead end. The fall would always kill you, if the fiend didn't. To have any chance of surviving, you had to head down the stairs and take your chances from there.

He pushed forward, onto the catwalk. Out here he was alone, completely exposed.

Behind him, a door opened. The faceless fiend moved out onto the landing.

And followed him out onto the catwalk.

Behind Ellis Hoile, as he sat in the chair, the door rattled.

Out in the hallway, the killer cursed. Somebody had locked the door from inside.

The killer put down the axe, pulled out his key ring.

In the killing room, Ellis Hoile straddled two worlds.

In his visor, he stood on the steel catwalk as the virtual killer advanced toward him.

From behind the door he heard the jingle of keys. He heard the soft chunking sound of a key being inserted in the lock.

In the visor, the virtual killer raised his machete, as he strode forward.

In the corridor, the killer grasped the doorknob and turned the key.

With the fiend bearing down on him, he jumped from the catwalk.

He was falling, falling . . .

As always, the fall was fatal.

The visor screen went red at the exact moment that the angry killer grasped the knob and turned the key in the lock.

Twelve thousand volts surged up the cable, through the terminals, into the metal doorknob where Stephen Leviste had taped them: the doorknob which the killer now gripped.

The charge leapt through the door and through flesh and bone with the ripping sound of a thunderclap, rolling thunder that crashed and crashed and dimmed the lights.

Then it ended.

The yellow bar graph had reset to zero.

Ellis Hoile pulled off the visor and rose to his feet.

The body lay sprawled out in the corridor. For a moment or two Ellis Hoile stood over it, looking down into a face where fear and fury and surprise commingled in an expression that was as permanent as death.

It was the face of Jon Wreggett.

Ellis Hoile turned back into the room. He found Stephen Leviste looking out from the vent opening.

"Was that it?" the boy said.

"Done."

Kate's voice, from behind the boy: "Are you all right?"

"I'm fine."

"Let's get out of here."

"Right," said Ellis Hoile. He moved the straight-backed wooden chair to the wall, so that he could clamber up into the duct.

Then he remembered.

He crossed the room, to the computer. His fingers found the power switch.

He flipped it down.

The monitor screen died.

He turned his back on the dormant machine. He climbed out, through the duct, and up into the world.